A RITE of SWORDS

(BOOK #7 IN THE SORCERER'S RING)

MORGAN RICE

D0110740

ISBN: 978-1-939416-57-5

Books by Morgan Rice

THE SORCERER'S RING
A QUEST OF HEROES (BOOK #1)
A MARCH OF KINGS (BOOK #2)
A FEAST OF DRAGONS (BOOK #3)
A CLASH OF HONOR (BOOK #4)
A VOW OF GLORY (BOOK #5)
A CHARGE OF VALOR (BOOK #6)
A RITE OF SWORDS (BOOK #7)
A GRANT OF ARMS (BOOK #8)
A SKY OF SPELLS (BOOK #9)
A SEA OF SHIELDS (BOOK #10)
A REIGN OF STEEL (BOOK #11)

THE SURVIVAL TRILOGY
ARENA ONE (Book #1)
ARENA TWO (Book #2)

the Vampire Journals
turned (book #1)
loved (book #2)
betrayed (book #3)
destined (book #4)
desired (book #5)
betrothed (book #6)
vowed (book #7)
found (book #8)
resurrected (book #9)
craved (book #10)

"What is it that you would impart to me?
If it be aught toward the general good,
Set honor in one eye and death in the other,
And I will look on both indifferently,
For let the gods so speed me as I love
The name of honor more than I fear death."

--William Shakespeare
Julius Caesar

CHAPTER ONE

Thorgrin rode on the back of Mycoples as she flew across the sprawling countryside of the Ring, heading south, somewhere towards Gwendolyn. Thor clutched the Destiny Sword as he looked down and saw below, sprawled out, the endless expanse of Andronicus' million-man army, covering the Ring like a plague of locusts. He felt the Sword throb in his palm and knew what it was urging him to do. Protect the Ring. Drive out the invaders. It was almost as if the Sword were commanding him—and Thor was only too happy to oblige.

Very soon, Thor would circle back and make each and every one of the invaders pay. Now that the Shield was restored, Andronicus and his men were trapped; no more Empire reinforcements could filter in, and Thor would not rest until he had killed each and every one.

But now was not yet the time for killing. Thor's first order of business was his one true love, the woman he had pined for ever since had had left these borders: Gwendolyn. Thor ached to lay his eyes upon her once again, to hold her, to know she was alive. Inside his shirt his mother's ring burned, and he could hardly wait to offer it to Gwen, to profess his love, to propose. He wanted her to know that nothing had changed between them, regardless of whatever had happened to her. He still loved her just as much—even more—and he needed her to know that.

Mycoples rumbled gently, and Thor could feel the vibration through her scales. Mycoples, he sensed, was eager to reach Gwendolyn, too, before anything happened to her. Mycoples ducked and weaved in and out of clouds, flapping her great wings, and she seemed content being here, inside the Ring, carrying Thor. Their bond was only growing stronger, and Thor felt that Mycoples shared his every thought and wish. It was like riding an extension of himself.

Thor's thoughts shifted from Gwendolyn as he flew in and out of the clouds. The former Queen's words dominated his thoughts, kept returning to him, as much as Thor preferred to shut them out. Her revelation had pained him beyond what he could imagine. Andronicus? His father?

It couldn't be. A part of Thor hoped it was just another cruel mind game of the former Queen, who, after all, had hated him from the start. Perhaps she had wanted to implant false thoughts in his mind to disturb him, to keep him away from her daughter, for whatever reason. Thor wanted desperately to believe that.

But deep down, as she had spoken the words, they had resonated within Thor's body and soul. He knew them to be true. As much as he would like to think otherwise, the second she had uttered it, he knew that Andronicus was, indeed, his father.

The thought hung over Thor like a nightmare. He had always hoped and prayed, somewhere in the back of his mind, that King MacGil was his father and that somehow Gwen was not truly his daughter, so that they could be together. Thor had always hoped that the day he learned who his father truly was, all would make sense in the world, that his destiny would become clear.

To learn that his father was not a hero was one thing. He could accept that. But to learn that his father was a monster—the worst of all monsters—the man, more than anything, who Thor wanted dead—it was too much to process. Thor carried Andronicus' bloodline. What did that mean for Thor? Did that mean that he, Thor, was destined to become a monster, too? Did that mean he had some evil streak lurking in his veins? Was he destined to become like him? Or was it possible that he could be different from him, despite their shared blood? Did destiny travel through the blood? Or did each generation make its own destiny?

Thor also struggled to understand what this all meant for the Destiny Sword. If the legend was true—that only a MacGil could wield it—did that mean Thor was a MacGil? If so, how could Andronicus possibly be his father? Unless Andronicus, somehow, was a MacGil?

Worst of all, how could Thor ever share this news with Gwendolyn? How could he tell her that he was the son of her most-hated enemy? Of the man who had her attacked? Surely, she would hate Thor. She would see Andronicus' face every time she saw Thor's. And yet Thor had to tell her—he couldn't keep this secret from her. Would it ruin their relationship?

Thor's blood boiled with rage. He wanted to flail out at Andronicus for being his father, for doing this to him. As they flew,

Thor looked down and scanned the land. He knew Andronicus was down there somewhere. Soon enough, he would meet him face to face. He would find him. Confront him. And he would kill him.

But first, he had to find Gwendolyn. As they crossed over the Southern Forest, Thor sensed she was close. He had a sinking feeling in his chest that something awful was about to happen to her. He urged Mycoples faster and faster, feeling that any moment could be her last.

CHAPTER TWO

Gwendolyn stood alone on the upper parapets of the Tower of Refuge, dressed in the black robes the nuns had given her, already feeling as if she had been here forever. She had been greeted in silence, only one nun, her guide, speaking, just once, to instruct her about the rules of this place: there was to be no speaking, no interacting with any of the others. Each woman lived here in her own, separate universe. Each woman wanted to be left alone. This was a tower of refuge, a place for those seeking healing. Gwendolyn would be safe here from all the harms of the world. But also alone. Utterly alone.

Gwendolyn understood all too well. She wanted to be left alone, too.

She stood there now, atop the tower, looking out at the sweeping view of the treetops of the Southern Forest of the Ring, and felt more alone than ever before. She knew she should be strong, that she was a fighter. A King's daughter, and wife—or nearly wife—to a great warrior.

But Gwendolyn had to admit that, as much as she yearned to be strong, her heart and her spirit were still wounded. She missed Thor dearly and feared he would never return for her. And even if he did, once he found out what had happened to her, she feared he would never want to be with her again.

Gwen also felt hollowed-out knowing that Silesia had been destroyed, that Andronicus had won, and that everyone she cared about had already been captured or killed. Andronicus was everywhere now. He completely occupied the Ring and there was nowhere left to turn. Gwen felt hopeless, exhausted; far too exhausted for someone her age. Worse of all, she felt as if she had let everyone down; she felt as if she had lived too many lifetimes already, and she did not want to see any more.

Gwendolyn took a step forward, up onto the ledge, on the very edge of the parapet, beyond where one was supposed to stand. She lifted her arms slowly and held her palms out to her side. She felt a cold gust of wind, the freezing winds of winter. They knocked her off balance and she swayed on the edge of the precipice. She looked down and saw the steep plummet below.

Gwendolyn looked up to the sky, and thought of Argon. She wondered where he was, trapped in his own universe, serving his punishment, for her sake. She would give anything to see him now, to hear his wisdom one last time. Maybe that would save her, make her turn around.

But he was gone. He, too, had paid a price, and could not come back.

Gwen closed her eyes and thought one last time of Thor. If only he were here, that could change everything. If only she had *one* person left alive in the world who truly loved her, maybe that would give her a reason to go on living. She peered into the horizon, hoping beyond reason to see Thor. As she looked into the fast-moving clouds, she thought she heard dimly, somewhere on the horizon, the roar of a dragon. It was so distant, so soft, she must have imagined it. It was just her mind playing tricks on her. She knew no dragon could be here, inside the Ring. Just as she knew Thor was far away, lost forever in the Empire, in some place from which he would never return.

Tears rolled down Gwen's cheeks as she thought of him, of the life they could have had. Of how close they had once been. She pictured the look on his face, the sound of his voice, his laughter. She had been so sure they would be inseparable, that they would never be torn apart by anything.

"THOR!" Gwendolyn threw back her head and cried, swaying on the ledge. She willed for him to come back to her.

But her voice echoed on the wind and faded. Thor was a world away.

Gwendolyn reached down and held the amulet Thor had given her, the one that had saved her life once. She knew that her one chance had been used. Now, there were no more chances.

Gwendolyn looked down over the ledge and saw her father's face. He was surrounded by white light, smiling at her.

She leaned forward and hung one foot over the edge, closing her eyes to the breeze. She hovered there, caught between two worlds, between the living and the dead. She was balanced perfectly, and she knew the next gust of wind would decide for her which direction she would go.

11

Thor, she thought. *Forgive me.*

CHAPTER THREE

Kendrick rode before the vast and growing army of MacGils, Silesians, and liberated countrymen of the Ring as they all burst out of the main gates of Silesia and onto the wide road, heading east, for Andronicus' army. Beside him rode Srog, Brom, Atme and Godfrey, and behind them, Reece, O'Connor, Conven, Elden, and Indra, amongst thousands of warriors. As they rode, they passed the charred bodies of thousands of Empire soldiers, black and stiff from the breath of the dragon; others lay dead from the mark of the Destiny Sword. Thor had unleashed waves of destruction, as if a single-man army. Kendrick took it all in, and was in awe at the scope of Thor' destruction, the power of Mycoples and the Destiny Sword.

Kendrick marveled at the turn of events. But days ago, they had all been imprisoned, under Andronicus' yoke, forced to admit defeat; Thor had been still in the Empire, the Destiny Sword but a lost dream, and there had been little hope of their returning. Kendrick and the others had been crucified, left to die, and it had seemed as if all were lost.

But now they rode as free men, as soldiers and knights once again, invigorated by Thor's arrival, the momentum now turned to their side. Mycoples had been a godsend, a force of destruction raining down from the sky; Silesia now stood as a free city, and the countryside of the Ring, instead of being filled with Empire soldiers, was littered with Empire corpses. The road leading east was lined with Empire bodies as far as the eye could see.

Yet as encouraging as all of this was, Kendrick knew that a half-million of Andronicus' men lay in waiting on the other side of the Highlands. They had beaten them back temporarily, but they had hardly wiped them out. And Kendrick and the others were not content to sit on their heels and wait in Silesia for Andronicus to regroup and attack once again—nor did they want to allow them a chance to escape and retreat back to the Empire. The Shield was up, and as badly outnumbered as Kendrick and the others were, at least now they had a fighting chance. Now, Andronicus' army was on the run, and Kendrick and the others were determined to continue the string of victories that Thor had begun.

Kendrick glanced back over his shoulder at the thousands of soldiers and free men riding with him and saw the determination on their faces. They had all tasted slavery, tasted defeat, and now he could see how much they all appreciated what it felt like to be free men once again. Not just for themselves, but for their wives and families. Each and every one of them was embittered, emboldened to make Andronicus pay and make sure he did not attack again. These were an army of men ready to fight to the death, and they rode as one. Everywhere they rode, they liberated more and more men, releasing them from their bonds and absorbing a sprawling and ever-growing army.

Kendrick himself was still recovering from his time upon the cross. His body was still not as strong as it was, and there still lingered the ever-present pain in his wrists and ankles from where those coarse ropes had dug into him. He looked over at Srog and Brom and Atme, his neighbors on the cross, and saw that they, too, were not as strong as they had once been. The crucifixion had taken its toll on all of them. Yet still they all rode proudly, emboldened. There was nothing like a chance to fight for your life, a chance for vengeance, to make you forget your injuries.

Kendrick was overjoyed to have his younger brother Reece and the other Legion brothers back from their quest, riding by his side once again. It had torn him apart to watch the slaughter of the Legion back in Silesia, and having these men back home restored some of his grief. He had always been close to Reece growing up, protective of him, taking the role of a second father to him during all those times when King MacGil had been too busy. In some ways, being only his half-brother had allowed Kendrick to become even closer to Reece; there was no burden on them to be close, and they became close out of choice. Kendrick had never been able to be close to his other younger brothers—Godfrey had spent his time with misfits in the tavern, and Gareth—well, Gareth had been Gareth. Reece had been the only other one of the siblings who had embraced the battlefield, who had wanted to take up the life that Kendrick had chosen, too. Kendrick could not be more proud of him.

In the past, when Kendrick had ridden with Reece he had always been protective, keeping one eye on him; but since his return, Kendrick could see that Reece had become a true, hardened warrior himself, so he no longer felt the need to be so watchful of him. He wondered what sort of travails Reece must have undergone in the Empire to have transformed him to as hardened and skillful a warrior as he had become. He was looking forward to sitting down with him and hearing his stories.

Kendrick was overjoyed that Thor was back, too, and not just because Thor had liberated them, but also because he liked and respected Thor immensely and cared about him as he would a brother. Kendrick still replayed in his mind the image of Thor returning and wielding the Sword. He could not get over it. It was a vision he had never expected to see in his lifetime; indeed, he had never expected to see *anyone* wield the Destiny Sword, much less Thor, his own squire, a small, humble boy from a farming village on the periphery of the ring. An outsider. And not even a MacGil.

Or was he?

Kendrick wondered. He kept turning over in his mind the legend: only a MacGil could wield the Sword. Deep in his own heart, Kendrick had to admit that he'd always hoped that he himself would be the one to wield it. He'd hoped it would be the ultimate stamp on his legitimacy as a true MacGil, as the firstborn son. He had always dreamed that somehow, one day, circumstances would allow him to try.

But he had never been afforded that chance, and he did not begrudge Thor his achievement. Kendrick was not covetous; on the contrary, he marveled at Thor's destiny. He could not understand it, though. Was the legend false? Or was Thor a MacGil? How could he be? Unless Thor, too, was King MacGil's son. Kendrick wondered. His father had been known to sleep with many women outside of his marriage—which was indeed how he himself had been sired.

Was that why Thor had rushed out in Silesia, after speaking to his mother? What had they discussed, exactly? His mother wouldn't say. It was the first time she had kept a secret from him, from all of them. Why now? What secret was she withholding? What could she have said that had made Thor run off like that, leaving them all without a word?

15

It made Kendrick think of his own father, his own lineage. As much as he wished otherwise, he burned at the idea that he was illegitimate, and for the millionth time he wondered who his true mother was. He had heard various rumors throughout his life of different women that his father, King MaGil, had slept with, but he had never known for certain. When everything settled down—if it ever did—and the Ring returned to normal, Kendrick resolved to find out who his mother was for sure. He would confront her. He would ask her why she had let him go, why she had never been a part of his life. How she had met his father. He really just wanted to meet her, to see her face; to see if she looked like him; and to have her tell him that he was indeed legitimate, as legitimate as anyone else.

Kendrick was pleased that Thor had flown off to retrieve Gwendolyn, yet a part of him also wished Thor had stayed. Charging into battle, vastly outnumbered against tens of thousands of Andronicus' men, Kendrick knew they could use Thor and Mycoples now more than ever.

But Kendrick was born and bred a warrior, and he was not one to sit back and wait for others to fight his battles for him. Instead, he did what his instinct commanded him to do: ride out and conquer as much of the Empire army as he could, with his own men. He did not have special weapons like Mycoples or the Destiny Sword, but he had his own two hands, the same he had used since he was a boy. And that had always been enough.

They ascended a hill and as they reached its crest, Kendrick looked out over the horizon and saw in the distance a small MacGil city, Lucia, the first city east of Silesia. Empire corpses lined the road, and clearly Thor's wave of destruction had ended here. On the distant horizon, Kendrick could see a battalion of Andronicus' army retreating, riding east. He presumed they were heading back to Andronicus' main camp, to the safety of the other side of the Highlands. The main body of the army was retreating—but they had left behind a smaller division to hold Lucia. Several thousand of Andronicus' men were stationed in the city, standing guard before it. Also visible were its citizens, enslaved by the soldiers.

Kendrick remembered what had happened to them back in Silesia, how they had been treated, and his face reddened with a desire for vengeance.

16

"ATTACK!" Kendrick screamed.

He raised his sword high and behind him came the invigorated shouts of thousands of soldiers.

Kendrick kicked his horse, and all of them raced as one down the hill, heading for Lucia. The two armies were preparing to face off, and though they were equally matched in terms of numbers, they were not, Kendrick knew, matched in terms of heart. This remnant division of Andronicus' army were invaders on the run, while Kendrick and his men were ready to fight for their very lives to protect their homeland.

His battle cry rose to the heavens as they charged for the gates of Lucia. They came so fast and quick that several dozen Empire soldiers standing guard turned and looked at each other in confusion, clearly not expecting this attack. The Empire soldiers turned, ran inside the gates, and furiously turned the cranks to lower the portcullis.

But not fast enough. Several of Kendrick's archers, leading the way, fired and killed them, their arrows landing expertly through their chests and backs, finding the joints in their armor. Kendrick himself hurled a spear, as did Reece beside him. Kendrick found his target—a large warrior taking aim with a bow—and was impressed to see Reece found his effortlessly, piercing a soldier through his heart. The gate remained open and Kendrick's men did not hesitate. With a great battle cry, they charged through, aiming for the heart of the city, not pausing to shy from confrontation.

There arose a great clang of metal as Kendrick and the others raised swords and axes and spears and halberds, and met the thousands of Empire soldiers who raced out to greet them on horseback. The first to make impact, Kendrick raised his shield and blocked a blow, at the same time swinging his sword and killing two soldiers. Without hesitating, he wheeled around and blocked another sword slash, then thrust his sword into an Empire soldier's gut. As the man died, Kendrick thought of vengeance; he thought of Gwendolyn, of his people, of all the people of the Ring who had suffered.

Reece, beside him, swung his mace and impacted a soldier on the side of his head, knocking him off his horse, then raised his shield and blocked a blow coming at him from his side. He swung his mace around and took out his attacker. Elden, beside him, rushed forward with his great axe and brought it down on a soldier aiming for Reece, cutting straight through his shield and into his chest.

O'Connor fired several arrows with deadly precision, even at such close distance, while Conven threw himself into the battle and fought recklessly, lunging forward beyond all the other men, not even bothering to raise his shield. He instead swung with two swords, heading into the thick of the Empire soldiers, as if he wanted to die. But amazingly, he did not. Instead, he took out men to the left and right.

Indra followed not far behind. She was fearless, more so than most of the men. She used her dagger with skill and cunning, cutting like a fish through the ranks and stabbing Empire soldiers in the throat. As she did, she thought of her homeland, of how much her own people had suffered under the boot of the Empire.

An Empire soldier brought his axe down for Kendrick's head before he could dodge it, and he braced himself for the blow; but he heard a great clang, and saw his friend Atme beside him, stopping the blow with his shield. Atme then jabbed his short spear and stabbed the attacker in the gut. Kendrick knew he owed him his life, once again.

As another soldier charged forward with a bow and arrow aimed right for Atme, Kendrick charged in front and slashed his sword upwards, knocked the bow up high into the sky, the arrow sailing aimlessly over Atme's head. Kendrick then butted the soldier on the bridge of the nose with his sword hilt, knocking him off his horse, where he was trampled to death. Now they were even.

And so the battle went, on and on, each army going blow for blow, men falling on both sides, but more on the Empire side, as Kendrick's men, fueled with rage, pressed farther and farther into the city. Eventually, their momentum swept them through like a tide. The Empire men were strong warriors, but they were the ones who were used to attacking and were caught off guard; soon, they were unable to organize and hold back the swell of Kendrick's army. They were pushed back and fell in greater numbers.

After nearly an hour of intense fighting, the Empire losses became a full scale retreat. Someone on their side sounded a horn, and one by one, they began to turn and gallop away, trying to make it out of the city.

With an even greater shout, Kendrick and his men charged after them, chasing them all the way through Lucia and pursuing them out the rear gates.

Whoever remained of the Empire battalion, still hundreds strong, rode for their lives in organized chaos, racing for the horizon. There arose a great shout within Lucia from the freed MacGil captives. Kendrick's men slashed their ropes and liberated them as they went, and the captives wasted no time in rushing to the horses of the fallen Empire soldiers, mounting them, stripping the corpses' weapons, and joining Kendrick's men.

Kendrick's army swelled to nearly double its size, and the thousands of them chased after the Empire soldiers, riding up and down the hills as they closed in on them. O'Connor and the other archers managed to pick some of them off, bodies falling here and there.

The chase went on, Kendrick wondering where they were heading, when he and his men crested a particularly high hill and he looked down to see one of the largest MacGil cities east of Silesia— Vinesia—nestled between two mountains, sitting in the valley. It was a substantial city, far greater than Lucia, with thick stone walls, and enforced iron gates. It was here, Kendrick realized, that the remnants of the Empire battalion fled, as the city stood protected by tens of thousands of Andronicus' men.

Kendrick paused with his men atop the hill and took in the situation. Vinesia was a major city, and they were vastly outnumbered. He knew it would be foolhardy to try, that the safest course would be to return to Silesia and be grateful for their victory here today.

But Kendrick was not in the mood for safe choices—and neither were his men. They wanted blood. They wanted vengeance. And on a day like today, odds no longer mattered. It was time to let the Empire men know what the MacGils were made of.

"CHARGE!" Kendrick yelled.

A shout arose, and thousands of men rushed forward, charging recklessly down the hill, toward the great city and the greater opponent, prepared to give up their lives, to risk it all for honor and for valor.

CHAPTER FOUR

Gareth coughed and wheezed as he stumbled his way across the desolate landscape, his lips chapped from lack of water, his eyes hollow with dark circles beneath them. It had been a harrowing few days, and he had expected to die more than once.

Gareth had escaped by the skin of his teeth from Andronicus' men in Silesia, hiding in a secret passageway deep within the wall and biding his time. He had waited, curled up like a rat inside the blackness, waiting for an opportune moment. He felt he had been there for days. He had witnessed everything, had watched with disbelief as Thor had arrived on the back of that dragon, had killed all those Empire men. In the confusion and chaos that ensued, Gareth had found his chance.

Gareth had slunk out through the back gate of Silesia while no one was looking, and had taken the road south, making his way along the edge of the Canyon, sticking mostly to the woods so as not to be detected. It did not matter—the roads were deserted anyway. Everyone was off east, fighting the great battle for the Ring. As he went, Gareth noted the charred bodies of Andronicus' men lining this road, and knew the battles here, down south, had already been fought.

Gareth made his way ever farther south, his instinct driving him back towards King's Court—or what remained of it. He knew it had been ravaged by Andronicus' men, that it likely lay in ruins, but still, he wanted to go there. He wanted to get far away from Silesia and go to the one place he knew he could take safe harbor. The one place everyone else had abandoned. The one place where he, Gareth, had once reigned supreme.

After days of hiking, weak and delirious from hunger, Gareth had finally emerged from the woods and spotted King's Court in the distance. There it was, its walls still intact, at least partially, though charred and crumbling. All around were the corpses of Andronicus' men, evidence that Thor had been here. Otherwise it sat empty, with nothing left but the whistling of the wind.

That suited Gareth just fine. He did not plan on entering the city anyway. He had come here for a small, hidden structure just outside the city walls. It was a place he had frequented as a child, a circular, marble structure, rising just a few feet above ground and adorned with elaborately carved statues about its roof. It had always looked ancient, sitting low like that, as if it had sprung up from the earth. And it was. It was the crypt of the MacGils. The place where his father had been buried—and his father before him.

The crypt was the one structure Gareth knew would be left intact. After all, who would bother to attack a tomb? It was the one place left where he knew no one would ever bother to look for him, where he could seek shelter. It was a place where he could hide, be left utterly alone. And a place where he could be with his ancestors. As much as Gareth hated his father, oddly enough, he found himself wanting to be closer to him these days.

Gareth hurried across the open field, a cold gust of wind making him shiver as he wrapped his ragged cloak tight around his shoulders. He heard the shrill cry of a winter bird, and looked up to see the huge, awful black creature circling high overhead, surely, with each cry, anticipating his collapse, its next meal. Gareth could hardly blame it. He felt on his last legs, and he was sure he appeared to be a prime meal for the bird.

Gareth finally reached the building, grabbed the massive iron door handle with two hands, and yanked with all his might, the world spinning, nearly delirious from exhaustion. It creaked and took all his strength to pry it wide.

Gareth hurried into the blackness, slamming the iron door. It echoed behind him.

He grabbed the unlit torch on the wall, where he knew it was mounted, struck its flint and lit it, affording himself just enough light to see by as he descended the steps, deeper and deeper into the blackness. It became colder and draftier the deeper he went, the wind finding its way down, whistling through small cracks. He could not help but feel as if his ancestors were howling at him, rebuking him.

"LEAVE ME!" he screamed back.

His voice echoed again and again off the crypt's walls.

"YOU WILL HAVE YOUR PRIZE SOON ENOUGH!"

Yet still the wind persisted.

Gareth, enraged, descended deeper, until finally he reached the great marble chamber, excavated with its ten-foot ceilings, where all his ancestors lay entombed in marble sarcophagi. Gareth marched solemnly down the hall, his footsteps echoing on the marble, toward the very end, where his father lay.

The old Gareth would have smashed his father's sarcophagus. But now, for some reason, he was beginning to feel an affinity for him. He could hardly understand it. Perhaps it was the opium wearing off; or perhaps it was because he knew that he himself would be dead soon, too.

Gareth reached the tall sarcophagus and hunched over it, leaning his head down. He surprised himself as he began to cry.

"I miss you father," Gareth wailed, his voice echoing in the emptiness.

He cried and cried, tears pouring down his face, until finally his knees grew weak and he slumped down in his exhaustion alongside the marble, sitting on the floor, leaning against the tomb. The wind howled as if in response, and Gareth lay down the torch, which burned lower and lower, a tiny flame decreasing in the blackness. Gareth knew that soon all would be blackness and that soon, he would join all those he loved the most.

CHAPTER FIVE

Steffen trekked somberly on the lonely forest road, slowly making his way from the Tower of Refuge. It broke his heart to leave Gwendolyn there like that, the woman whom he had been sworn to protect. Without her, he was nothing. Since meeting her, he had felt that he had finally found a purpose in life: to watch over her, to devote his life to paying her back for allowing him, a mere servant, to rise in the ranks; and most of all, for being the first person in his life not to detest and underestimate him based on his appearance.

Steffen had felt a sense of pride in helping her reach the Tower safely. But leaving her there had left him feeling hollow inside. Where would he go now? What would he do?

Without her to protect, his life felt aimless once again. He couldn't go back to King's court or to Silesia: Andronicus had defeated them both, and he recalled the destruction he saw as he'd fled from Silesia. The last he remembered, all his people were captives or slaves. There would be no virtue in returning. Besides, Steffen didn't want to cross the Ring again and be that far from Gwendolyn.

Steffen walked aimlessly for hours, winding through the forest trails, gathering his wits, until it had occurred to him where to go. He followed the country road north, up to a hill, the highest point, and from this lookout spotted a small town perched on another hill in the distance. He headed for it, and as he reached it, he turned back and saw this town had what he needed: a perfect view of the Tower of Refuge. If Gwendolyn ever tried to leave it, he wanted to be close by to make sure he was there to accompany her, to protect her. After all, his allegiance was to her now. Not to an army or a city, but to her. She was his nation.

As Steffen arrived in the small, humble village, he decided he would stay here, in this place, where he could always watch the Tower, and keep an eye out for her. As he passed through its gates, he saw it was a nondescript, poor town, another tiny village on the farthest outskirts of the Ring, so hidden in the southern forest that Andronicus' men had surely not even bothered to come this way.

Steffen arrived to the gaping stares of dozens of villagers, faces etched with ignorance and a lack of compassion, looking at him with mouths agape and the familiar scorn and derision he had received ever since he had been born. As they all scrutinized his appearance, he could feel their mocking eyes.

Steffen wanted to turn and run, but he forced himself not to. He needed to be close to the Tower, and for Gwendolyn's sake, he would put up with anything.

One villager, a burly man in his forties, dressed in rags as the others, turned and headed meanly toward him.

"What have we here, some sort of deformed man?"

The others laughed, turning and approaching.

Steffen kept calm, expecting this sort of greeting, which he had received his entire life. He'd found that the more provincial people were, the more joy they took in ridiculing him.

Steffen leaned back and assured himself that his bow was at the ready over his shoulder, in case these villagers were not just cruel, but violent. He knew, if he had to, he could take out several of them in the blink of an eye. But he wasn't here for violence. He was here to find shelter.

"He might be more than just a regular freak, is he?" asked another, as a large and growing group of menacing villagers began to surround him.

"From his markings I'd say he is," said another. "That looks like royal armor."

"And that bow—it's a fine leather."

"Not to mention the arrows. Gold-tipped, are they?"

They stopped but a few feet away, scowling down threateningly. They reminded him of the bullies who tormented him as a child.

"So, who are you, freak?" one of them said down to him.

Steffen breathed deeply, determined to stay calm.

"I mean you no harm," he began.

The group broke out laughing.

"Harm? You? What harm could you do us?"

"You couldn't harm our chickens!" laughed another.

Steffen flushed red as the laughter grew; but he would not allow himself to be provoked.

"I need a place to stay and food to eat. I have calloused hands and a strong back for working. Set met to a task, and I will mind myself. I don't need much. As much as the next man."

Steffen wanted to lose himself in menial work again, as he had all those years in the basement serving King MacGil. It would take his mind off things. He could perform hard labor and live a life of anonymity, as he had been prepared to do before he had ever met Gwendolyn.

"You call yourself a man?" one of them called out, laughing.

"Maybe we can find some use for him," another called out.

Steffen looked at him hopefully.

"That is, fighting against our dogs or chickens!"

They all laughed.

"I'd pay a grand amount to see that!"

"There's a war out there, in case you haven't noticed," Steffen said back coolly. "I'm sure, even in a provincial and rudimentary town like this, you can use a hand to maintain provisions."

The villagers looked at each other, baffled.

"Of course we know of the war," one said, "but our village is too small. Armies won't bother coming here."

"I don't like the way you talk," another said. "All fancy-like? Sounds like you had some schooling. You think you're better than us?"

"I'm no better than the next man," Steffen said.

"That much is obvious," laughed another.

"Enough of the banter!" cried one of the villagers in a serious tone.

He stepped forward and pushed the others aside with a strong palm. He was older than the others and looked to be a serious man. The crowd quieted in his presence.

"If you mean what you say," the man said in his deep, brusque voice, "I can use an extra set of hands on my mill. Pay is a sack of grain a day and a jug of water. You sleep in the barn, with the rest of the village boys. If that's agreeable to you, I will have you on."

Steffen nodded back, satisfied to finally see a serious man.

"I ask for nothing more," he said.

"This way," the man said, parting his way through the crowd.

Steffen followed him, and was led to a huge, wooden gristmill, all around which were teenagers and men. Each of them, sweating and covered in dirt, stood in the muddy tracks and pushed a massive wooden wheel, each grabbing a spoke and walking forward with it. Steffen stood there, surveyed the work, and realized it would be backbreaking labor. It would do.

Steffen turned to tell the man he would accept, but the man had already gone, assuming he would. The villagers, with a few final heckles, turned back to their affairs while Steffen looked ahead at the wheel, at the new life that lay ahead of him.

For a glimmer in time, he had been weak, had allowed himself to dream. He had imagined a life of castles and royalty and rank. Had seen himself being an important person, the hand of the Queen. He should have known better than to think so high. He, of course, was not meant for that. He never had been. What had happened to him, meeting Gwendolyn, had been a fluke. Now, his life would be relegated to this. But this, at least, was a life he knew. A life he understood. A life of hardship. And without Gwendolyn in it, this life would be just as well for him.

CHAPTER SIX

Thor urged Mycoples faster as they raced through the clouds, getting ever closer to the Tower of Refuge. Thor felt with every ounce of his being that Gwen was in danger. He felt the vibration running through his fingertips, throughout his entire body, telling him, *warning* him. Go faster, it whispered to him.

Faster.

"Faster!" Thor urged Mycoples.

Mycoples roared softly in return, flapping her great wings harder. Thor had not even needed to utter the words—Mycoples understood everything, before he even said it—but he spoke the words anyway. They made him feel better. He was feeling helpless. He sensed that something was very wrong with Gwen, and that every second counted.

They finally broke through a patch of clouds and as they did, Thor was flooded with relief as he saw it come into view, in the distance: the Tower of Refuge. It was an ancient and eerie piece of architecture, a perfectly round, skinny tower shooting straight up into the sky, reaching nearly as high as the clouds. Built of an ancient, shining black stone, Thor could sense the power coming off it, even from here.

As they flew closer, suddenly he spotted something up high, atop the tower. It was a person. She was standing on the ledge, hands out, palms by her sides. Her eyes were closed, and she was swaying in the wind.

Thor knew immediately who it was.

Gwendolyn.

His heart pounded as he saw her standing there. He knew what she was thinking. And he knew why. She thought he had given up on her, and he could not help feeling as if it were his fault.

"FASTER!" Thor screamed.

Mycoples flapped her wings even harder, and they flew so fast it took Thor's breath away.

As they neared, Thor watched Gwen step backwards, off the ledge, back onto the safety of the roof, and his heart flooded with relief. Without even seeing him, on her own, she had changed her mind and decided not to jump.

Mycoples roared and Gwen looked up and spotted Thor for the first time. Their eyes locked, even from this great distance, and he watched the shock flood her face.

Mycoples landed on the roof and the moment she did, Thor jumped off, barely waiting for her to set down, and ran to Gwendolyn.

Gwen turned and stared at him, eyes open in complete surprise. She looked as if she were staring at a ghost.

Thor ran for her, his heart pounding, flooded with excitement, and reached out his arms. They embraced and held each other tightly as Thor picked her up and squeezed her. He spun her around again and again.

Thor heard her crying in his ear, felt her hot tears pouring down his neck, and he could hardly believe he was really here, holding her, here in the flesh. This was real. This was the dream he had seen in his mind's eye, day after day, night after night, when he had been deep in the Empire, when he had been sure he would never return, would never set eyes on Gwendolyn again. And here he was now, holding her in his arms.

Having been away from her for so long, everything about her felt new. It felt perfect. And he vowed he would never take another moment with her for granted again.

"Gwendolyn," he whispered in her ear.

"Thorgrin," she whispered back.

They held each other for he did not know how long, then slowly they pulled back and kissed. It was a passionate kiss, and neither of them backed away.

"You're alive," she said. "You're here. I can't believe you're here."

Mycoples snorted and Gwendolyn looked up over Thor's shoulder, as Mycoples flapped her wings once. Gwen's face flushed with fear.

"Do not be afraid," Thor said. "Her name is Mycoples. She is my friend. And she will be your friend, too. Let me show you."

Thor took Gwen's hand and led her slowly across the parapet. He could feel Gwen's fear as they approached. He understood. After all, this was a real, live dragon, and this was closer than Gwen had ever been to one in her life.

Mycoples stared back at Gwen with her huge, red glowing eyes, snorting gently, flapping her wings and arching back her neck. Thor sensed something like jealousy. And perhaps, curiosity.

"Mycoples, meet Gwendolyn."

Mycoples turned her head away, proudly.

Then suddenly she turned back and as she did, she stared right into Gwendolyn's eyes, as if seeing right through her. She leaned in, so close that her face was nearly touching Gwendolyn's.

Gwen gasped in surprise and awe—and perhaps fear. She reached up, her hand trembling, and lay it gently on Mycoples' long nose, touching her purple scales.

After several tense seconds, Mycoples finally blinked and lowered her nose and rubbed it against Gwen's stomach in a sign of affection. Mycoples kept rubbing her nose against Gwen's stomach, as if she were fixated on it, and Thor could not understand why.

Then, just as quickly, Mycoples turned her head away and looked off into the horizon.

"She's beautiful," Gwen whispered.

She turned and looked at Thor.

"I gave up hope that you would return," she said. "I did not think you would."

"Nor did I," Thor said. "Thinking of you is what sustained me. It gave me reason to survive. To return."

They embraced again, holding each other tightly as the breeze caressed them, then finally, they pulled back.

Gwendolyn looked down and noticed the Destiny Sword on Thor's hip and her eyes widened. She gasped.

"You brought back the Sword," she said. She looked up at him in disbelief. "*You* are the one to wield it."

Thor nodded back.

"But how…" she began, then trailed off. Clearly, she was overwhelmed.

"I do not know," Thor said. "I was just able to."

Her eyes opened with hope as she realized something else.

"Then the Shield is up again," she said hopefully.

Thor nodded back solemnly.

"Andronicus is trapped," he said. "We have already liberated King's Court and Silesia."

Gwendolyn's face rose in relief and joy.

"It was you," she said, realizing. "You freed our cities."

Thor shrugged modestly.

"It was Mycoples, mostly. And the Sword. I just went along for the ride."

Gwen beamed.

"And our people? Are they safe? Did any survive?"

Thor nodded.

"They are mostly alive and well."

She beamed, looking younger again.

"Kendrick awaits you in Silesia," Thor said, "as do Godfrey, Reece, Srog, and many, many others. They are all alive and well, and the city is free."

Gwendolyn rushed forward and hugged Thor, holding him tight. He could feel the relief flooding through her.

"I thought it was all gone," she said, crying softly, "lost forever."

Thor shook his head.

"The Ring has survived," he said. "Andronicus is on the run. We will return, and we will wipe him out for good. And then we will rebuild."

Gwendolyn suddenly turned her back to him and looked away, staring out at the sky, wiping away a tear. She wrapped her cloak tight around her shoulders, and her face filled with apprehension.

"I don't know if I can return," she said, hesitantly. "Something happened to me. While you were away."

Thor turned and faced her, holding her shoulders.

"I know what happened to you," he said. "Your mother told me. There is nothing to be ashamed of," he said.

Gwendolyn looking at him, her eyes filling with surprise and wonder.

"You *know*?" she asked, shocked.

Thor nodded.

"It means nothing," he said. "I love you as much as ever. Even more. Our love—that is what matters. That is what is unbreakable. I shall avenge you. I shall kill Andronicus myself. And our love, it will never die."

Gwen rushed forward and hugged Thor tight, her tears pouring down his neck. He could feel how relieved she was.

"I love you," Gwen said in his ear.

"I love you, too," he answered.

As Thor stood there, holding her, his heart pounded with trepidation. He wanted now, at this moment, more than ever, to ask her. To propose. But he felt he could not until he had first told her his secret, until he told her who his father was.

The thought of it filled him with shame and humiliation. Here he was, having just vowed to kill the very man they both hated most. And with his very next words, how could he announce that Andronicus was his father?

Thor felt sure that if he did, Gwendolyn would hate him forever. And he could not risk losing her. Not after all that happened. He loved her too much.

So instead, his hands trembling, Thor reached into his shirt and pulled out the necklace, the one he'd found among the dragon's treasures, with a rope made of gold and a shining golden heart, laden with diamonds and rubies. He held it up to the light, and Gwen gasped at the sight.

Thor came up behind her, and clasped it around her neck.

"A small token of my love and affection," he said.

It hung beautifully on her, the gold shining in the light, reflecting everything.

The ring burned in his pocket, and Thor vowed to give it to her when the time was right. When he could muster the courage to tell her the truth. But now was not that time, as much as he hoped that it could be.

"So you see, you can return," Thor said, stroking her cheek with the back of his hand. "You *must* return. Your people need you. They need a leader. The Ring, without a leader, is nothing. They look to you for guidance. Andronicus still inhabits half the Ring. Our cities still need to be rebuilt."

He looked into her eyes and could see her thinking.

"Say yes," Thor urged. "Return with me. This Tower is no place for a young woman to live out the rest of her days. The Ring needs you. *I* need you."

Thor held out a hand and waited.

31

Gwendolyn looked down, wavering.

Then finally, she reached out and placed a hand in his. Her eyes turned lighter and lighter, glowing with love and warmth. He could see her slowly coming back to the old Gwendolyn he once knew, filled with life and love and joy. It was as if she were a flower, being restored before his eyes.

"Yes," she said softly, smiling.

They embraced and he held her tight and vowed never to let her go again.

CHAPTER SEVEN

Erec opened his eyes to find himself lying in Alistair's arms, looking up at her crystal-blue eyes, which shone down with love and warmth. She wore a small smile at the corner of her lips, and he felt the warmth radiating off her hands, and through his body. As he checked himself, he felt entirely healed, reborn, as if he had never been injured. She had brought him back from the dead.

Erec sat up and looked into Alistair's eyes with surprise, finding himself wondering once again who she really was, how she could have such powers.

As Erec sat up and rubbed his head, he immediately remembered: Andronicus' men. The attack. The defense of the gulch. The boulder.

Erec jumped to his feet and saw his men all looking back towards him, as if awaiting his resurrection—and his command. Their faces were filled with relief.

"How long have I been unconscious?" he turned and asked Alistair, frantic. He felt guilty he had abandoned his men for so long.

But she smiled back at him sweetly.

"But for one second," she said.

Erec could not comprehend how that could be. He felt so restored, as if he had slept for years. He felt a new bounce in his step as he jumped to his feet and turned and ran for the entrance to the gulch and saw his handiwork: the huge boulder which he had smashed now stopped it up, and Andronicus' men could no longer get through. They had achieved the impossible and had fended off the much larger army. At least for now.

Before he could celebrate, Erec heard a sudden scream come from up above and looked up: there, atop the cliff, one of his men screamed, then tumbled backwards, end over end, and landed on the ground, dead.

Erec looked down and saw a spear impaled in the man's body, then looked back up to see a host of activity, shouts and screams erupting everywhere. Before his eyes, dozens of Andronicus' men appeared at the top, fighting hand-to-hand with the Duke's men, going blow for blow, and Erec realized what had happened: the

Empire commander had split his forces, sending some through the gulch, and sending others straight up the mountain face.

"TO THE TOP!" Erec commanded. "CLIMB!"

The Duke's men followed him as he ran straight up the mountain face, sword in hand, scrambling up the steep ascent of rock and dust. Every several feet he slipped and reached out with his palm, scraping it against the stone, grabbing hold, doing his best not to fall backwards. He ran, but the face was so steep it was more climb than run; each step was hard fought, armor clanging all around him as his men huffed and puffed their way, like mountain goats, straight up the cliff.

"ARCHERS!" Erec screamed.

Down below, several dozen of the Duke's archers, scaling the mountain, stopped and took aim straight up the cliff. They unleashed a volley of arrows and several Empire soldiers screamed and hurled backwards, tumbling down along the side of the cliff. One body came hurling down at Erec; he dodged and barely avoided it. One of the Duke's men was not so lucky, though—a corpse hit him and sent him flying backwards to the ground, screaming, dead beneath its weight.

The Duke's archers dug in and stationed themselves up and down the mountain, firing every time an Empire soldier popped his head over the edge of the cliff to keep them at bay.

But the fighting up there was tight, hand-to-hand, and not all of the arrows hit their mark: one arrow missed, accidentally lodging into the back of one of the Duke's own men. The soldier screamed and arched his back, and an Empire soldier took advantage and stabbed him, knocking him backwards, screaming down the cliff. But as the Empire soldier was exposed, another archer landed an arrow in his gut, taking him out, too, his corpse falling face-first over the edge.

Erec redoubled his efforts, as did those around him, sprinting with all he had straight up the cliff. As he neared the top, just feet away, he slipped and began to fall; he flailed, reached out, and grabbed hold of a thick root emerging from the stone. He held on for his life, dangling from it, then pulled himself up, regained his footing, and continued to the top.

Erec reached the top before the others and raced forward with a battle cry, sword raised high, eager to help defend his men, who were holding their positions at the top but getting pushed back. There were but a few dozen of his men up here, and each was embroiled in hand-to-hand combat with Empire soldiers, outnumbered two to one. With each passing second, more and more Empire soldiers kept appearing at the top.

Erec fought like a madman, charging and stabbing two soldiers at once, freeing up his men. There was no one faster in battle than he, not in the whole Ring, and with two swords in hand, slashing every which way, Erec drew on his unique skills as champion of the Silver to fight back the Empire. He was a one-man wave of destruction as he spun and ducked and slashed, heading ever deeper right into the thick of Empire soldiers. He dodged and head-butted and parried, and went so fast that he opted not to use his shield.

Erec tore through them like a wind, downing a dozen soldiers before they barely had a chance to defend themselves. And the Duke's men, all around him, rallied.

Behind him, the rest of the Duke's men also reached the top, Brandt and the Duke leading the way, fighting by Erec's side. Soon, the momentum turned, and they found themselves pushing back the Empire men, corpses piling up all around them.

Erec squared off with the final Empire soldier left at the top, and he drove him backward then leaned back and kicked him, sending him off the Empire side, screaming as he tumbled backwards.

Erec and his men all stood there, catching their breath; Erec walked forward, across the broad landing, to the very edge of the Empire side of the cliff. He wanted to see what lay below. The Empire had stopped sending men up here, wisely, but Erec had a sinking feeling that they might still have some in reserve. His men came up beside him and looked down, too.

Nothing in Erec's wildest imagination prepared him for what he saw below. His heart sank. Despite the hundreds of men they had managed to kill, despite the fact that they had successfully sealed off the gulch and taken the high ground, there still remained below tens of thousands of Empire soldiers.

Erec could scarcely believe it. It had taken everything they had to get this far, and all the damage they had done had not even put a dent in the endless armor of the Empire. The Empire would just send more and more men up here. Erec and his men could kill dozens more, perhaps even hundreds. But eventually, the thousands would get through.

Erec stood there, feeling hopeless. For the first time in his life, he knew he was about to die, here, on this ground, on this day. There was no way around it. He did not regret it. He had put up a heroic defense, and if he were to die, there was no better way, or place. He gripped his sword and steeled himself, and his only hesitation was that Alistair should be safe.

Maybe he thought, in the next lifetime he would have more time with her.

"Well, we had a good run," came a voice.

Erec turned to see Brandt standing beside him, his hand on the hilt of his sword, also resigned. The two of them had fought countless battles together, had been outnumbered many times—and yet Erec had need never seen the expression on his friend's face that he saw now. It must have mirrored his own: it signaled that death was here.

"At least we shall go down with swords in our hands," said the Duke.

He echoed Erec's thoughts exactly.

Down below, the Empire's men, as if realizing, looked up. Thousands of them began to rally, to march in unison, heading for the cliff, weapons drawn. Hundreds of Empire archers began to kneel, and Erec knew it would only be moments until the bloodshed began. He braced himself and breathed deep.

Suddenly there came a screeching noise from somewhere in the sky, off on the horizon. Erec looked up and searched the skies, wondering if he was hearing things. Once, he had heard the cry of a dragon, and he thought perhaps it sounded like that. It had been a sound he had never forgotten, one he had heard during his training, during The Hundred. It was a cry he had never thought to hear again. It couldn't be possible. A dragon? Here in the Ring?

Erec craned his neck and, in the distance, through the parting clouds, he saw a vision that would be burned into his mind for the rest of his life: flying toward them, its great wings flapping, was a huge purple dragon with large, glowing red eyes. The sight filled Erec with dread, more so than any army could.

But as he looked closer, his expression turned to one of confusion. He thought he could see two people riding on the back of the dragon. As Erec narrowed his eyes, he recognized them. Were his eyes playing tricks on him?

There, on the back of the dragon, sat Thorgrin and behind him, gripping his waist, was King MacGil's daughter. Gwendolyn.

Before Erec could begin to process what he was seeing, the dragon dove down, plunging toward the ground like an eagle. It opened its mouth and screeched an awful sound, a sound so sharp that a boulder beside Erec began to split. The entire ground shook as the dragon plunged, opened its mouth, and breathed a fire unlike anything Erec had ever seen.

The valley filled with the shouts and cries of thousands of Empire soldiers, as wave after wave of fire engulfed them, the whole valley becoming lit with flames. Thor directed the dragon up and down the ranks of Andronicus' men, wiping out scores of them in the blink of an eye.

The remaining soldiers turned and fled, racing for the horizon. Thor hunted these down, too, directing his dragon to breathe more and more fire.

Within moments, all the men below Erec—the men he had been so sure would lead to his death, were themselves dead. There remained nothing of them but charred corpses, fire and flames, souls that once were. The entire Empire battalion was gone.

Erec looked up, mouth open in shock, and watched as the dragon rose high into the air, flapped its great wings, and flew past them. It headed north. His men erupted into a great cheer as it passed them.

Erec was speechless in admiration of Thor's heroics, his fearlessness, his control of this beast—and of the beast's power. Erec had been given a second chance at life—he and all of his men—and for the first time in a while, he was feeling optimistic. Now they could win. Even against Andronicus' million men, with a beast like that, they could actually *win*.

"Men, march!" Erec commanded.

He was determined to follow the trail of the dragon, the smell of sulfur, the blaze in the sky, wherever it led them. Thorgrin had returned, and it was time to join him.

CHAPTER EIGHT

Kendrick charged on his horse, surrounded by his men, the thousands of them massed outside Vinesia, the major city that Andronicus' battalion had retreated to. A tall, iron portcullis barred the city gates, its stone walls were thick, and thousands of Andronicus' men teemed inside and out, vastly outnumbering Kendrick's army. The element of surprise was no longer on his side.

Worse, coming into view from behind the city were thousands more of Andronicus' men, reinforcements, flooding the plains. Just when Kendrick thought they had them on the run, the situation had been quickly reversed. In fact, now the army marched towards Kendrick, orderly, disciplined, one massive wave of destruction.

The only alternative now was to retreat to Silesia, to hold it temporarily until the Empire took it once again, until they were all slaves once again. And that could never be.

Kendrick had never been one to retreat from a confrontation, even when outnumbered, and neither were any of the other brave warriors here of MacGil's army, of Silesia, of the Silver. They would all, Kendrick knew, fight with him to the death. And as he tightened his grip on the hilt of his sword, he knew that was precisely what he would have to do on this day.

The Empire men let out a battle cry, and Kendrick's men met it with a louder one of their own.

As Kendrick and his men raced down the slope to meet the oncoming army, knowing it was a battle they could not win but determined to wage it anyway, Andronicus' men picked up speed and raced towards them too. Kendrick felt the air rushing through his hair, felt the vibration of the sword hilt in his hand, and knew it was a matter of time until he found himself lost in that great clang of metal, in that great, familiar rite of swords.

Kendrick was surprised to hear something like a screech high above; he craned his neck to look up into the sky and saw something bursting through the clouds that made him look twice. He had seen it once before—Thor appearing on the back of Mycoples—yet still the sight took his breath away. Especially because this time, Gwendolyn rode on the back, too.

Kendrick's heart swelled as he watched them dive and realized what was about to happen. He grinned wide, raised his sword higher, and charged faster, realizing for the first time that victory on this day would, after all, be theirs.

*

Thor and Gwen flew on the back of Mycoples, weaving in and out of the clouds, her great wings flapping faster and faster as he urged her on. He sensed danger below for Kendrick and the others, dove down low, and broke through the clouds. Before him there opened up a bird's eye view of the landscape: amidst the rolling hills of the Ring he saw the vast expanse of Andronicus' division, racing for Kendrick's men on the open plains.

Thor urged Mycoples down.

"Dive!" he whispered.

She dove low, so close to the ground that Thor could nearly jump off, then opened her mouth and breathed fire, the heat of it nearly singing Thor. Waves and waves of fire rolled through the plains, and there came the terrified shouts of Empire men. Mycoples wreaked destruction unlike anything the men had ever seen, setting miles of the countryside alight, and thousands of Andronicus' men fell.

Whoever survived turned and fled. Thor would leave the rest of them for Kendrick to take care of.

Thor turned towards the city and saw thousands more Empire soldiers within. He knew Mycoples could not maneuver in such a confined area, with its steep, narrow walls, and that it would be too risky to set her down there. Thor saw hundreds of soldiers aiming at the sky with arrows and spears, and he feared the damage they might do to Mycoples at such short range. He didn't like it at all. He felt the Destiny Sword throbbing in his hand and knew this was a battle he would have to wage himself.

Thor directed Mycoples down to the front of the city, outside the huge iron portcullis.

As she set down, he leaned over and whispered into Mycoples' ear: "The gate. Burn it down and I will take it from there."

Mycoples sat there and squawked back at him, flapping her wings in defiance. Clearly, she wanted to stay with Thor, to fight by his side inside the city. But Thor would not give her the chance.

"This is my battle," he insisted. "And I need you to take Gwen to safety."

Mycoples seemed to concede. Suddenly, she leaned back and breathed fire on the iron gate, until finally it melted away to nothing.

Thor leaned over to Mycoples.

"Go!" he whispered to her. "Take Gwendolyn to safety."

Thor jumped off her back and as he did he felt the Destiny Sword throbbing in his hand.

"Thor!" Gwen called out.

But Thor was already racing to the melted gates. He heard Mycoples take off and knew she was taking Gwen to safety.

Thor sprinted through the open gates and into the courtyard, right into the heart of the city, into the mass of thousands of men. The Destiny Sword vibrated in Thor's hand like a living thing, bearing him as if he were lighter than air. All he had to do was hold on.

Thor felt his arm and wrist and body moving, slashing and attacking in every direction, the sword ringing through the air as it cut through men like butter, killing dozens in a single stroke. Thor spun and unleashed damage in every direction. At first, the Empire tried to attack him back; but after Thor cut through shields, through armor, through other weapons as if they were not even there, after he killed row after row of men, they realized what they were up against: a magical, unstoppable whirlwind of destruction.

The city broke into chaos. The thousands of Empire soldiers turned and tried to flee the city, to get away from Thor. But there was nowhere to go. Led by the sword, Thor was too fast, like lightning spreading through the city. The soldiers, panic-stricken, ran into the city walls, into each other, stampeding to get out.

Thor did not let them escape. He sprinted through every corner of the city, the sword bearing him with a speed unlike any he had ever known, and, as he thought of Gwendolyn, and what Andronicus had done to her, he killed soldier after soldier, exacting vengeance. It was time to rectify the wrongs that Andronicus had beset upon the Ring.

Andronicus. His father. The thought burned through him like a fire. With each sword slash, Thor imagined killing him, wiping out his ancestry. Thor wanted to be someone else, *from* someone else. He wanted a father he could be proud of. Anyone but Andronicus. And if he killed enough of these men, maybe, just maybe, he could be free of him.

Thor fought in a daze, wheeling in every direction, until finally he realized he was slashing at nothing. He looked around, and saw that every soldier, every single one of Andronicus' thousands, lay on the ground, dead. The city was filled with bodies. There was no one left to kill.

Thor stood alone in the city square, breathing hard, the Sword glowing in his hand, and not a soul stirred.

Thor heard a distant cheer; he snapped out of it, ran out the city gate and saw, in the distance, Kendrick's men, charging, pursuing the remnants of the army, pushing them back.

As Thor sprinted out the city gate, Mycoples saw him and descended, waiting for his return, Gwen still on her back. Thor mounted the dragon, and they rose once again up into the air.

They flew over Kendrick's army and Thor saw them from above, like ants below him. They cheered in victory as he flew over them. Finally they were in front of Kendrick's army, in front of the great mass of men and horses and dust. Up ahead were the scattered remnants of Andronicus' legions.

"Down," Thor whispered.

They dove and came upon the rear of Andronicus' men, and as they did Mycoples breathed fire, wiping out one row after the next, the great wall of fire going ever faster. Screams arose, and soon Thor wiped out the entire rear guard.

Finally, there was no one left to kill.

They continued flying, crossing the expansive plains, Thor wanting to be sure there was no one left. In the distance Thor saw the great mountain range, the Highlands, dividing east the East from the West. Between here and the Highlands there was not a single Empire soldier alive. Thor was satisfied.

The entire Western Kingdom of the Ring had been liberated. It had been enough killing for one day. The sun began to set, and whatever lay ahead, on the Eastern side of the Highlands, could lay there for now.

Thor circled and flew back towards Kendrick. The countryside raced below him and soon he heard the shouts and cheers of the men, looking up at the sky, cheering his name.

He set down before the army, dismounting and helping Gwendolyn down.

They were embraced by the huge group, all of them rushing forward, a great cheer of victory rising up as the soldiers pressed in from all sides. Kendrick, Godfrey, Reece and his other legion brothers, the Silver—everyone Thor had ever known and cared about rushed forward to embrace him and Gwendolyn.

They were all, finally, united. Finally, they were free.

CHAPTER NINE

Andronicus stormed through his camp and in an impulsive fit of rage, reached out with his long claws and severed the head of the young soldier who happened, to his great misfortune, to be standing nearby. As he marched, Andronicus decapitated one soldier after the next, until finally his men got the idea, and ran to stay clear of him. They should have known better than to be near him when he was in a mood like this.

Soldiers parted ways as Andronicus stormed through his camp of tens of thousands, all keeping a healthy distance. Even his generals stayed safely away, trailing behind him, knowing better than to get anywhere near him when he was this upset.

Defeat was one thing. But a defeat like this—it was unprecedented in the history of the Empire. Andronicus had never experienced defeat before. His life had been one long string of victories, each more brutal and satisfying than the next. He did not know what defeat felt like. Now he did. And he did not like it.

Andronicus ran over and over in his mind what had happened, how things had gone so wrong. Only yesterday it had seemed as if his victory was complete, as if the Ring were his. He had destroyed King's Court and had conquered Silesia; he had subjugated all the MacGils and humiliated their leader, Gwendolyn; he had tortured their greatest soldiers high up on the crosses, had already murdered Kolk, and had been about to execute Kendrick and the others. Argon had meddled in his affairs, had snatched Gwendolyn away before he could kill her, and Andronicus had been about to rectify that, to get her back and execute her, along with all the others. He had been a day away from complete victory and greatness.

And then everything had changed, so quickly, for the worse. Thor and that dragon had appeared on the horizon like a bad apparition, had descended like a cloud, and with their great flames and Destiny Sword had managed to wipe out entire divisions of men. Andronicus had witnessed it all at a safe distance; he'd had the good battle sense to retreat here, to this side of the Highlands, while his scouts continued to bring him back reports throughout the day of the damage Thor and the dragon had done. Down south, near Savaria, an entire battalion was wiped out; in King's Court and Silesia it was just as bad. Now the entire Western Kingdom of the Ring, once under his control, was liberated. It was inconceivable.

He stewed as he thought of the Destiny Sword. He had gone to such lengths to get it away from the Ring, and now it had returned here and with it, the Shield was back up. That meant he was trapped in here with the men he had; he could leave, of course, but he could not get any more reinforcements inside. He estimated he still had a half-million soldiers here, on this side of the Highlands, more than enough to outnumber the MacGils; but against Thor, the Destiny Sword and that dragon, numbers no longer mattered. Now the odds, ironically, were against *him*. It was a position he had never been in before.

As if things could not get even worse, his spies had also brought him reports of unrest back at home, in the Empire's capitol, of Romulus conniving to take his throne away from him.

Andronicus growled with rage as he stormed through his camp, debating his options, looking for someone, anyone to blame. He knew as a commander that the wisest thing to do, tactically, would be retreat and leave the Ring now, before Thor and his dragon found them, to salvage whatever forces he had left, board his ships, and sail back to the Empire in disgrace to retain his throne. After all, the Ring was but a speck in the huge expanse of the Empire, and every great commander was entitled to at least one defeat. He would still rule ninety-nine percent of the world, and he knew he should be more than satisfied with that.

But that was not the way of the Great Andronicus. Andronicus was not one to be prudent or content. He had always followed his passions, and though he knew it was risky, he was not ready to leave this place, to admit defeat, to allow the Ring to slip from his grasp. Even if he had to sacrifice his entire Empire, he would find a way to crush and dominate this place. No matter what it took.

Andronicus could not control the dragon or the Destiny Sword. But Thorgrin…that was a different matter. His son.

Andronicus stopped and sighed at the thought. How ironic: his very own son, the last remaining obstacle to his domination of the world. Somehow, it seemed fitting. Inevitable. It was always, he knew, the people closest to you that hurt you the most.

He recalled the prophecy. It had been a mistake, of course, to let his son live. His great mistake in life. But he'd had a weak spot for him, even though he knew the prophecy declared it might lead to his very own demise. He had let Thor live, and now the time had come to suffer the price.

Andronicus continued storming through the camp, trailed by his generals, until finally he reached the periphery and came across a tent smaller than the others, the one scarlet tent in a sea of black and gold. There was only one person who had the audacity to have a different color tent, the only one his men feared.

Rafi.

Andronicus' personal sorcerer, the most sinister creature he had ever encountered, Rafi had counseled Andronicus every step of the way, had protected him with his malevolent energy, had been more responsible for his rise than any other. Andronicus hated to turn to him now, to admit how much he needed him. But when he encountered an obstacle not of this world, a thing of magic, it was always Rafi who he turned to.

As Andronicus approached the tent, two evil beings, tall and thin, hidden in scarlet cloaks, glowing yellow eyes protruding from behind their hoods, stared back. They were the only creatures in this entire camp who would dare not to bow their heads in his presence.

"I summon Rafi," Andronicus declared.

The two creatures, without turning, each reached over with a single hand and pulled back the flaps of the tent.

As they did, a horrible odor came out at Andronicus, making him recoil.

There was a long wait. All the generals stopped behind Andronicus and watched in anticipation, as did the entire camp, who all turned to see. The camp grew thick with silence.

Finally, out of the scarlet tent emerged a tall and skinny creature, twice as tall as Andronicus, as skinny as a branch from an olive tree, dressed in the darkest of scarlet robes, with a face that was invisible, hidden somewhere in the blackness behind its hood.

Rafi stood there and stared back, and Andronicus was able to see only his unblinking yellow eyes looking back, embedded in his too-pale flesh.

A tense silence ensued.

Finally, Andronicus stepped forward.

"I want Thorgrin dead," Andronicus said.

After a long silence, Rafi chuckled. It was a deep, disturbing sound.

"Fathers and sons," he said. "Always the same."

Andronicus burned inside, impatient.

"Can you help?" he pressed.

Rafi stood there silently, for too long, long enough that Andronicus considered killing him. But he knew that would be frivolous. Once, in a rage, Andronicus had tried to impetuously stab him, and in mid-air, the sword had melted in his hand. The hilt had burned his hand, too; it had taken months to recover from the pain.

So Andronicus just stood there, gritting his teeth and bearing the silence.

Finally, beneath his hood, Rafi purred.

"The energies that surround the boy are very strong," Rafi said slowly. "But everyone has a weakness. He has been elevated by magic. He can be brought down by magic, too."

Andronicus, intrigued, took a step forward.

"Of what magic do you speak?"

Rafi paused.

"A kind you have never encountered," he answered. "A kind reserved only for a being like Thor. He is your issue, but he is more than that. He is more powerful even than you. If he lives to see the day."

Andronicus fumed.

"Tell me how to capture him," he demanded.

Rafi shook his head.

"That was always your weakness," he said. "You choose to capture, not to kill him."

"I will capture him first," Andronicus countered. "Then kill him. Is there a way or not?"

There came another long silence.

"There is a way to strip him of his power, yes," Rafi said. "With his precious Sword gone, and his dragon gone, he will be just like any other boy."

"Show me how," Andronicus demanded.

There was a long silence.

"For a price," Rafi finally replied.

"Anything," Andronicus said. "I'll give you anything"

There came a long, dark chuckle.

"I think one day you will come to regret that," Rafi answered. "Very, very much."

CHAPTER TEN

As Romulus marched down the meticulously paved road, made of golden bricks, leading to Volusia, the Empire capital, soldiers dressed in their finest snapped to attention. Romulus walked in front of the remainder of his army, reduced to but a few hundred soldiers, dejected and defeated from their bout with the dragons.

Romulus seethed. It was a walk of shame. His entire life he had always returned victorious, paraded as a hero; now he returned to silence, to a state of embarrassment, bringing back, instead of trophies and captives, soldiers who had been defeated.

It burned him up inside. It had been so stupid of him to go so far in pursuit of the Sword, to dare do battle with the dragons. His ego had led him on; he should have known better. He had been lucky to escape at all, much less with any of his men intact. He could still hear his men's screams, still smell their charred flesh.

His men had been disciplined and had fought bravely, marching to their deaths on his command. But after his thousands dwindled before his eyes to a few hundred, he knew when to flee. He had ordered a hasty retreat, and the remnant of his forces had slipped into the tunnels, safe from the breath of the dragons. They had stayed underground and had made it all the way back to the capital on foot.

Now here they were, marching through city gates that rose a hundred feet into the sky. As they entered this legendary city, crafted entirely of gold, thousands of Empire soldiers crisscrossed in every direction, marching in formations, lining the streets, snapping to attention as he passed. After all, with Andronicus gone, Romulus was the *de facto* leader of the Empire, and the most respected of all warriors. That is, until his loss today. Now, after their defeat, he did not know how the people would view him.

The defeat could not have come at a worse time. It was the moment when Romulus was preparing his coup, preparing to seize power and oust Andronicus. As he wound his way through the meticulous city, passing fountains, meticulously paved garden trails, servants and slaves everywhere, he marveled that instead of returning, as he had envisioned, with the Destiny Sword in hand, with more power than he'd ever had, he was instead returning in a position of weakness. Now, instead of being able to claim the power that was rightly his, he would have to apologize before the Council and hope not to lose his position.

The Grand Council. The thought of it twisted him inside. Romulus was not one to answer to anyone, much less to a council made up of citizens who had never wielded a sword. Each of the twelve provinces of the Empire sent two representatives, two dozen leaders from every corner of the Empire. Technically, they ruled the Empire; in reality, though, Andronicus ruled as he wished, and the Council did as he said.

But when Andronicus had left for the Ring, he had given the Council more authority than they'd ever had; Romulus assumed Andronicus had done this to protect himself and keep Romulus in check, to make sure he had a throne left to come back to. His move had emboldened the Council; they now acted as if they had real authority over Romulus. And Romulus had to, for the time being, suffer the indignity of having to answer to these people. They were all hand-picked cronies of Andronicus, people Andronicus had entrenched to assure his throne would never die. The Council searched for any excuse to strengthen Andronicus and weaken any threat to him—especially Romulus. And Romulus' defeat left them a perfect opening.

Romulus marched all the way to the shining capitol building, a huge, black, round building that rose high into the sky, surrounded by golden columns, with a shining golden dome. It flew the banner of the Empire, and embedded over its door was the image of a golden lion with an eagle in its mouth.

As Romulus climbed its hundred golden steps, his men waited at the base of the plaza. He walked alone, taking the steps to the capitol doors three at a time, his weapons clanking against his armor as he went.

It took a dozen servants to open the massive doors at the top of the steps, each fifty feet high, made of shining gold with black studs throughout, each embossed with the seal of the Empire. They opened them all the way, and Romulus felt the cold draft rip through, bristling the hairs on his skin as he marched into the dim interior. The huge doors slammed shut behind him, and he felt, as he always did when entering this building, as if he were being entombed.

Romulus strutted across the marble floors, his boots echoing, clenching his jaw, wanting to be done with this meeting and on to more important things. He had heard a rumor of a fantastical weapon, right before coming here, and needed to know if it was true. If so, it would change everything, shift the balance entirely in his power. If it really existed, then all of this—Andronicus, the Council—would no longer mean anything to him. In fact, the entire Empire would finally be his. Thinking of this weapon was the only thing keeping Romulus confident and assured as he marched up yet another set of steps, through another set of huge doors, and finally into the round room that held the Grand Council.

Inside this vast chamber was a black, circular table, empty in its center, with a narrow passageway for one to enter. All around it sat the Council, in twenty-four black robes, sitting sternly around the table, all old men with graying horns and scarlet eyes, dripping red from too many years of age. It was humiliating for Romulus to have to face them, to have to walk through the narrow entry into the center of the table, to be surrounded by the people whom he had to address. It was humiliating to be forced to turn every which way to address them. The entire design of this room, this table, was just another one of Andronicus' intimidation tactics.

Romulus stood there in the center of the room, in the silence, for he did not know how long, burning up. He was tempted to walk out, but he had to check himself.

"Romulus of the Octakin Legion," one of the councilmen formally announced.

Romulus turned and saw a skinny, older councilmen, with hollow cheeks and graying hair, staring back at him with scarlet eyes. This man was a crony of Andronicus, and Romulus knew he would say anything to curry Andronicus' favor.

The old man cleared his throat.

"You have returned to Volusia in defeat. In disgrace. You are bold to come here."

"You have become a reckless and hasty commander," another councilmen said.

Romulus turned to see scornful eyes staring back at him from the other side of the circle.

"You have lost thousands of our men in your fruitless search for the Sword, in your reckless confrontation with the dragons. You have failed Andronicus and the Empire. What have you to say for yourself?"

Romulus stared back, defiant.

"I apologize for nothing," he said. "Retrieving the Sword was of importance to the Empire."

Another old man leaned forward.

"But you did *not* retrieve it, did you?"

Romulus reddened. He would kill this man if he could.

"I nearly did," he finally answered.

"*Nearly* doesn't mean a thing."

"We encountered unexpected obstacles."

"Dragons?" remarked another councilman.

Romulus turned to face him.

"How foolhardy could you be?" the councilman said. "Did you really think you could win?"

Romulus cleared his throat, his anger rising.

"I did not. My goal was not to kill the dragons. It was to retrieve the Sword."

"But again, you did not."

"Even worse," another said, "you have now unleashed the dragons against us. Reports are coming in of their attacks, all throughout the Empire. You have started a war we cannot win. It is a great loss for the Empire."

Romulus stopped trying to respond; he knew it would only lead to more accusations and recriminations. After all, these were Andronicus' men, and they all had an agenda.

"It is a pity that the Great Andronicus himself is not here to chastise you," said another councilmember. "I feel sure that he would not let you live the day."

He cleared his throat and leaned back.

"But in his absence, we must await his return. For now, you will command the army to send legions of ships to reinforce the Great Andronicus in the Ring. As for you, you will be demoted, stripped of your arms and your rank. Stay in the barracks and await further orders from us."

Romulus stared, disbelieving.

"Be glad that we don't execute you on the spot. Now leave us," said another councilman.

Romulus bunched his fists, his face turning purple, and stared down each of the councilmen. He vowed to kill each and every one of them. But he forced himself to refrain, telling himself that now was not the time. He might get some satisfaction out of killing them now, but it would not yield his ultimate goal.

Romulus turned and stormed from the room, his boots echoing, walking through the door as the servants opened it then slammed it shut behind him.

Romulus marched out of the capitol building, down the hundred golden steps and to his group of waiting men. He addressed his second-in-command.

"Sir," the general said, bowing down low, "what is your command?"

Romulus stared back, thinking. Of course he could not obey the Council's orders; on the contrary, now was the time to defy them.

"It is the command of the Council that all Empire ships at sea return home to our shores at once."

The general's eyes opened wide.

"But sir, that would leave the Great Andronicus abandoned inside the Ring, with no way of returning home."

Romulus turned stared at him, his eyes going cold.

"Never question me," he replied, steel in his voice.

The general bowed his head.

"Of course, sir. Forgive me."

His commander turned and rushed off, and Romulus knew he would execute his orders. He was a faithful soldier.

Romulus smiled inwardly to himself. How foolish the Council had been to think that he would defer to them, would carry out their orders. They had vastly underestimated him. After all, they had no one to enforce his demotion, and until they got around to figuring that out, Romulus, while he had power, would execute enough commands to prevent them from gaining power over him. Andronicus was great, but Romulus was greater.

A man stood on the periphery of the plaza, wearing a glowing green robe, his hood pulled down, revealing a wide, flat yellow face with four eyes. The man had long skinny hands, fingers as long as Romulus' arm, and stood patiently. He was a Wokable. Romulus did not like to deal with this race, but in certain circumstances he was compelled—and this was one of those times.

Romulus walked over to the Wokable, feeling its creepiness from several feet away as the creature stared back with its four eyes. It reached out with one of its long fingers and touched his chest. Romulus stopped cold at the contact from the slimy finger.

"We have found what you have sent us for," the creature said. The Wokable made an odd gurgling noise in the back of its throat. "But it will cost you dearly."

"I will pay anything," Romulus said.

The creature paused, as if deciding.

"You must come alone."

Romulus thought.

"How do I know you are not lying?" Romulus asked.

The creature leaned in and came the closest it could to a smile. Romulus wished it hadn't. It revealed hundreds of sharp, small teeth in its rectangular jaw.

"You don't," it said.

Romulus looked into all of its eyes. He knew he should not trust this creature. But he had to try. The prize it dangled was too great to ignore. It was the prize Romulus had been searching for all his life: the mythical weapon that, legend had it, could lower the Shield and allow him to cross the Canyon.

The creature turned its back and began to walk away, and Romulus stood there, watching it.

Finally, he followed.

CHAPTER ELEVEN

Gwendolyn rode on the back of Mycoples, behind Thor, holding him tight, the wind rushing through her hair. It was cold, but it felt so refreshing. She was beginning to feel alive again.

In fact, Gwendolyn had never felt so happy as she did now. All felt right in the world again. She could feel her baby, kicking in her stomach, and could sense its joy at being near Thor. Gwen burned with excitement to tell Thor the news, but she was waiting for the perfect moment. And ever since they had left the Tower of Refuge, they had not had a moment to talk.

It had been a whirlwind of battle and adventure, the two of them flying on Mycoples, Gwendolyn watching in awe as the beast wiped out scores of Andronicus' men. She felt no pity for them. On the contrary, she felt satisfied, felt her desire for vengeance slowly being fulfilled. With each Empire soldier they killed, with each city and town they liberated, she felt wrongs being made right. After all the defeats, after watching her homeland destroyed, it felt good to finally be victorious.

After liberating Vinesia, Kendrick and his men began to make their way back to Silesia. Gwendolyn and Thor decided to fly back on their own and meet them there. With Mycoples, they were so much faster than the horses and had plenty of time to spare. Thor had directed Mycoples to take them on an aerial tour of the Western Kingdom. As they flew, Gwen looked down with satisfaction to see scores of Andronicus' men wiped out, lining the ground everywhere from the Highlands to the Canyon. The Western Kingdom, she was relieved to see, was completely free.

Of course, half the Empire army remained on the other side of the Highlands, but Gwendolyn was not worried about that now. Seeing the tremendous damage Thor had inflicted on this day, it was obvious to her that they could wipe out the remnant of Andronicus' men in another day. Andronicus would have no choice now but to surrender, or to go down in defeat.

For the first time in she could not remember how long, there was no longer need to worry. Now it was time to celebrate. Mycoples flapped her great wings and Gwendolyn examined her in awe, still hardly able to conceive that she was riding on the back of a dragon.

She clutched onto Thor as they took a romantic ride throughout the Ring, looking down at the mountains and valleys and rolling hills, seeing them for the first time from this perspective. They reached the Canyon and in the far distance she could spot the sparkling yellow of the Tartuvian on the horizon. They turned and flew along the Canyon's edge, and her breath was taken away viewing it from this perspective, its swirling mists aglow in the setting suns. It seemed as vast as the world.

They turned and headed for Silesia, and Gwen's heart fluttered at the thought of being reunited with all her people. Before Thor's arrival, she had been so nervous to return, to face her people. But now, she no longer felt shame; on the contrary, she felt filled with joy and even pride. Argon's words of wisdom had finally sunk in, and she finally realized that what happened to her had nothing to do with who she was, that it did not define her. Her entire life was ahead of her, and she had the power to choose whether she would let herself live happily or let her life be ruined. She had decided she was going to live. That was the best revenge. She would not let anything bring her down.

All the different colors sparkled in the mist below, and it was the most romantic ride she'd ever taken, beyond her wildest dreams. She was, most of all, overjoyed to be sharing this with Thor. She couldn't wait until they landed, until they finally had time alone together, to tell him the amazing news that she was pregnant. She sensed Thor had something to tell her, too, and couldn't help but wonder if he was going to propose to her. She smiled at the thought of it, giddy with excitement. There was nothing in the world she wanted more.

They flew over King's Court and Gwendolyn's heart dropped to see the remnant of this glorious city, its charred walls, abandoned homes, toppled fountains, and statues. But its walls, at least, still stood; they were charred and crumbling in places, but they had not all collapsed. Gwen felt determined, filled with a sense of purpose. She vowed to herself that she would rebuild King's Court. She would make it greater than it ever was, even in her father's time. It would be a shining bastion of hope, a beacon for all to see. They would see that the Ring had survived, and that it would continue to survive for centuries.

They flew ever farther north, and finally, Silesia came into view, its shining red stone rising up into the air, sparkling in the horizon. Its upper and lower cities were visible even from here, and Gwen's heart beat faster as she saw Kendrick and all the men returning from the victory, flooding through the city gates and into the huge city square.

Thor urged Mycoples on, and they dove down, landing right in the city center. As they did, a great cheer arose amongst the men, and Mycoples arched her neck and squawked with pride.

Thor dismounted, then took Gwen's hand and helped her down, and as their feet touched the ground they were met with the cheers of thousands. The thick crowd ecstatically waved their hats and chanted Thor's and Gwendolyn's names. She could see the love and devotion on all their faces as they rushed forward and embraced her from every side. She realized they were thrilled to have her back. And the feeling filled her heart. She had thought they might look at her with shame or disappointment. She had been so wrong. They still loved her as much as they always had; perhaps even more.

Gwen felt home again. This was her place, here, with these people, helping them. Not in a Tower of Refuge, isolating herself from the world. She needed to embrace the world. Argon had been right.

"My sister!" came the voice.

Gwen's heart lifted as she turned to see her youngest brother, Reece, standing before her, alive. He had made it back from his quest in the Empire. She had never expected to see him standing before her again.

He rushed forward and embraced her, and she hugged him back. He looked older, more battle-hardened, more mature.

"I'm so happy you're alive," she said.

The mood in the air was beyond festive, beyond jovial—it was elation. It was as if everyone here had been born again. She embraced her brother Godfrey, her brother Kendrick, and then one person after the next stepped up and embraced her, an endless stream of well-wishers. As she stood there beside her brothers, she could not help but think of her father and her other siblings. Here they stood, she, Kendrick, Godfrey and Reece, four out of six of them. Gareth had been lost to them all. And Luanda, as always, stayed apart, could not seem to get over her jealousy of Gwendolyn. But at least there were four of them, and she felt as close to Kendrick and Godfrey and Reece as she ever had. She felt, finally, as if they had all become a close family. It was ironic that it had to happen after their father had passed away.

The rally turned into a massive celebration, all the liberated Silesians so happy to be alive, to be out from under Andronicus' thumb. Godfrey wasted no time: he directed a group of men, with the help of Akorth and Fulton, toward hidden taverns, and soon casks of ale were rolled out into the courtyard. Shouts and cheers rose up from among all the citizens, and Gwendolyn felt herself lifted up on someone's shoulders. She was up high in the air, crying out in delight, while Thor was placed on someone's shoulders beside her. There came another great shout and cheer, as the two of them were paraded throughout the city. Musicians appeared, clanging cymbals, playing flutes and trumpets and drums, playing traditional, happy songs. People broke into dance.

Gwendolyn was lowered and Thor found her, locking arms with her and spinning her around in their traditional dance. Gwen screamed with laughter as he circled with her, first in one direction, then another, the two of them dancing amongst thousands of others, spinning wildly, linking arms, then letting go. They switched partners, and Gwen found herself linking arms with Godfrey, then Kendrick, then Reece, then Elden, then O'Connor, then Srog, then back to Thor.

They all danced and danced as the sun began to set, punctuating the air with cheers, as wineskins were passed around, with frothing mugs of ale. People drank and sang and cheered and danced some more, and to Gwen's surprise, Silesia was once again filled with the sounds of joy and laughter.

As the sky darkened, torches were lit everywhere, lighting up the night, and the dancing and celebration continued on as if the day had just begun. Gwen looked over and saw a makeshift stage being rolled over, a large wooden plank on wheels, a good ten feet high. As it reached the center of the square, her brother Godfrey jumped up on it with a shout, accompanied by Akorth and Fulton and several more of Godfrey's friends whom she recognized from the taverns. They all climbed onto the stage with mugs of ale in both hands, drinking heavily, to the shouts and cheers of thousands.

The crowd gathered around as Godfrey and Akorth and Fulton came forward and addressed them.

"I think it's time for a play, my fellow brothers and sisters, do you not?" Godfrey called out.

There came a huge shout of approval in return.

"But my Lord, what should the play be about?" Akorth bellowed in the exaggerated voice of a bad actor. Gwendolyn laughed.

"I say ... it's a play about Andronicus!" Fulton chimed in.

There came boos from the drunk and rowdy crowd.

"And who shall play him?" Godfrey called out.

"Why I am the tallest and fattest of you all, so I think the role would fall on me," Akorth answered, leaning forward and scowling down at the crowd with an exaggerated look, mocking Andronicus.

The crowd roared in delight, and Gwendolyn laughed with them. It felt so good to laugh. She felt a release of all her pent-up emotions, watching the exaggerated faces of the bad actors, all of them mocking Andronicus together. She felt safe again, felt as if she were no longer alone, as if they were all in this together. It felt so good to be alive and free again, and making fun of her worries made them all seem insubstantial.

Thor came up beside her, slipped an arm around her waist, and pulled her tight, laughing with her. She loved the feel of his hand on her stomach; it made her think of their child. As she watched the sun set against this ancient, shining red city, she wanted to freeze this moment of joy and laughter, to make it never end. Finally, all was right in the world. She only wished it would stay this way forever.

*

Reece laughed heartily as he stood there in the crowd, beside his Legion brothers, Thor, Elden, O'Connor, and Conven, and watched Godfrey and Akorth and Fulton on the stage. It had been the first time he had laughed in he did not know how long, and he could not stop laughing as he watched Akorth mimic Andronicus.

"I think I shall play McCloud!" Fulton boomed out to the audience.

They all booed, and Fulton hid his face in his hands, then pulled out a handkerchief and covered one of his eyes in an eye patch.

"Oh I forgot, I am now missing one eye!" he yelled out, mocking McCloud, and the entire crowd roared in laughter.

"The MacGils have beaten me back, so with no other hope, I'll join Andronicus!" Fulton yelled. He hurried across the stage and linked arms with Akorth, and together, they strutted across the stage, one tripping over the other, to waves of laughter.

"Then that shall make it easier to kill you both!" Godfrey yelled, rushing forward with a mock sword, and stabbing each one of them.

The crowd roared and screamed in approval as Akorth and Fulton collapsed on stage; all the other actors jumped in, pretending to stab them.

Reece laughed with the others, the ale going to his head. After all those months of travel, it felt so good to be home. After all the travails they went through in the Empire, a part of him had never expected to make it home alive, and he was still in shock. He was so used to being in a hostile environment, to being in battle-mode, that it felt great just to have a night to rest on his heels, to not have to worry about being attacked. ·

But while his friends screamed with laughter and watched the play, transfixed, Reece was distracted. Other things preoccupied his thoughts, and he broke off from the group, scanning the crowd, as he had ever since returning, looking for any sign of the woman who preoccupied his thoughts.

Selese.

Ever since he had returned to the Ring, Reece had been able to think of little else. He recalled that she lived in a small village not far from here, but he had also heard the reports and knew that all those villages had been attacked. He knew most villagers had died; yet he had also heard a few had escaped and had made it here, to Silesia, to seek refuge. He prayed she was among the survivors, that somehow she had made it, that she was here with the others, and that she still remembered him.

Most of all, he hoped she cared for him even a fraction as much as he'd cared for her.

Thoughts of Selese had sustained him throughout his quest, and he vowed that if he ever returned alive he would find her, tell her how much he cared for her. Now that he was home, he felt he had no time to waste.

Reece hurried through the crowd, searching all the faces, eager for any sign of her. But no matter how hard he looked, stumbling through rows of people, he saw no sign of her.

His heart sank as he pushed his way through the crowd of thousands, swarming about to and fro. With the sky growing darker, it was even harder to make out the faces gleaming in the dim torchlight. They all started to blur after a while.

Reece began to feel hopeless. Selese had probably not made it, he told himself. And even if she had, she would likely still not be interested in him.

The smell of food filled the air, and Reece turned to see long banquet tables being carried out in rows, heaped with all kinds of meats and cheeses and delicacies. As the servants set them out, the masses descended on them. Reece, stomach growling, ambled over, grabbed a chunk of meat, and tore into it. He had not realized how hungry he was, and as he devoured a chicken leg and a handful of potatoes, and took a long draw on his mug of ale, he felt rejuvenated.

Reece stood there, staring vacantly up at the play, not really watching and wondering what had ever become of Selese.

Suddenly, he felt a tap on his shoulder.

Reece turned around, and his heart stopped.

Standing there, a smile on her lips, clasping her hands nervously and looking up at him, unsure, was the most beautiful woman he'd ever seen.

Selese.

There she stood, looking at him with such love in her sparkling eyes, delight in her face at seeing him.

Reece, caught off guard, had to blink several times, wondering if it was real or just a figment of his imagination.

"I've been looking for you everywhere," she said. "I found your Legion brothers, and they told me I might find you at the banquet table."

"Did they?" Reece said, still staring into her smiling eyes, hardly able to speak. He wanted to tell her so many things at once, how much he loved her, how he had never stopped thinking of her.

But instead he stood there, frozen with nervousness. The words would not come out. As he stood there awkwardly, silently, she began to look unsure, as if wondering whether he were interested in even speaking with her.

"I've wanted to speak to you since you left my village," she said. "I tried to find you, and I learned you were gone."

"Yes, in the Empire," Reece said. "On a quest for the Sword. We only just came back. I did not think I would come back at all."

"I'm glad you did," she said.

He looked at her, wondering.

"Why?" he asked. "I thought, back in the village, you had said you didn't like me."

She cleared her throat and worry crossed her brow.

"I thought more about what you'd said to me. About how you love me. About how I said it was crazy."

He stared back at her, nodding.

"But the thing is, I didn't mean it," she added. "You're not crazy. Those feelings you felt, I feel them, too. You see, I didn't come to Silesia for safe harbor. I came here to find you."

Reece felt his heart soaring as he heard her words, hardly able to process them. She was saying the very same things that had been on his mind.

He raised a hand and ran it along her cheek.

"On my quest, I thought of you and nothing else," he said. "You are what sustained me."

She smiled wide, her eyes aglow.

"I prayed every day for your safe return," she said.

The music rose again, and couples broke out dancing at the sound of the harp and the lyre.

Reece smiled and held out a hand.

"Will you dance with me?" he asked.

She looked down and smiled, and lay her hand in his. It was the softest feel of his life, and his fingers felt electrified at the touch.

"There is nothing I would love more."

CHAPTER TWELVE

Luanda stood beneath the torchlight, against the stone wall on the periphery of the courtyard of Silesia, watching the festivities, and seething. There was her sister, Gwendolyn, in the center of it all, as she had always been since they were kids, adored by everyone. It was just like it had been growing up: she, Luanda, the oldest, had been passed over by their father, who had showered all his affections on his youngest daughter. Her father had treated her, Luanda, as if she'd barely existed. He had always reserved the best of everything for Gwendolyn. Especially his love.

Luanda burned as she thought of it now, as she watched Gwendolyn, the charmed one, and it brought back fresh memories. Now here they were, so many years later, their father dead, and Gwendolyn still in the center of it all, still the one who was celebrated, adored by everyone. Luanda had never been very good at making friends, had never had the charisma or personality or natural joy for life that Gwendolyn had. She did not have the kindness or graciousness either; it just wasn't natural to her.

But Luanda didn't care. In place of Gwendolyn's kindness and charm and sweetness, Luanda had outright ambition, even aggression when she needed it. She displayed all the aggressive qualities of her father, while Gwendolyn displayed all the sweet ones. Luanda did not apologize for it; in her view, that was how people got ahead. She could be blunt and direct and even mean when she had to be. She knew what she wanted and she got things done, no matter who or what got in her way. And for that, she had always assumed people would admire and respect her.

But instead, she had piled up a long list of enemies along the way—unlike Gwen, who had a million friends, who had never sought anything, and yet who somehow managed to get it all. Luanda watched one person after another cheer for Gwendolyn, hoist her up on their shoulders, watched her with Thorgrin, her perfect mate, while here she was, stuck with Bronson, a McCloud, maimed from his father's attack. It wasn't fair. Her father had treated her like chattel, had married her off to the McClouds to further his own political ambitions. She should have refused. She should have stayed here at home, and she should have been the one to inherit King's Court when her father died.

She was not prepared to give it up, to let it go. She wanted what Gwendolyn had. She wanted to be queen, here in her own home. And she would get what she wanted.

"They treat her as if she's a Queen," Luanda hissed to Bronson, standing by her side. He stood there stupidly, like a commoner, with a smile on his face and a mug of ale in his hand, and she hated him. What did he have to be so happy about?

Bronson turned to her, annoyed.

"She *is* a Queen," he said. "Why shouldn't they?"

"Put down that mug and stop celebrating," she ordered, needing to let her anger out at someone.

"Why should I?" he shot back. "We're celebrating after all. You should try it—it won't hurt you."

She glowered back at him.

"You are a stupid waste of a man," she scolded him. "Do you not even realize what this means? My little sister is now Queen. We will all now have to answer to her. Including you."

"And what's wrong with that?" he asked. "She seems nice enough."

She screamed, reached up, and shoved Bronson.

"You'll never understand," she snapped. "I, for one, am going to do something about it."

"Do what?" he asked. "What are you talking about?"

Luanda turned and began to storm off, and Bronson hurried to catch up with her.

"I don't like that look in your eye," he said. "I know that look. It never leads to anything good. Where are you going?"

She glared back at him, impatient.

"I will speak to my mother, the former Queen. She still holds a good deal of power. Of all people, she should understand. I am her firstborn, after all. The throne deserves to be mine. She will establish it for me."

She turned to go but felt a cold hand on her arm as Bronson stopped her and stared back. He was not smiling now.

"You're a fool," he said back coldly. "You are not the woman I once knew. Your ambition has changed you. Your sister has been more than gracious to us. She took us in when we fled from the McClouds, when we had nowhere to go. Do you not remember? She trusted us. Would you return the favor this way? She is a kind and wise Queen. She was chosen by your father. *Her.* Not you. You would only make a fool of yourself to meddle in the affairs of King's Court."

Luanda glowered back, about to explode.

"We are not in King's Court anymore," she hissed. "And these affairs you speak of—these are *my* affairs. I am a MacGil. The *first* MacGil." She raised a finger and jabbed him in the chest. "And don't you ever tell me what to do again."

With that, Luanda turned on her heel and hurried across the courtyard, down the steps to lower Silesia, determined to find her mother and to oust her sister once and for all.

*

Luanda stormed through the corridors of the castle in Lower Silesia, twisting and turning her way past guards until she finally reached her mother's chamber. Without knocking or acknowledging the attendants, she barged in.

The former Queen sat there, her back to Luanda, in a tall wooden chair, flanked by two attendants and Hafold, staring out a small window into the blackness of night. Through the window, Luanda could see all the torches lining lower Silesia, a thousand sparks of light, and could hear the distant cries of celebration.

"You never learned to knock, Luanda," her mother said flatly.

Luanda stopped in her tracks, surprised that her mother knew it was her.

"How did you know it was me?" Luanda asked.

Her mother shook her head, her back still to her.

"You always had a certain gait about you. Too rushed. Too impatient. Like your father."

Luanda frowned.

"I wish to speak with you in private," she said.

"That never amounts to anything good, does it?" her mother retorted.

After a long silence, finally her mother waved her hand; her two attendants and Hafold left, crossing the room and slamming the oak door behind them.

Luanda stood there in the silence and then hurried forward, walking around to the other side of her mother's chair, determined to face her.

She stood across from her and looked down and was surprised to see how much her mother had aged, had dwindled, since she'd last seen her. She was healthy again since the poisoning, yet she looked much older than she ever had. Her eyes had a deadness to them, as if a part of her had died long ago, with her husband.

"I'm happy to see you again mother," she said.

"No you're not," her mother said back, staring at her blankly, coldly. "Tell me what it is you want from me."

Luanda was irked by her, as always.

"Who is to say that I want anything from you other than to say hello and wish you well? I am your daughter after all. Your firstborn daughter."

Her mother blinked.

"You've always wanted something from me," her mother said.

Luanda clenched her jaws, steeling herself. She was wasting time.

"I want justice," Luanda finally said.

Her mother paused.

"And what form should that take?" her mother asked carefully.

Luanda stepped forward, determined.

"I want the throne. The queenship. The title and rank my sister has snatched from me. It is mine by right. I am firstborn. Not she. I was born to you and father first. It is not right. I've been passed over."

Her mother sighed, unmoved.

"You were passed over by no one. You were given first choice of marriage. You chose a McCloud. You chose to leave us, to have your own queenship elsewhere."

"My father chose McCloud for me," Luanda countered.

"Your father asked you. And you chose it," the Queen said. "You chose to be Queen in a distant land rather than to stay here with your own. If you had chosen otherwise, perhaps you would be queen now. But you are not."

Luanda reddened.

65

"But that is not *fair!*" she insisted. "I am *older* than she!"

"But your father loved her more," her mother said simply.

The words cut into her like a dagger, and Luanda's whole body went cold. Finally, she knew her mother had spoken the truth.

"And who did *you* love more, mother?" Luanda asked.

Her mother looked up at her, held her gaze for a long time, expressionless, as if summing her up.

"Neither of you, I suppose," she finally said. "You were too ambitious for your own good. And Gwendolyn…." But her mother trailed off with a puzzled expression.

Luanda shivered.

"You don't love anyone, do you?" she asked. "You never did. You're just an old, loveless woman."

Her mother smiled back.

"And you are powerless," she replied. "Or else you would not be visiting an old, loveless woman."

Luanda stepped forward, impassioned.

"I *demand* that you give me my throne! Order Gwendolyn to hand power to me!"

Her mother laughed.

"And why would I do that?" she asked. "She makes a better Queen than you ever would."

Luanda turned red and felt her whole body on fire.

"You shall regret this mother," she seethed, her voice filled with rage.

Luanda turned and stormed from the room, and the last thing she heard before she slammed the door were her mother's final words, haunting her:

"When you reach my age," she said, "you will find there are few things left in life that you do not regret."

CHAPTER THIRTEEN

Thor stood somberly beside his Legion brothers—Reece, Elden, O'Connor, and Conven, along with the dozen other Legion who survived Andronicus' invasion—all of them lined up, holding torches. Late in the night, the festivities winding down, they stood amongst a huge crowd in the city square, Gwen facing them as a heavy silence overcame the crowd. Behind him an immense funeral pyre was erected. It stood a dozen feet high and stretched a hundred feet, and on it were laid all the brave souls who had been murdered by Andronicus' men.

Among them, Thor had been pained to learn, was his former commander, Kolk, along with dozens of his Legion brothers and Silver. It weighed heavily on his heart, to think all these brave warriors had died defending the Ring while he had not made it back in time to help. If only he had found the Sword sooner, he thought, perhaps none of this would have happened.

Gwendolyn had called for this funeral service, in the midst of the celebrations, to mark and remember the dead, all those who had fallen defending the city. Thor was so proud of her, standing up there, before these thousands, all looking to her with hope, all looking to her as their leader.

She bowed her head and thousands followed suit. In the thick silence, all that could be heard were the flickering of the torches and the howling of the wind. In her somber expression, Thor could see her own suffering in her face. She could truly empathize with those in grief, and Thor knew that whatever words she was about to utter would not be empty ones.

"In the midst of our greatest joy," Gwendolyn began gravely, her voice booming out, the voice of a leader, "we must pause to honor our greatest tragedy. These brave souls gave their lives to defend our country, our city, our honor. You fought side-by-side with them. We were the lucky ones to survive. They were not."

She breathed.

"May their souls be taken by the gods, and may we make a place for each of them in our memory. They fought for a cause which we carry on. The Empire still remains within our borders and each one of us must fight to the death until we have driven out the invaders from our precious Ring for good."

"HEAR, HEAR!" screamed the crowd as one, the chant of thousands rising up to the midnight air.

She turned and held her torch high, and Thor followed with the others. They gravely approached the pyre, then each leaned forward and set their flames to the wood.

In moments the flames spread throughout the night, creating a massive fire and lighting the city square. The flames rose high in the cold night, and Thor could feel the heat even from here. He forced himself not to recoil, forced himself to stare into the fire, to remember all the brothers he had lost, to remember Kolk. He owed Kolk a great deal: he had accepted him into the Legion, even if grudgingly, and had helped train him. They'd had their differences, but Thor never wanted to see him dead. On the contrary, Thor had been looking forward to seeing Kolk's expression when he returned with the Sword in hand. It was yet another reason for vengeance.

As the fire blazed towards the heavens, Thor saw the distraught faces of his remaining Legion brothers. None were more distraught than Conven, whose faced was still etched with grief for the loss of his twin brother.

Gwendolyn rejoined Thor by his side, and as they all stood there in the silence, staring into the flames with thousands of others, Aberthol, using his cane, stepped forward and emerged from the crowd. He turned and faced them, clearing his throat against the crackling of the immense flames.

"Tonight is the Winter Solstice. From this day forward, each day grows a little lighter, a little longer. We have turned the corner, and it is no coincidence that our salvation has come on this day. It was written in the stars. We are on the road to renewal, to rebirth. We will build all that once was, once again. But we must always remember the destruction. For only from the ashes can there grow the strongest tree.

"The Ring has suffered under the weight of hundreds of years of battle," he said. "This is not the first funeral for brave warriors. Nor will it be the last. But these brave young souls here today died fending off an invasion on a scale unlike any other their forefathers had known. Their deeds shall be recorded in the Annals of the MacGils, and shall be remembered for all time."

"HEAR, HEAR!" shouted the crowd.

Aberthol paused.

"Remember that you carry a piece of them with you now," he continued. "Do not think your life is permanent. The greatest illusion we all live under is the permanence of life. You are mortal, like they. Do not hesitate to meet your enemy, to live a life of valor. Let us transform our grief. Let us take up their cause, seek justice, and transform these funeral rites into a rite of swords."

"HEAR, HEAR!" shouted the crowd.

Bells tolled, Aberthol retreated, and as he did, the crowd began to disperse. Thor and the others slowly turned and followed. Small bonfires were erected all throughout the city square, as people broke off into smaller groups, the mood of the night's festivities having turned somber as they remembered their dead at midnight.

The crowd broke off into small groups, and people huddled on the ground before their bonfires, passed around wineskins, roasted desserts, and told stories. Others fell asleep where they sat or lay, exhausted from the day of battle, from the heat of the fires, and from bellies filled with food and wine.

Thor broke off into a small group with Gwendolyn, Kendrick, Godfrey, Reece, Elden, O'Connor, and Conven. Reece was accompanied by Selese, and Elden by Indra. Thor was happy to see Reece with the girl he had not stopped talking about throughout their quest.

The group settled comfortably on the ground, around the flames of a small fire. Gwen sat next to Thor and he draped an arm around her, pulling her in close, her fur mantle soft on his palm. Krohn came up close and lay his head in Gwen's lap and Thor stroked his head and handed him another piece of meat. Krohn ate happily. Thor had forgotten how attached Krohn was to Gwen, and he did not know if Krohn was happier to see him or her.

As they all sat around the fire, a drink was passed around which Thor had never seen. Thor looked down as a cup of foaming white liquid, warm to the touch, was placed in his hands. It was welcome in the cold night.

"Koonta," Srog explained to the curious group. "The drink of the Silesians."

Thor held it in both his hands and raised it to his lips. It was spicy and warm, frothing at the top, and it tasted like vanilla mixed with rum. It was delicious, and as Thor drank, it warmed his throat and chest. It also went right to his head, and he immediately realized he'd drunk too much. Everyone around him did the same.

Thor looked up to see two of the surviving Legion members approach and stand over their group.

"Can we join you?" one of them asked.

Thor had remembered meeting these Legion members once, briefly, when he had first joined: Serna and Krog. Serna, the one who addressed them, was a tall, broad soldier, about Thor's age, with long brown hair and piercing brown eyes, wide and narrowly shaped. He looked prematurely aged, hollow circles under his eyes, and Thor knew that if he had been one of the few who had survived, he must be a good warrior indeed. The other, Krog, was several years older, short, with darker skin, a shaved head and a large hoop earring in his left ear. He wore a vest with no sleeves, even in the cold, and his muscles were visibly bulging through it. He was unsmiling, and Thor could see that he was a man who lived for war.

They both looked down at Thor with respect, and indeed, Thor noticed everyone looking at him differently since his return.

"Please do," Thor said, always one to be gracious and hospitable. He slid over and made room; they came and sat beside him.

They nodded in greeting at the other Legion in the circle, who nodded back. After so much time spent together with Reece, Elden, O'Connor, and Conven, it felt a bit odd to see their group expand, especially after the loss of Conval. But it felt good, too. After all, they were all Legion, and they all needed to stick together—especially until the Legion could be replenished with a new crop of warriors.

Serna and Krog's eyes fell to the Destiny Sword at his belt, and they looked at Thor as if he were a god.

"Is it heavy?" Serna asked.

The others all turned and looked at Thor, as all eyes fell to the Destiny Sword. It was the first time he had been asked about it, and he was not quite sure how to respond. He hadn't really thought about it that much—it had just felt natural.

Thor shook his head.

"Actually, it is lighter than my other swords," Thor replied. "It feels weightless."

"But twenty men could not wield it," Krog said. "It is heavy. It is just not heavy in *your* hands."

"That is because you are the one meant to wield it," Kendrick added.

Thor shrugged.

"I don't know why," Thor answered humbly. "It is as much a mystery to me as to anyone else."

"It is because you carry a great destiny," Aberthol said, leaning forward from across the fire, face aglow in the flames.

"What destiny is that?" Thor asked, eager to understand more.

Aberthol shook his head.

"No one knows," he said. "The Sword has been written and sung about for seven generations of MacGil Kings, but the truth is, no one really knows its origin, or what it means. All that is known is that it maintains the Shield. And that you're the only one in recorded history, of all the generations, of all the kings, to have wielded it."

The group stared at Thor in awe, and he felt self-conscious. He did not savor all the attention.

"All I have done is try to serve the Ring," Thor replied.

"And you have served it well, indeed, my friend," Kendrick said, reaching over and clasping a hand on his shoulder.

"I am not done yet," Thor said. "Not while Andronicus remains. Tomorrow, as the sun breaks, I shall fly Mycoples and wield the Sword, and battle whatever remains of Andronicus' army. I shall not give him time to regroup and escape on his ships."

"And we shall join you," Kendrick chimed in.

"We may not be as fast as you," Atme added, "or as powerful as Mycoples. But we have men, and we have swords, and we will kill whomever we can."

Thor nodded.

"Then I shall welcome your accompaniment," Thor said.

"And when it's done?" O'Connor chimed in. "What shall we do when there are no more wars left to wage?"

"Rebuild," Gwendolyn said.

They all looked to her with respect.

"King's Court will be resurrected," she added. "It will stand and shine once again."

"And Silesia," Srog chimed in.

"We shall rebuild the Legion, too," Brom said.

"I, for one, shall welcome a rest from battle," Elden said. "We have not stopped battling since we crossed the Canyon. I will return to my hometown and see if my father is alive. Maybe help rebuild his home there."

He turned to Indra, sitting beside him.

"I hope you will join me," he added.

She just shrugged.

"Domestic life is not for me," she said. "I would rather be waging battle."

Elden looked disappointed.

Kendrick turned to Sandara, who sat beside him, staring into the flames with her perfect posture, so noble. Of the Empire race, she seemed so foreign to the group.

"I hope that you shall stay with me here," Kendrick said softly to her.

She glanced over at Kendrick, then looked away.

"I do not deserve the honor, my Lord," she replied.

"You do, more than anyone," Kendrick replied. "You saved all of our lives. Stay with me, and you shall have a life fit for a queen."

"I am but a simple slave girl, indentured to Andronicus," she replied.

"Indentured no more," Kendrick corrected. "You are free now. Your home is here, within the Ring. If you choose."

She lowered her eyes.

"I have witnessed Andronicus' men wreak devastation on many peoples, many lands," she said. "I will only be free when I see him dead. Until that day, I am still a slave. I fear he will return here."

"Never," Kendrick insisted.

"You heard Thor," Reece added. "Andronicus will be crushed tomorrow."

But Sandara did not seem convinced, and a heavy silence fell over the group.

"There are others who I wish would return here," Gwendolyn said. "Steffen is missing. He helped give me safe passage to the Tower of Refuge, and I have not seen him since."

"We shall send out a party for him," Kendrick said. "We shall find him and bring him back."

"Argon, too," Gwen added. "He risked his life for me, and now he has paid the price. He is gone, and I do not know where—or if he shall ever return."

Thor thought of that, and it pained him. He missed Argon terribly, and he wanted see him, to ask about the Sword, to ask about his destiny—and most of all, to ask about his father. Thor thought he could almost hear Argon, faintly in the back of his mind, in glimpses in his dreams; yet he seemed farther away than ever. Thor wondered where he was now, if he was trapped, if he would ever come back again. He felt orphaned without him.

Gwendolyn leaned in, and Thor held her shoulder tight; he looked over into her crystal eyes, glowing in the firelight, and leaned in and kissed her. He felt alive in that kiss. As he held it, his heart pounded with anticipation. He felt the ring burning in his pocket, and more than ever, he wanted to ask her, to give it to her.

But first, he knew, he had to tell her. She had to know about the monster he hailed from. The more he thought about it, the more he began to tremble.

"You're shaking," Gwen said.

"I'm just cold," Thor lied.

She smiled, leaned in and whispered in his ear: "Then follow me."

She got up wordlessly, and Thor took her hand and allowed himself to be led into the black night, between the fires, anywhere Gwen would take him.

*

Thor and Gwendolyn entered the ancient halls of Srog's castle in Upper Silesia, guards stiffening to attention as they passed down corridors lit by torchlight. They walked hand in hand, Gwen leading them as they twisted and turned down one hall then the next, up a flight of steps, until finally an attendant opened the door to the guest chamber.

As they stepped inside, Thor looked up at the ancient arched ceilings, all stone, at the roaring fire in the huge marble fireplace, at the massive four-poster bed, at the torchlight along the walls, and he was grateful to Srog for his hospitality. They had been given a room fit for a King and Queen. Of course, Gwendolyn *was* Queen, but Thor did not feel entitled to any of this. In his mind, he was still just a boy from another small village on the periphery of the Ring.

Walking into a room like this, though, made him feel like a king. He had always envisioned bigger things for himself; but now that they were *here*, before his eyes, he could hardly believe it. This all didn't seem real. Here he was, with Gwendolyn, the Queen, wielding the Destiny Sword, with his own dragon waiting for him in the castle grounds. He had managed not just to join the Legion, but to become the head of it; he had not just earned the respect of the Silver, but had become the one they looked up to most. He had dreamed big for himself, but never that big. And now that it was all here, it was hard to process. He still expected someone to wake him up and tell him he was dreaming.

As Gwendolyn took his hand, her soft, smooth skin warm in his palm, he knew this was real; he felt as if it were the first time he had ever touched her. And as he held her, he realized his joy had nothing to do with this room or this castle or any of it—it was all about Gwendolyn's love. As surreal as everything else felt, her love, and his love for her, felt natural to him. It grounded him.

As they approached the pile of furs before the fireplace, Gwendolyn leading him with a smile, Thor found himself feeling nervous, as if it were the first time he had ever been with her. They had been apart for so long, and so much time and distance had grown between them, in a way it was like meeting her again for the first time. He felt a fluttering in his stomach, and the old fear of saying the wrong thing.

Thor thought back and remembered when he'd first met her, how tongue-tied he had been; in a strange way, a part of him was feeling that way again now. He had to admit, he was still intimidated by her beauty, by her charm, by her graciousness—by everything about her. He could not help but feel she was of a greater class than he, that she was so much greater than he would ever be.

As they lay down together, Gwen leaned in and kissed Thor, and he kissed her back. They held the kiss for a long time, the fire crackling beside them, Thor feeling the heat of it on his face. He took her into his arms, and the two of them lay side-by-side on the furs.

Gwendolyn smiled over at him, and he felt his entire world restored in that smile.

Yet Thor was still nervous, for another reason. As Gwendolyn looked into his eyes, he wondered if somehow she recognized who his father was. He blinked and looked away, self-conscious, and hoped not. He knew his thoughts were foolish, that it was impossible, yet still, it plagued him. He had to get it off his chest, to tell her. At the same time, he didn't want to ruin the moment.

Gwen looked away, and Thor sensed there was something she wanted to tell him, too. He was not quite sure what it was, but he knew her well enough to know there was something she was withholding. He could see it in the slight tremble in her lip. It made him wonder. Did she know of his father? Or was it something else?

As he studied her, he could not imagine the horrors she had endured at the hand of Andronicus. Yet here she was, still happy, smiling. He admired her more than he could say. She was stronger than him—stronger than all of them.

"What's wrong?" Gwendolyn finally asked. "You seem quiet."

Thor shook his head. He was afraid to speak, afraid to tell her. He knew he had to, but he just could not summon the courage. He was too ashamed.

"I…I…just miss you," he stammered.

It was true, he had missed her; but it was not what was on the forefront of his mind.

"I missed you, too," she smiled back. "It felt like you were away for a lifetime. You don't seem like the same boy that left. You seem more like…a man," she smiled.

Thor understood. He felt older himself. Much, much older.

"The Empire…" he began, then stopped. "It was so foreign…everything about it so different, so exotic… The things I've seen…" he trailed off.

She took his hand and brought it to her lips.

"Another time," she said softly. "There will always be wars and battles, but now is *our* time. It seems to be a very rare thing. Let us cherish it. Now is the time for us."

Thor felt his heart swell at her words. She leaned in, and they kissed again. She held him tight, and he held her back tighter, and they rolled on the furs, the lights flickering in this beautiful chamber.

He let himself go. All the worries of the world began to fade from his mind. Everything else slipped away, and he thought of nothing but Gwendolyn. Of their love. He had found a place in the world.

CHAPTER FOURTEEN

Luanda rode through the night, Bronson beside her, galloping down the dark roads leading out of Silesia and heading east, towards the Highlands. Luanda had never thought she'd find herself heading back in this direction. When she had fled the McClouds that day, she had vowed to never return, vowed to live and die the rest of her life on the MacGil side.

But things had changed, beyond what she could have foreseen. With her father dead and Gwendolyn in power, Andronicus' invasion had altered her life in a way she had never expected. There was clearly no place for her anymore on the MacGil side of the Ring, no spot for her to rule, no way for her not to have to answer to her little sister. She hadn't been born first to answer to her. It wasn't fair. If a queenship would not be given to her, then Luanda would have to take one for her own.

Luanda screamed and kicked her horse, and they raced deeper into the night, Bronson riding reluctantly at her side a few feet behind. She recalled their argument, before they had left Silesia. Bronson had always been so innocent, so gullible; ironic, considering his father was such a manipulative monster. She had needed Bronson to come along with her, so she had fed him a lie, and he had bought it. After that disastrous meeting with her mother, she had lied to Bronson, had told him that her mother had asked her to broker a truce, to be the one to approach Andronicus with an offer for surrender. That a truce would spare the lives of thousands of men and hasten Andronicus' departure. And that Luanda, being a member of the royal family yet not holding any official position, would be the perfect person to make the offer.

Bronson had looked back at her, puzzled, not knowing Luanda to be so selfless. He had bought it, and had agreed to accompany her, thinking it was for a good cause. He had suggested they take a group of soldiers to accompany them, but Luanda had refused, insisting they go alone. She could not have any MacGil soldiers around her with what she was about to do.

As they navigated their horses through the narrow mountain pass leading up the Highlands, they crested a peak and Luanda saw in the distance the lights from thousands of torches, representing what could only be Andronicus' camp. The sight gave her pause. Her plan was a desperate one, she knew, but once she formulated a plan, she stuck to it, no matter what. She would find Andronicus and cut a deal: she would deliver Thor into his lap, and in return, he would make her queen of all the Ring. It was a deal, she knew, he would not refuse.

Luanda's eyes flashed as she kicked her horse and charged down the steep mountain slope, racing down into the McCloud side of the Ring, bearing down on Andronicus' camp. Bronson, ignorant of her scheme, rode along beside her, still thinking he was going to broker a peace deal for Gwendolyn. Bronson could be useful, if she used him in the right way. She knew that when he found out he would be upset—but by then it would be too late. She would be Queen, and he would have no choice but to go along with her. At the end of the day, it didn't matter how she got there. All that mattered was that she became Queen.

As the two of them entered the Empire camp, the road narrowed and took them into the thick of the camp of soldiers. It was tense here, torchlight on either side of them, Empire soldiers staring them down. Luanda could feel the uneasiness in the air and knew this would be the trickiest part. She had to convince them to bring them to bring her to Andronicus; she had to command them with all the authority she could muster—or else risk being captured by the enemy.

"I don't know that this is a good idea," Bronson said beside her. She could hear fear in his voice as they headed deeper into the Empire camp.

"Andronicus may kill us—even if we are offering him a peace deal. Maybe we should turn back."

Luanda ignored him and rode deeper into the thick of the camp, toward the brightest glow in the center, the largest tent, which she knew could only be Andronicus'.

Suddenly, several Empire officers blocked their way, forcing their horses to a stop. She turned and saw they were barred from behind, too.

Luanda faced the officers before her, and looked down at them with her haughtiest look. After all, she was the firstborn daughter of a king, and she knew how to appear regal.

"Bring us to Andronicus," she commanded. "We bring him an offer of surrender."

Luanda phrased her words in a deliberately ambiguous way, so they would not know whose surrender was being offered—and so that Bronson would not know, either.

The Empire officers exchanged a puzzled glance with each other, then looked up at her; she could see from their expressions that her haughty, aristocratic manner was working, throwing them off guard.

They finally parted, grabbed the reins of her horses, and led them at a walk toward a huge tent. Andronicus' tent.

The officers forced Luanda and Bronson to dismount, then led them on foot. The torches burned even brighter here, the crowd grew thicker, and a banner flapped in the cold night air with an enormous emblem on it, a lion with an eagle in its mouth. Luanda's heart pounded as they approached the tent, realizing that now she was at their mercy. She prayed her scheme worked.

They were stopped a few feet away from the tent when the flap opened and out came the largest and most vicious creature on two legs Luanda had ever set eyes upon. She spotted the shrunken heads on his necklace, saw his horns, saw the menacing way he bore himself, and knew without a doubt this was the Great Andronicus.

Despite herself, as she looked up at him, she gasped.

Andronicus smiled down at both of them, as if objects of prey had landed in his lap.

Luanda swallowed, and suddenly wondered if this had been a very bad idea.

CHAPTER FIFTEEN

Thorgrin stood atop the highest knoll of the low country of the Western Kingdom of the Ring, looking out at the road, as he always had since he was a boy, waiting for the King's men to arrive. He watched the road, sparkling in the morning mist, and had a sweeping view of his hometown, sitting there, looking as it always had. Except this time, as he looked closer, he saw it was abandoned. It appeared as if he were the only one left in the world.

Thor looked back to the road, and there came a great rumbling, as there appeared a dozen horse-drawn carriages, all made of a burnished gold, glistening in the sun. They galloped his way. The sound grew louder, clouds of dust rising, and his heart beat quicker as he raced down the hill to greet them.

Thor stood in the middle of the road as the horses came to a stop just a few feet away. He stood there in the silence, staring back at all the brave warriors, their faces covered beneath their helmets, everything shining in the early morning sun. The horses stood there, breathing hard, prancing.

As Thor looked up at the soldier sitting on the lead horse, the soldier raised his visor and Thor was shocked at what he saw.

The warrior bore his features. He looked exactly like him, but younger.

Thor realized: it was his son.

"Father," the warrior said down to Thor.

Thor looked up at the boy, perhaps ten years old, but tall for his size, sitting erect, proud. He could see Gwendolyn's fair features in his face, his hair. Thor looked up at him with such pride. His son sat there, gleaming in golden armor, holding a golden halberd, looking proudly down at his father, with the bearing of a true warrior. He had Thor's same gray eyes, a strong, noble jaw, and he sat straight on his horse, as if unafraid of a thing in the world.

Thor took a step forward, awestruck.

"Tell me," Thor said, hardly able to speak, "what is your name?"

The boy opened his mouth to speak, but before he could finish, Thor blinked, and found himself standing before a lake, Gwendolyn at his side. She looked at him sweetly, leaned in, kissed him, and took his hand. She looked down at the waters below and he did, too. In their reflection, Thor was shocked to see that Gwendolyn was pregnant.

Thor turned and examined her, and her stomach was flat. But when he turned back to the water, her belly was huge. He could not understand.

Thor reached down toward the water, as if to touch the reflection, and as he did, he found himself suddenly pulled in, sucked beneath the waters.

Thor was tossed and turned, flailing in swirling rapids, gasping for air. He looked over and saw that beside him, floating downriver, was Conval, eyes wide open, a corpse, and beside Conval, Kolk. More corpses floated by, bearing the faces of everyone he'd ever known and loved.

Thor blinked, and found himself flying on the back of Mycoples. He looked below and saw Andronicus' men, spread out as far as the eye could see. He commanded Mycoples to dive but she stopped in midair, flapping her great wings, refusing to go any further. He sensed she was telling him something: that if he went any closer, he would die.

But Thor urged Mycoples on, and grudgingly, she dove down. But she dove too fast, and Thor found himself falling off her, tumbling through the air, end over end. He flailed towards the ground, towards Andronicus' men, their spears sticking straight up in the air. Thor braced himself as the spears impaled him. He shrieked.

Thor opened his eyes to find himself lying in a boat, on a bed of spears, looking up as the sky floated past him. The sea turned into a river, foaming, carrying him through crashing rapids. There was no color in this place: everything was a muted gray and brown, and he looked over and saw he had passed a small castle, though something about it was not quite right, as if it were melted or twisted in some way.

As he looked in the upper parapet, he saw a woman whom he knew to be his mother. She stood there, looking down him, arms out by her side.

"Mother!" Thor screamed, floating past her quickly. "Save me!"

"Come home, my son," she pleaded. "Your duty is done. Come home with me."

81

"Mother!" Thor screamed, reaching for her.

Thor woke sweating. He sat upright, breathing hard and looked over, disoriented.

Gwendolyn lay beside him on the pile of furs. Thor started to calm down and remember their night together. He was safe. It was all just a dream.

Thor's face was covered in sweat, despite the fact that the fire had died long ago. Krohn whined and jumped down from Gwendolyn's lap and came over and licked him. Thor closed his eyes and collected himself, wondering about the nature of dreams. It took him a while to come back to himself. It had all seemed too real.

Thor looked over and studied Gwendolyn in her sleep. Her eyes were closed and she looked angelic. He looked down at her stomach, saw that it was flat, and wondered.

He shook his head. Of course, it was just a dream, just a fanciful vision of the night. He had to teach himself not to pay so much attention to his dreams. But try as he did, he was beginning to find that it was getting harder to separate what was real from what was imagined.

Thor could not fall back asleep. His heart pounding, he gently rose from the furs.

He looked outside and could see that it was still dark out. The sky had not yet broke, and torches still flickered in the corners of the room. All was still. Surely Silesia was sleeping off the great revelries of the night.

But Thor could no longer sleep. He crossed the room, put on his robe, and walked barefoot across the cold, stone floor. As he went, Krohn followed, staying by his side. He quietly opened the great arched door and gently closed it behind him.

Thor walked down the corridor, Krohn on his heels, twisting and turning, making his way to the parapets, to clear his head and get fresh air. He passed several guards, still at attention, who stiffened as he went.

He finally turned down a narrow corridor, walked through a low doorway, and stepped out onto one of the upper balconies of the castle.

A cold gust of wind hit his face and woke him. It was refreshing, just what Thor needed. He walked forward to the thick stone railing and looked out at the city of Silesia. There was still the occasional torch flickering, but all was silent and still. Down below was a huge mess from all the food and wine that had been eaten and drunk. It looked as if a parade had swept through the city and not cleaned up.

Thor breathed deep, trying to wipe out the visions of his dreams. But their residue clung to him, like an evil fog.

"The burdens of the night," came a voice.

Thor spun, recognizing the old man's voice, and was comforted to see standing there, not far from him, Aberthol. He held a staff and looked out over the parapets, too. The scholar of MacGil kings, Gwendolyn's teacher, he was a man who meant so much to the MacGil family, and whom Thor respected greatly.

"I am sorry," Thor said. "I did not see you or I would have paid my respects."

Aberthol smiled.

"You were not looking for me. You came, surely, for another reason. Besides, men are barely seen at my age. It is the young who steal the vision."

Thor felt comforted at the sound of his voice; this man had seen it all, had been so close to King MacGil, to Gwendolyn. He had a grandfatherly tone that made Thor feel that everything would be all right, no matter what. He also reminded him of Argon somewhat, and made him miss Argon dearly. Thor resolved once again to find Argon, wherever he was, and bring him back.

"You flee from the terrors of the night," Aberthol said. "I see from the look in your eye. I know it, because I flee from them, too. I rarely sleep well. I am up most nights, poring over books, as I have been nearly my entire life. They calm me. It is my way."

He sighed.

"One day you will learn to walk the horrors of the night," he continued. "Staying awake keeps them at bay, but then again, our waking hours create them to begin with."

As Thor studied Aberthol, the ancient lines of his face, he wondered if he could be of help, be a source of answers for him for all the questions that were burning in his mind. After all, Aberthol was a scholar, and he knew the history of the Ring better than anyone.

"Can I share a secret with you?" Thor asked.

Aberthol studied him, and finally nodded.

"Many men share secrets with me," he said. "Gwendolyn's father did, and the King MacGil before him. My head is filled with bones and secrets."

Thor stood there, hesitating. On the one hand, he wasn't sure if he could trust him; but on the other, he desperately needed to talk to someone, to release the burden he carried inside.

"My father," Thor said, and paused. "I…do not descend from a great king. My father is…a monster. My father . . . is Andronicus."

Aberthol looked back for the longest time, gravely, and Thor's heart pounded as he wondered if he were being judged.

Finally, to Thor's surprise, Aberthol nodded and replied: "I know."

Thor was shocked; he stared back, dumbfounded.

"You *know*? How? Why didn't you tell me?"

"It wasn't for me to tell," Aberthol replied. "It was for you to find out, when the time was right. Your lineage is common knowledge among certain of the Ring's elite, among those few of us old enough to know what really happened in the early days."

"But you've never told anyone?" Thor asked, shocked.

Aberthol smiled.

"Like I said, secrets stay locked with me."

"But is it possible?" Thor pressed. "Maybe it is a mistake. Maybe he is not really my father."

Aberthol slowly shook his head.

"If it gives you solace to think that, then do. We all live with our fantasies, with our dreams that sustain us. But if it is the truth you want, then you must know that Andronicus is indeed your father."

Thor felt himself grow cold.

"How is that possible?" Thor repeated. "I wield the Destiny Sword. Legend has it that only a MacGil can wield it. Is the legend false?"

Aberthol shook his head.

"It is true. Your father is indeed a MacGil. And you are indeed a MacGil."

Thor's eyes opened wide, confused.

"Andronicus?" he asked. "A MacGil?"

Aberthol sighed.

"He is. As much of a MacGil as any of the others. In the beginning, at least. You see, Andronicus was not always the monster that he is now. He was once, simply, the eldest brother of the King MacGil you knew and loved."

Thor was breathless; his mind reeled.

"I did not know that King MacGil had an older brother," he said.

Aberthol nodded.

"King MacGil had two brothers. Andronicus, the eldest, and Tirus, the youngest. These three brothers were as close as three brothers could be. Andronicus was of a fair and good nature and virtue. One of the bravest and noblest members of the Silver."

Thor could hardly believe it.

"The Silver? Andronicus? How is it possible?"

Aberthol shook his head.

"The day of the Great Divide. That story is long, and for another time. Suffice it to say that there is within all of us a very fine line between the good and the dark. This line becomes even finer when you reach supreme power. Andronicus wanted power, more power than he was entitled to. He made a choice. A pact. He succumbed to dark forces. He abandoned the Ring. He gained great power in the Empire, and he became someone else. *Something* else. Over time, he has changed to become what he is now, unrecognizable to the man he once was."

Aberthol stepped forward.

"You must understand," he said compassionately, "your father, the *true* Andronicus, he was a good man. A MacGil. He was of a good nature. *That* is your true father—not the man he became. There is a propensity to change in all of us. Some of us fight it better than others. He was not strong enough; he gave into it. But that doesn't mean you will. You can be stronger than your father."

Thor stood there, his mind reeling, trying to process at all. It all made him feel sick to his stomach. It also made him realize that he and Gwendolyn were cousins; it made him realize that he was cousins, too, to Reece and Kendrick and Godfrey. Perhaps that was why they had felt so close. He wondered if they knew.

"Does anyone else know?" Thor asked tentatively.

Aberthol shook his head.

"Nobody," he said. "The ones who did have all died. Except the former queen and myself. And now, of course, you."

"I hate him," Thor said, seething. "I hate my father. I don't care who he was; I care only for who he is now. I want to kill him. I *will* kill him."

Aberthol laid a hand on Thor's shoulder.

"Whether you kill him or not, it will not change who *you* are. You must choose to rise above all of these feelings. You must choose to focus on what is positive. After all, your lineage has two strains, of course. Your mother's blood runs deep in you, and in your case, that is more important than your father's. You just have to see that, and to embrace it."

Thor studied Aberthol.

"Do you know who my mother is?" he asked, nervously.

Aberthol nodded back.

"It is not for me to say. But when you meet her, you will understand. As powerful as Andronicus is, she is far more powerful. And your fate and destiny is linked with hers. Indeed, the entire fate of our Ring is linked to hers. The power of the Destiny Sword is nothing next to the power she can impart to you. You must find her. And you must not delay any further."

"I would love to meet her," Thor said, "but I must destroy Andronicus first."

"You will never destroy Andronicus," he said. "He lives within you. But you can find your mother, and save yourself. Until you meet her, you will never be complete."

Aberthol suddenly turned and strutted away, walking off the parapets, his cane echoing as he went.

Thor turned and looked out at the blackness of Silesia. In the distance, he could hear the howling winds of the Canyon. Somewhere out there, somewhere in the beyond, lay his father. And his mother. Thor needed to see them both.

His mother, to embrace.

And his father, to kill.

CHAPTER SIXTEEN

Luanda stood inside Andronicus' tent, alone, trembling inside and trying not to show it. She had never been before a man so physically large and imposing, and who exuded such a sinister feeling. She glanced about his tent and saw all the spikes protruding along its edge, each crowned with a severed head, each with eyes open, frozen in a death mask of agony.

Andronicus purred from somewhere deep in his chest and smiled down at her, clearly feeling at home.

She cleared her throat and tried to remember why she had come, tried to muster the courage to speak.

"I've come to make you an offer," she finally managed to say, trying her best to stand proud, to make her voice sound confident. But despite herself, she could hear the tremor in her own voice and hoped she did not give away her fear.

"*You*, make *me* an offer?" he asked.

He threw his head back and laughed, and the grating sound set her hairs on edge. It was the laugh of a monster, deep and hollow and filled with cruelty.

Luanda was caught off guard; she had expected to find Andronicus a broken and humbled man, prepared to either flee the Ring or surrender. She had not expected to find him so confident. He seemed more than unafraid—he seemed certain of victory. She could not understand it.

"Yes," she said, clearing her throat, "an offer. I can deliver your enemy to you, Thorgrin. In return, you will name me Queen of the Ring, and put me in control of all that is."

Andronicus smiled wide, surveying her.

"Will I?" he asked.

He stared her up and down, and there came a dark and growling noise from deep within his chest.

"You would betray your own people, then?" he asked. "Sell them all for the right to rule?"

He paused, staring right through her; his eyes twinkled, as if perhaps he approved of her.

"I like you," he said. "You are a girl after my own heart."

"I am the best chance you have," she said defiantly, mustering her old confidence. "You are surrounded. And with his dragon and his Destiny Sword, Thor is decimating your armies. If you reject my offer, then by tomorrow Thor will have wiped out all your men. If you accept it, then by tomorrow, Thor will be in your custody."

He examined her.

"And just how do you propose to deliver Thorgrin to me?" he asked.

She had been expecting this question, and she breathed deep, prepared.

"They trust me," she replied. "I am a MacGil. I am family. I will send them a message telling them I have brokered a truce. That you have agreed to surrender. That Thorgrin must come alone to accept your surrender. When he does, you can capture him."

Andronicus surveyed her.

"And why would they trust a traitor like you?" Andronicus asked.

She reddened, insulted by his words.

"They will trust me, because I'm family. And I am *not* a traitor. The Ring is mine by right. I am firstborn."

Andronicus shook his head.

"Family, most of all, are least to be trusted."

She bunched her fists, defiant, feeling her plan slipping away.

"They will trust me," she said, "because they have no reason not to. And because they are a trusting people. And most of all, because it makes sense: they, of course, believe you will surrender. Who would think otherwise? You are completely surrounded. Half your men have been wiped out. Your surrender would be expected. My message should come as no surprise to them."

"And when Thor arrives here," he said, "just how do you propose I capture him? He who, as you say, has wiped out half my men?"

Luanda shrugged.

"That is not my problem. I will deliver the lamb to slaughter. I am sure you have your own ways of treachery."

Andronicus looked her up and down, and as he did, she felt her heart pounding. Luanda wanted to be queen so bad she could taste it. Even more, she wanted to one-up her little sister; there was a small part of her that felt bad—but there was a much bigger part of her that felt entitled, that felt bad for herself. She could not imagine living in a kingdom where her little sister ruled over her, and if that meant selling out her own people, so be it. After all, they didn't deserve it after what they had done to her.

Luanda shivered as Andronicus stepped closer, reached out and lay his long claws on her shoulder. She felt his slimy palms run over her bare skin, run up and down her throat.

"King MacGil should be proud of his issue," he said. "Yes, very proud indeed."

He sighed.

"I will accept your offer. And you will have your queenship."

Luanda's heart was pounding so fast, it was all a blur as she was ushered out of the tent, two guards coming up behind her and herding her out. The next thing she knew she was back outside, in the cold night, Bronson coming up beside her as they walked quickly away, back through the camp and towards their horses.

"What happened!?" Bronson asked impatiently.

Luanda walked quickly, her heart thumping, trying to gather her thoughts—and trying to figure out how best to word it to Bronson. She knew she had to say the right things if she were going to manipulate Bronson successfully.

"It went very well," she said, choosing her words carefully. "Andronicus has agreed to surrender."

Bronson looked at her, puzzled.

"I have a hard time believing that," he replied. "He agreed to surrender? As easily as that?"

Luanda wheeled on Bronson and put on her fiercest face and voice, desperate to convince him.

"Andronicus is outnumbered," she said coldly. "In another day he will be dead. He was grateful for the chance. I was right. You were wrong. He has conditions: his army must be allowed to leave the Ring unharmed. He will forfeit himself as a prisoner. And he will surrender only to Thor, and to Thor alone. He has asked us to bring our offer to Thor at once, before the attack at dawn. This is our chance to make peace, to save lives, and to oust his men once and for all."

Bronson stared back at her, and she could see his mind working, see him thinking it through. He was smart, but not nearly as smart as her, and his gullible streak worked in her favor.

"Well," he said, "I guess that sounds like a fair offer. All he's asking for is for his men to leave safely. As you say, it will spare a lot of lives on both sides, and liberate the Ring. It sounds reasonable. I can't imagine that Thor and Gwendolyn would not want to agree to this. You have done well to serve the Ring as you have. What you have done here is selfless. You have saved many lives, and your family will be proud. You were right, and I was wrong."

Inside, Luanda smiled. She had deceived him.

"Go then," she urged. "Be our messenger. Deliver the message to Thor and the others. I will await you here. Ride throughout the night and don't stop until you deliver them the good news. The fate of the Ring now rests on your shoulders."

She waited, hopeful. She knew, being the chivalrous fool that he was, that if she appealed to his sense of honor and duty, he would be blind to reason.

Bronson nodded solemnly, mounted his horse, and took off at a gallop, racing through the night.

She watched his horse disappear into the blackness, and she smiled openly at the night.

Finally, she would be Queen.

CHAPTER SEVENTEEN

Steffen felt his palms go raw as he stood before the huge mill, pushing on the wooden crank with all the other laborers. It was backbreaking labor, what he was used to, and it made him blot out the worries of the world. He had been given just enough grain and water to get by, sleeping on the floor like an animal with all the other indentured servants. It was not a life: it was an existence. The rest of his life, as it had been once before, would be filled with labor and pain and monotony.

But Steffen no longer cared. This was the sort of life he had led in King's Castle, working for King MacGil in the basement, tending the fires. That had been a harsh life, too, and really an extension of his entire life, of his home life, of his parents, who had been so ashamed of him because of how he looked, who had beat him and kicked him out of the house. His entire life had been one long bout of pain and bullying and scorn.

Until he had met Gwendolyn. She had been the only person he had ever known who had looked at him as something other than a deformed creature; who had actually had faith in him, who had actually cared for him. The time he had spent protecting her he valued as the most meaningful days of his life. For the first time, it had lent his life purpose and meaning; it had made him dream, for a brief moment, that maybe he could be something more than an object of loathing, that maybe everyone in his life had been wrong, and that he did have some value after all.

When Gwen had entered the Tower of Refuge and that door had slammed shut behind her, he felt as if a door had been closed on his own life. It had sunk a dagger into his heart. He respected, and even understood, her decision; but it had been the worst day of his life. He had stood there and waited outside the Tower for he did not know how long, hoping beyond hope that Gwen might change her mind, might come back out those doors. But they had remained closed, like a coffin on his heart.

With no direction or purpose left in his life, Steffen had wandered and had come here, to this small village high on this hilltop, and he checked over his shoulder once again, as he did every hour since his arrival, at the Tower of Refuge, keeping it in sight at all times, hoping beyond all expectation that he might see Gwendolyn walk out those doors, that he might have a chance to take up his old life again.

But watch as he did, there was no activity at the tower, no one in or out, day and night.

Steffen suddenly heard the crack of a whip and felt a sharp shooting pain across his back; he realized he had been whipped again by his boss. The sting of the whip snapped him out of his thoughts and made him focus on his duty before him. He looked around and saw he had cranked out more grain than any of the other servants, and his face reddened: it was unfair that he was being whipped, while the others were passed over.

"Work harder, you creature, or I'll throw you to the dogs!" the man barked at Steffen.

There came the rise of laughter all around him, as the other laborers turned and mocked him, mimicking his bent figure. Steffen looked away, forcing himself to stay calm. He had received much worse than these provincial villagers could dole out, and at least the pain and humiliation kept his mind off Gwendolyn, off of dreaming of a life that was too big for him.

Bells tolled, ringing loudly in the small town, and all the workers stopped, turned and looked. The bells tolled again and again, urgently, and villagers began to crowd around the town center, looking up at the bell keeper.

"News from the North!" the man yelled out. "The Empire has been driven from the Western Kingdom of the Ring! We are free again!"

A great cheer rose up among the villagers; they turned and grabbed each other and danced. They passed around wineskins and drank long and hard.

Steffen watched it all, shocked. The Empire driven out? The Western Kingdom free? It didn't make sense. When he had left Silesia it had all been in ruins, all his people enslaved. There had seemed to be no hope for any of them.

"Thorgrin has returned, a dragon with him, and the Destiny Sword! The Shield is up! The Shield is restored!" the bell keeper announced.

There came another shout and cheer, and Steffen's heart lifted with cautious optimism, as his thoughts turned back to Gwendolyn. Thor was back. That meant she would now have a reason to leave the Tower. A reason to return to Silesia. There might be a role for him once again.

Steffen turned and looked at the tower and saw no activity. He wondered. Had she somehow left?

"I saw him fly this way, the other day, the boy on the dragon, holding the Sword. I'm telling you!" one villager, a youth, insisted to another. "I saw him fly to that cursed tower. He landed on its roof!"

"You were seeing things!" an old, stern woman said. "Your imagination got the best of you!"

"I swear that I wasn't!"

"You've been dreaming too much, lad!" mocked an old man.

There came laughter, as all the others mocked the boy; he reddened and slinked away.

But as Steffen heard his words, they made perfect sense to him: Thor's first stop *would* be Gwendolyn. He loved her, and she mattered to him most. That was what these simple villagers could never understand. Steffen knew the words to be true, and his heart swelled with a sudden optimism. Of course, if he'd returned, the first place Thor would go would be to the Tower of Refuge, to see Gwendolyn—and to take her away. Likely, back to Silesia.

Steffen smiled for the first time since he had arrived here. Gwendolyn was free of that place. He smiled wider, realizing his life was about to change again. He no longer needed to be in this village, and he no longer needed these people. He no longer needed to seclude himself, to resign himself to a life of pain and labor and misery. He had a chance at life again; his fleeting dream was coming back. Maybe, after all, he was meant for a noble life.

"I said get back to work, you imp!" screamed the taskmaster, as he raised his whip high and aimed it for Steffen's face.

This time, Steffen lunged forward, drew his sword and slashed the whip in half before it reached him. He then reached out, snatched the remnant of the whip from the taskmaster's hand, and slashed the taskmaster himself across the face.

The taskmaster screamed, clutching his face with both hands, shouting and yelling at the pain.

Other villagers took notice and suddenly charged Steffen from every direction. But Steffen was a warrior with skills beyond what these provincial men would ever know, and he used the whip to lash them all, spinning and ducking and weaving from their blows; in moments, they were all on the ground, crying out in pain from the lashes.

Yet more men came charging, more serious men, with more serious weapons, and Steffen knew he had to get more serious as well; before they could get any closer, Steffen reached back, notched an arrow and raised his bow, aiming it at the lead man, a fat fellow wearing a shirt too small.

As he raised it up high, the fat man, wielding a club, suddenly stopped in his tracks, along with the men beside him.

A crowd gathered, everyone keeping a cautious distance from Steffen.

"Anyone comes closer to me in this dung-eating town," Steffen called out, "and I will kill you all. I will not warn you twice."

From the crowd there emerged three burly men, wielding swords and charging for Steffen. Without blinking, Steffen took aim and fired off three arrows, and pierced each man through the heart. They each fell to the ground, dead.

The town gasped.

Steffen notched another arrow and stood there at the ready, waiting.

"Anyone else?" he asked.

This time the villagers stood frozen, all with a new respect for Steffen. No one dared move an inch.

Steffen reached down, grabbed his sack of grain and of water, slung them over his shoulder and turned his back on them, taking the road out of the village and heading for the forest. He was on edge, listening carefully, waiting to see if anyone pursued him—but not a sound could be heard in that place.

Not a single person dared insult him now.

CHAPTER EIGHTEEN

Romulus strutted down the forest trail, following the Wokable, which walked with a strange gait in its glowing green robe, prancing through the forest so quickly that it was hard to follow. If there was anything Romulus distrusted more than this Wokable, it was this place, Charred Wood, which he had always avoided at all costs, given its reputation. The trees here grew short and fat, the gnarled branches spreading over the trails in every direction, and they were alive in ways that other trees weren't. They were rumored to have swallowed men whole. As Romulus looked over warily, he saw small sets of teeth embedded in some of the trunks, opening and closing lazily.

He quickened his pace.

Charred Wood was a place of darkness and gloom, and as they went it grew thicker, the wood growing dense in a thicket of tangled branches and thorns. It was a place permeated by fog and filled with all things evil, a place you came when you wanted just the right poison to assassinate someone, or needed just the right potion to place a curse.

Now Romulus needed this place, as much as he had hoped to avoid it. He had relied his whole life on strength, on his battle skills; yet what he needed now was not strength alone. He was battling in a new realm, a realm of politics and subtle treachery, a realm in which the sword alone could not slay your opponent. He needed a weapon greater than a sword. He needed an edge over all of them. And the key lay deep inside this twisted forest.

For years, Romulus had embarked on his own secret mission, on a hunt for the legendary weapon rumored to hold the power to lower the Shield. Of course, keeping the Destiny Sword in the Empire would have been the simplest option; but with that gone now, Romulus had to turn once again to the weapon. For years he had been chasing wild rumors of its existence, following trails here and there only to discover another false lead.

This time, it felt different. This time, the lead had come after the torture and assassination of a long string of people, until the trail had finally led to this Wokable. It could not have come at a better time; if Romulus did not find it, the Grand Council—or Andronicus—would kill him. But if he truly held the weapon to lower the Shield, he would be invincible. The others would rally around him, and there would be nothing left to stop him from ruling the Empire.

They twisted and turned down yet another trail, through a tangle of thorns, the fog growing thick. The Wokable put on gloves, several feet long, to shield his long fingers from the thorns. Romulus, though, tore them from his way with his bare hands. He felt the thorns piercing his skin, drawing blood, but he did not care; he actually enjoyed the pain.

They cut through the thorn bushes and carved a path deeper into the forest, and just as Romulus was starting to wonder if this Wokable was leading him astray, finally, the path opened up into a small circular clearing.

There sat a small, circular grass knoll, perhaps ten feet high, a mound of earth really. In its center was a low, arched door, covered in grass, almost imperceptible. There were no windows and was no other entryway. It looked like a dome of earth.

Romulus paused, sensing the evil behind that door.

The Wokable turned and looked at him, with its flat, yellow face and four eyes, making an odd purring noise of satisfaction that set Romulus on edge. It smiled, baring its hundreds of tiny, sharp teeth.

"Your precious weapon lies within that knoll."

Romulus stepped forward to go to it, but the Wokable reached out with its long, bony fingers and laid them on his chest, stopping him. It was surprisingly strong.

"You must wait until you are summoned."

Romulus sneered. He was not one to wait for anyone.

"And if I don't?" Romulus demanded.

The Wokable opened its mouth again and again, flashing its rows of teeth, expressing displeasure.

"Then your endeavor will be cursed."

Romulus glowered. He was not one to cower to signs and omens; he went whenever and however he wanted, on his own terms.

Romulus strutted across the clearing, grabbed the small door and yanked it open with such strength that he tore it off its hinges. He stepped fearlessly into the blackness of the hollowed-out grassy knoll, ducking as he went.

The inside was dark, an evil residue hanging in the air, clinging to his skin. The place was lit by a small candle, flickering at the far end, and it took a moment for his eyes to adjust.

As he walked into the center, he spotted a small, circular table. Seated before it was an old man, bald, long strands of white hair dangling down the sides of his head, wearing a green velvet cloak, the collar pulled high. His back was to him and he hummed a strange tune.

Romulus waited, unsure what to make of it all. He hoped this wasn't another dead end, as he saw no weapon in this place.

"I have no time to waste," Romulus said. "Give me what I have come for."

There came a long silence.

"You come before I summon you," the old man said, his ancient voice raspy.

Romulus sneered.

"I wait for no one," he said.

"That will be your downfall," the man said.

Romulus glowered.

"Give me what I came for. If not, you will suffer the wrath of the great Romulus."

There came a low chuckle, like a rumble, and Romulus felt he was being mocked.

In a rage, Romulus rushed forward, knocked over the table, came around and confronted the old man. He drew his sword and stabbed him, but he looked down and saw the sword was only going through air, harmless.

He looked at the man's face and he stood back, aghast. The man's cheeks were long and bony, his face drawn, and in place of eyes were two empty sockets.

The old man smiled, his face crinkling into a million lines, and Romulus, despite himself, shivered.

"You look death in the face," the old man said. "How does it look?"

Romulus stood there, speechless. Finally, he gathered enough courage to say: "I come for the weapon. The weapon that will lower the Shield."

The old man smiled.

"It can only be wielded by the worthy. Are you worthy?"

"I am second only to Andronicus in the entire Empire. I am the Great Romulus."

"Yes…" the man said slowly. "For now, anyway. Soon, you will be first."

Romulus' heart soared at the words.

"Tell me more," he demanded.

"Your fate has yet to be determined. The weapon may change it. But the price will be great."

"I will pay your price," Romulus said hastily. "Give it to me!"

The man rose and walked past Romulus, crossing the room to the far wall as he reached into the blackness. Romulus's heart pounded as he waited in anticipation to see what the weapon could be. Was it a sword? A javelin? Some other weapon?

Romulus was confused as the man returned holding a simple, black velvet cloak. He held it up, and lay it in Romulus' hands.

"What is this?" Romulus asked, annoyed.

"Your sacred weapon," came the reply.

Romulus looked at it, confused, wondering if he were being mocked.

"This is no weapon," he said. "It is a cloak."

"Not all weapons have blades," the old man said. "This weapon is more powerful than any you have ever known."

"I will try it on," Romulus said, preparing to wear it.

The old man reached out and grabbed his arm. Romulus was surprised by the strength of his grip, his bony hand so strong he could not even free himself of it. He realized this encounter was magical, of a strength he did not understand, and for the first time in his life, he felt afraid.

"Put that cloak on now, and you will die," the old man said.

Romulus examined it in wonder.

"Wear it only when you cross the bridge to the Canyon. It will make you invisible and allow you to penetrate the Shield, to enter the Ring. You must cross by yourself. In order to destroy the Shield for good, you will need to bring a MacGil with you back across the Canyon, while wearing the cloak. When a MacGil sets foot on land outside the Canyon, together with you, wearing this cloak, then the Shield will come down for good."

Romulus surveyed the cloak in awe. He sensed it was the truth.

Finally, after all these years, he held in his hand the key to bringing down the Shield, to taking the Ring. There was no obstacle left in his path. Finally, power would be his.

CHAPTER NINETEEN

Thor sat on the upper parapets of the castle, the Destiny Sword in his lap, twisting and turning it, examining it in the early morning light. The Sword sparkled, illuminated in all different colors, long and smooth, nearly translucent, made of a metal he could not understand. The hilt, solid gold, felt like butter in his palm, making his hand mold to it completely, as if he had always held it, as if he and the Sword were one. Along the edge of the hilt were embedded small rubies, and the blade was engraved with an ancient inscription he did not understand.

As he studied it, Thor wondered. The Sword felt positively ancient, and he wondered who had forged it, who had wielded it in the past, how it had gotten here. He wondered about its history. He wondered about its future. He wondered about his own future. He reflected on all they had gone through to get the Sword, on their quest, crossing the Canyon, crossing the Tartuvian, the hostile Empire, its jungles and deserts and mountains and slave cities and dragons…

All for this. This blade, this piece of metal that he held in his hand. He thought of the lives lost, and saw the faces of his friends, floating in the water. He thought of all the dead in the Ring, of Andronicus' invasion…all for this Sword. What was it about this singular weapon?

Thor thought of all the Empire warriors he had killed with it since his return. As he had wielded it, it had felt more like it had been wielding him. He did not understand it. And Thor feared things he did not understand.

Most of all, he contemplated Aberthol's ominous words, which rang in his head, which had kept him up all night, which had drawn him back up here, to these parapets, before dawn, to find solace, time to reflect: the legend that the wielding of the Sword would be short-lived.

Did that mean he would be defeated? That he would die soon? Without the Sword, who would he be? What would become of the Shield? Of the Ring?

Thor knew he had powers in his own right. Yet none of his powers matched those of the Sword. Already, he felt one and the same with it. He felt invincible now. What could possibly bring him down?

Thor felt the ring in his pocket, determined to propose to Gwendolyn as soon as she woke. First, though, he needed to tell her. The time had come. Before he embarked on a mission to kill his father, Gwendolyn must know who he was.

How would she react? Badly, he feared. Would that mean the end of their relationship?

Thor looked up at the breaking light of dawn, the Sword glistening, making his grey eyes sparkle, and he thought of the day's battle ahead. Today was the day he would destroy the remainder of Andronicus' army—and Andronicus himself. His own father. He did not know how he felt about that. He wanted him dead, more than anything in the world. But he also, he had to admit, wanted a father in this world. A part of him felt conflicted about murdering his own father. Why was this destiny thrust upon him?

Thor knew that when the time came, he would not hesitate. He would kill him. But he wished it could be otherwise, wished he could have a different sort of father. He wished he had a father he could meet for the first time in a fatherly embrace—not in an act of violence.

"There you are," came a voice.

Thor wheeled to see Gwendolyn standing at the entrance to the parapets, smiling, sleepy, her hair tousled, Krohn by her side, looking at him with love. Gwen approached and Krohn hurried over and jumped on him, licking him.

Thor smiled, re-sheathed the Sword, walked over, and met Gwendolyn in an embrace, happy to have this welcome distraction from his dark thoughts.

"Dawn breaks," she said, "and all our men await you down below, in the Great Hall. It is a big day of battle and they want to convene with you before you begin your attack."

Thor nodded. He had expected as much, and he turned and walked with Gwendolyn.

The two of them left the parapets, re-entered the castle and marched down the halls, Krohn beside them. They held hands silently

101

as they walked, Thor's heart thumping in his chest, with so many things he wanted to tell her. He needed to tell her that he wanted to be with her forever. That he wanted her to have his mother's ring. And who his true father was.

But his heart pounded more and more, and he found himself unable to say any of these things. Their time was too rushed.

Finally, as they descended a flights of steps and turned a corridor, Thor mustered the courage. It was now or never.

"Gwendolyn, there is something I must tell you," he said, his voice shaking.

She looked at him with a worried glance.

He opened his mouth to speak, and as he was about to utter the words, suddenly, two huge doors opened. Thor and Gwendolyn turned and saw before them the Great Hall, a huge chamber, a hundred feet wide and high, lined with the arms and banners of all the great warriors. In its center sat a long, rectangular table, and around this, there sat and stood hundreds of warriors. All of them looked to Thor expectantly.

Thor paused at the door, as Gwendolyn looked at him, waiting.

Now, he knew, was not the right time.

"We shall talk afterwards," he said.

He turned and took her hand, and the two of them entered the hall together. As they did, the men stood and banged the hilts of their swords on the table, a cacophony of noise, and a sign of respect.

"Thorgrinson!" they chanted.

As Thor approached, finally they quieted down. He was embraced by Kendrick, Srog, Godfrey, Reece, Elden, O'Connor, and Conven, along with several other brave warriors. The new Legion members were there too, Serna and Krog, as well as dozens of members of the Silver and of MacGil's army. It was a large and formidable force.

"Thorgrinson," Srog said as the crowd quieted. "Silesia's soldiers await your disposal. And thousands more await us outside this hall."

"And all of the Silver, and all of MacGil's army," Kendrick added. "You are the army's leader now."

Thor shook his head, as he clasped Kendrick's shoulder.

"You are their leader," he said. "I am but a simple boy with a dragon and a sword, and I shall do whatever I can in service to the Ring."

Kendrick smiled.

"We will accompany you, when you attack Andronicus," Kendrick said, "we will ride alongside, on the ground below you. You will be faster, with your dragon, but we will ride hard, and will not be far behind. As you have Andronicus' men on the run, we will pursue on the ground, and finish off whatever men you cannot kill. As powerful as you are, even with your dragon and your sword, there are too many places—caves and nooks and crannies—where Andronicus' men can hide."

Thor nodded.

"I shall be honored to have you join me in battle. You are right: even with all the might in the world, I cannot do it alone. And I can think of no greater honor than to fight alongside this army."

"After today," Srog said, "Andronicus and his men will be no more. At the end of this day's battle, the Ring will be free and the Empire driven back to the sea!"

"HEAR, HEAR!" came the huge shout of approval from the knights in the room.

Thor surveyed their faces, all battle-hardened men, men he had grown up hearing of and respecting, and he felt honored to be in their presence.

Thor was about to respond when, suddenly, the doors to the room burst open, and in rushed a man Thor dimly recognized. All heads turned as he strutted into the room, out of breath, marching right up to the table.

It was Bronson. Luanda's husband.

"Forgive me, great soldiers, for intruding," Bronson announced, gasping, trying to catch his breath. He stood there, wearing an eye patch.

"I come carrying great news," Bronson said. "Urgent news. News that will affect this day's events. I've ridden all the way from the far side of the Highlands. I was sent here by Luanda. She has spoken to Andronicus, and he has offered his surrender!"

A surprised murmur broke out amongst the room, as the knights turned and murmured amongst themselves.

103

"Of course he wants to surrender," one shouted. "He's outnumbered! And a day from death!"

"I don't believe Andronicus would ever surrender!" another shouted.

"What choice does he have?" another called out.

"Silence!" Srog yelled, and eventually the hall quieted down enough for all eyes to focus back on Bronson.

"He said he will surrender personally," Bronson said.

"Under what conditions?" Kendrick asked.

"He said he will surrender to Thorgrin and to Thorgrin alone. And that his armies must be allowed to leave the Ring unharmed."

An agitated murmur broke out amongst the knights, as they looked at each other, puzzled.

"That sounds like a fair offer," Brom said. "He wants to save his men."

"That doesn't sound like Andronicus," said another.

"What choice does he have?" asked another. "He is probably being pressured by his generals. He has a half-million men and there is but one of him, and they have seen the damage Thor can do."

"Why should we agree?" called out another. "What do we gain by letting them go free? Now is the time to kill them all!"

"With Andronicus our prisoner, and the Shield up, we have nothing to fear from his men. We would save bloodshed, ours, too. No lives will be lost today. After all, he still has half a million men next to our ten thousand."

Arguing broke out amongst the men, as Thor stood there, listening, taking it all in.

"Even if we agree," said Kendrick, "for Thor to go alone, it doesn't seem right."

"And how do we know you are not lying?" Godfrey asked Bronson.

All eyes turned back to Bronson.

"Yes, how do we know we can trust you?" Reece asked. "After all, you are a McCloud."

"I am a MacGil now," Bronson insisted. "I reject the McClouds. I reject my father. After all, he is the one who has maimed me. I fought for you valiantly during the siege of Silesia, and I have no reason to stain my honor. I vow with every ounce of my being that I tell the

104

truth. I am a knight, as are you. We may have fought on other sides of battle, but we all adhere to the same code of honor."

Bronson spoke with the utmost sincerity and Thor could see he was not lying.

"What could Thor have to fear anyway?" Elden asked. "With Mycoples by his side and the Destiny Sword in hand, all of Andronicus' men could do him no harm."

"I say we accept his surrender," Srog said.

Kendrick slammed his fist on the table and the room quieted.

"The offer is Thor's and Thor's alone to accept or reject. It is his life that is risked for us all."

Thor stood there, listening, wondering. On the one hand, he would gladly risk his life for the Ring; on the other, something felt wrong to him. He was not sure what. Then again, as they'd said, what could Andronicus possibly do to him? With Mycoples and the Sword, he felt invincible.

"I would rather kill Andronicus than accept his surrender," Thor replied. "But if that is your wish, then I will honor it. I will go."

There came a cheer from the group of knights.

"I will accept his surrender," Thor said, "and I will make sure that every last one of his soldiers leaves the Ring."

"No!" Gwendolyn called out.

The room grew silent as they turned and looked at her.

"You must not go," she said to Thor. "It is not fair that you and you alone should risk your life."

Thor turned to her, touched by her concern.

"My lady," Srog said, "we do not wish to endanger Thorgrin, either. But how can he possibly be hurt?"

Gwendolyn shook her head.

"Send somebody else. Thorgrin had just returned from risking his life for the Ring. He has done enough."

The room fell silent, and Thor looked at Gwendolyn, overcome with love for her. But she still did not understand. For Thor, this was more than just about confronting an enemy: it was about confronting his *father*. And that was something she would never understand until he told her. The time had come.

He took Gwendolyn's hand, leaned over and kissed her fingers, and said softly:

"There's something I need to tell you. Let us talk alone."

Thor took Gwen's hand and guided her from the room, to the puzzled stares of hundreds. They walked down a corridor, until they came to the privacy of a small chamber. They stepped inside, and the attendants closed the door behind them.

"You can't trust him," she insisted, turning to him, impassioned. "Fight him. Kill him. But do not go alone to accept his surrender. Perhaps I'm being selfish. But I have had you taken away from me once already, and I did not think you would ever come back. My life felt like it was over. Now that you are here, I feel reborn again, and I can't have you risk your life again. I'm sorry. But let someone else go. Andronicus needn't only to surrender to you. He could surrender to anyone. I don't know what his fixation is with you. Please. Let anyone go but you."

Thor slowly shook his head.

"I love you, Gwendolyn," he said. "More than I could say. And I'm deeply touched by your care for me. But I must accept Andronicus' surrender. It may spare the lives of thousands of our men in battle. Those men's deaths will be on my own head. I must go. My honor compels me."

Gwendolyn began to cry.

"You cannot go," she insisted. "Not now. There's too much at stake. It is not just about you."

She cried, and Thor felt his heart breaking. He reached up and laid a hand on her shoulder and looked at her, confused.

"What do you mean?" he asked.

He sensed there was something she was not telling him, something she desperately wanted him to know, and he could not understand what it was.

"I sense you are withholding something from me," he said. "Tell me what it is. Why shouldn't I go?"

Gwendolyn looked at him, and he felt her about to say something—but then she turned abruptly, wiping tears away, and looked out the window instead.

"I am sorry for crying," she said. "It is not Queen-like."

Thor walked up to her and lay a hand on her shoulder.

"You are more Queen-like than anyone I've ever met," he said.

She smiled back at him.

Thor swallowed, his heart thumping, knowing that the time had come to tell her. He could withhold it from her no longer.

"Gwendolyn," he began, clearing his throat, "there's another reason I alone must go to meet Andronicus."

Thor swallowed hard, not wanting to say the words, but knowing he had to.

"It is more complicated than you think," he continued. "There is a reason why he wants to surrender to me, and to me alone."

She looked at him, puzzled.

"What are you speaking of?" she asked.

"You see," he began, then stopped. "I…have learned something. Something which…I wish I had never learned. There is nothing I can do to change it. And it compels me to take the action that I must."

"I don't understand," she said.

She looked at him, baffled, and Thor's heart was slamming, his throat dry. He was terrified that once he uttered the words, it would ruin their relationship forever.

"There is a reason why I must meet Andronicus…" he said, "…a reason why I must be the one to kill him."

"To avenge me?" Gwendolyn asked.

Thor swallowed.

"Yes, to avenge you," he said. "But for another reason as well."

She stared into his eyes, and he stood there, trembling, wanting to get out the words, forcing himself.

"You see, Gwendolyn…" he said, then stopped.

Finally, he took a deep breath and uttered the words:

"Andronicus is my father."

Gwendolyn stared at him, frozen, and blinked several times, completely shocked. It seemed as if, at first, she could not even process his words.

But then her stare widened, her eyes grew larger, and her mouth dropped open. She raised a hand to her open mouth, and involuntarily took several steps back, away from Thor.

107

Thor could see the horror and loathing in her expression, almost as if she were staring back at Andronicus himself. And his heart was crushed at the sight.

"It cannot be," she whispered.

Thor nodded grimly.

"It is. He is my father."

Fresh tears rolled down Gwen's cheeks as she stared at him with whole new eyes, as if staring at a monster. Thor could not help but feel as if things would never be the same between them.

"Gwendolyn—" he began.

"Leave me!" she snapped, her voice ugly, filled with venom and hate.

"LEAVE ME!" she screamed.

Thor looked back at her, saw the anger in her eyes, and felt his entire world collapsing. He had nothing left to live for.

Thor turned on his heel and left the room, no longer caring whether he lived or not. There was only one place left for him in the world now:

It was time to meet his father.

CHAPTER TWENTY

Gwendolyn stood in the castle chamber, looking out the window, watching Thor fly away with Mycoples, her great wings flapping against the breaking sky, silhouetted by the huge ball of the morning sun. Tears rolled down her cheeks as she tried to breathe again, overcome with a million conflicting emotions. She felt betrayed by Thor, by his revelation, betrayed to learn he was the son of Andronicus, the one person she hated most in the world. She felt betrayed that he had kept it from her. And she felt betrayed, once again, by the world.

Why did destiny have to be so cruel? In the entire universe, why couldn't anyone else—*anyone*—be Thor's father? Why did it have to be the one person who filled Gwendolyn's mind with hatred with a desire for vengeance?

Yet at the same time, she knew she was wrong to be upset with Thor. Thor could not be blamed for his lineage. Thor had never been anything but kind and loving and gracious to her, and she was blaming him for his bloodline. And of course, Thor had a mother, too, and his bloodline was not entirely from Andronicus.

She felt ashamed at having reacted the way she did. She felt torn with guilt and a sense of loss that she might have just unwittingly helped send Thor away, to the very battle which she had wanted to prevent him from going to.

As she watched him disappear in the horizon, she knew he was on his way to confront his father. And she knew that if Andronicus did not surrender, Thor would kill him if need be. She knew Thor felt the same hatred towards Andronicus as she did, and logically, she knew she was wrong to be upset with Thor. On the contrary, she should have been compassionate toward him and shown him sympathy: after all, she was sure he was suffering with this news himself.

Still, the profound impact of the revelation resonated within her, and there was nothing she could do about her gut reaction, about her lingering feelings. She reached down and felt her stomach, and it struck home on an even deeper level: after all, this news meant that she was carrying Andronicus' grandchild.

It made her want to cry and scream at the world. This child in her stomach, which she already loved more than she could say. Was she bringing a monster into the world?

Then again, Thor was hardly a monster. But Andronicus certainly was, and she knew that sometimes, traits skipped a generation.

Gwendolyn stood there, watching an empty sky. Thor had disappeared from view, and as she lingered, she felt a pressing sense of concern for his well-being, overriding all of her other emotions. After all, Thor was flying headlong into a meeting with the most dangerous man in the world, a meeting which she had urged him to, unwittingly. What if he never returned? It would weigh on her for the rest of her days. She already felt responsible.

She wanted to lean out the window and scream for Thor to come back. To scream that she was sorry. At the same time, she had to admit there was also a small part of her that wanted him to fly off and never return, that wanted all her troubles to fly away with him. She hated herself for thinking it, and she did not know what to feel, how to think.

She spotted a sudden commotion from the other side of the courtyard. She looked down and was confused at the sight: at the far end of Silesia, marching through the northern gate, there appeared an army, several thousand men, marching slowly, in perfect formation. At first, she could not understand what she saw. The markings of the army were not of the Empire; in fact, the armor resembled those of the MacGil armies. The colors, though, were different: a deep scarlet and blue, and the standard they carried had an emblem of a lone wolf.

The main body of the army stopped outside the gates, while a small contingent of a dozen well-dressed officers, bedecked in furs, rode out beyond them, entering Silesia. Clearly, they were coming with a message. Or a warning. Gwen could not tell if they were friendly or hostile. But her gut told her, from the way they carried themselves, that their intentions were hostile.

She did not understand what was happening, or who these people were. She thought back to all her schooling and remembered seeing that emblem and those colors in a book. She also had a vague memory, as a child, of her father taking them to visit his younger brother, the younger MacGil, in the Upper Isles. Gwen would never forget her time there. She could have sworn that banner, those colors, were flown there.

Could it be them? Her MacGil cousins? If so, what were they doing here now? Had they come to aid in her defense?

There had been a time when her father and his younger brother were as close as two brothers could be; but she remembered their falling out, their never speaking again, and she remembered her father warning them all about his brother. She could not imagine why they'd show up now, but for whatever reason, she doubted they had come to help.

Gwendolyn turned and hurried down the halls. Already they were filling with soldiers who also had spotted the army, the entire castle mobilizing, hurrying down to greet them. She hurried with them, descending the stone spiral staircase, her heart pounding, wondering what could be happening.

She had a sinking feeling that, whatever it was, it could not be good.

*

Gwendolyn stood in the center of the Silesian courtyard, flanked by Kendrick, Srog, Brom, Atme, Godfrey, Reece, and a dozen members of the Silver, all of them proudly holding their ground as they awaited the approach of the contingent of soldiers. The men all stood with their hands on the hilts of their swords, weapons at the ready.

"My lady, shall we summon the army?" Kendrick asked. She could hear the anxiety in his voice.

She watched the contingent approach, perhaps a dozen men, and did not see any of their hands on their weapons. She sensed that this army might be hostile, but that this contingent was not. Perhaps it was coming with a message—or an offer.

"No," she replied. "We have plenty of time for that. Let's hear them out."

"Are those the colors of the other MacGils?" Reece asked aloud. "Of the Upper Isles?"

"They appear so," Kendrick said. "But what are they doing here?"

"Perhaps they have come to abet our cause," Atme said.

"Or to prey on us at our weakest," Godfrey added.

All the same thoughts raced through Gwendolyn's mind as she stood there.

The men came closer, then finally stopped but a dozen feet before them. They dismounted.

One soldier walked out in front of the others, flanked by four men, looking right at Gwendolyn. He was a large and broad man, covered in the finest scarlet furs, and as he removed his helmet, Gwendolyn recognized his shaggy gray hair and pockmarked face immediately.

Her uncle: Tirus MacGil.

Tirus, close to her father's age, looked much older than the last time she had seen him, as a child. Now his beard was thick with gray, his face bore too many worry lines, and it did not carry the pleasant, carefree nature she remembered. Now his face was stern, humorless. He did not smile as he greeted her, as he used to when she had been a child, laughing in a carefree manner, picking her up and swinging her. Now, he approached with a stiff body, as an adversary might, his jaw locked and his brown eyes expressionless.

On the one hand, her heart leapt to see him, as he resembled her father so much, it made her miss him dearly. On the other hand, she felt a cold pit in her stomach, brought on by his demeanor and that of his soldiers, as she would when facing any other adversary.

Tirus stopped a few feet away from her, and stared back coldly. He did not bow or nod his head or offer to kiss her hand, even though she wore the royal mantle of Silesia and he surely must have known that she was queen. It was a sign of disrespect, and she took note.

"I've come to claim what is rightfully mine," he announced in a loud and booming voice, a voice meant not just for her but for everyone within earshot. "My eldest brother, King MacGil, is dead. By right, the kingship falls to me, his next eldest brother."

Gwen reddened. So that was what he was after. She should have known. Her father had warned her.

She cleared her throat, and addressed him back in an equally confident and formal manner:

"That is not the law of the Ring, as you very well know," Gwendolyn replied. "Our common law dictates the kingship fall to the named child of a deceased King."

"*Your* law," Tirus said. "Not mine. You alter your law as it suits you. We are of the Upper Isles, not the Ring proper, and we have our own law."

"My father did not alter any laws," she corrected, knowing her history all too well. All her years of reading were now paying off. "It has been the same law in use for seven generations of MacGil Kings, authored by Harthen MacGil and acknowledged by the Supreme Council before the formation of King's Court. If anyone seeks to alter the law, it is yourself."

Tirus reddened, clearly not expecting such a scholarly retort, clearly in over his head.

"You have too much schooling, girl," he said. "You always have. You are too smart for your own good. But you'll need more than books to rule a kingdom. Perhaps you know the technicalities of the law. But I come with real life. My eldest brother is dead, and I don't care what your law says—by right, control of the Ring should fall to me now. I have waited long enough, nearly a lifetime. I've come to take what I deserve. Whether your law grants it to me or not."

Tirus sighed.

"Because your father and I were once close," he added, "I've come with a kind and gracious offer. I will give you a chance to peacefully hand over the kingship to me. You have barely held it but a short time—you should not miss it too much. And you are a woman, after all—and a young woman at that. It was never meant for you. You will hand it over to me, and I will take all these responsibilities off your head. You could not possibly know how to rule a country anyway. As your ruler, I will treat you well. You will all have a place in my kingdom. Of course, I and my men will move our court here, and some of you may be displaced. But don't worry, we shall find you other homes. Your taxes will rise, and you will fight in service to me, but I will be a fair king."

"As fair as you are to your people now?" Kendrick asked.

Tirus turned and gave him a look of seething hatred.

"Our father took us to visit your lands many times," Kendrick added. "Children or not, we still had eyes. You were a brutal landlord.

Your people hated you. I saw no evidence of the kindness and fairness you boast of."

Tirus locked his jaws.

"You open your mouth when you should listen, boy," Tirus seethed. "You are barely weaned from your mother's breast. Let real men like me tell you what the world is like."

"You are full of bombast," Kendrick retorted. "Your fault is that you think yourself greater than you are."

Tirus turned purple, clutching the hilt of his sword. Clearly, he was not used to being spoken to this way. He must have been used to everyone deferring to him.

"And this comes from the bastard son of his father?"

Now Kendrick reddened.

"I am the *first* born of my father. The firstborn *son*, too. By right, that would give *me* the throne. But my father chose to give the throne to Gwendolyn—and I respect his decision. Unlike you, who seeks to seize what is not his."

"You are but a bastard," Tirus said, "and if your father had any sense he would have listened to me and killed you the day of your birth. It was another example of his great foolishness to keep you alive."

Kendrick gripped his hilt and took a step forward, and immediately, all the swords were drawn by knights on both sides of the contingents.

Gwendolyn reached out and lay a hand on Kendrick's wrist, and he turned and looked at her. She could see the fury in his eyes—she had never seen him so upset. But as he felt her calming hands, he stopped.

"Another time, brother," she said, emphasizing the word *brother*.

He calmed at her words, and relaxed his guard.

Gwen turned to Tirus, determined to get this weasel out of her city.

"Kendrick is my *true* brother," she said to Tirus. "He is as pure and true a brother to me as are all my siblings. And if he were to ask me for the kingship, I would gladly give it to him."

She sighed.

"But it was my father's wish that I should have it, and that is what Kendrick honors. That is what I honor, too, whether I cherish the role or not. You should honor your eldest brother's wishes, too. He was a good and kind brother to you. Do you think it would please him to witness this now?"

Tirus stared back, and she could see his jaws continually clenching and unclenching. Clearly, he was in over his head and had not expected it to be this difficult.

"My brother cared for nothing but the throne," Tirus said darkly. "And himself."

"Is that why you tried to assassinate him?" Godfrey chimed in. "I remember that feast that night, in your castle. The poison meant for our father killed your own son."

Tirus turned furious.

"I would give you a lashing boy, if I could."

"It was your father who tried to poison ours," a soldier, beside Tirus, called out. "That poison killed our brother."

"I have only four sons now of the five, thanks to him," Tirus added.

Gwendolyn looked closely at four of the soldiers standing beside Tirus, each with raised face visors, and she recognized them from her childhood. Her four cousins. They were all nearly the same age as her siblings, and she was surprised to see them all so grown up. They had become true knights. It was a shame they were sons to this man, because they had been good people once, as close as siblings.

"And what of your daughter?" Reece asked.

Tirus glared at him. Perhaps, in that glare, he recalled Reece's affections for her.

"She lives, too," he replied grudgingly.

"And is a daughter not worth mentioning then?" Gwendolyn asked. "Is that the sort of fairness you envision in your kingdom?"

Tirus scowled.

"Women are property," he replied. "Your father was a fool to name you queen, to try to elevate women to more than what they are."

Now it was Gwen's turn to redden; but she forced herself to keep a calm head.

"I *am* Queen," she said, "and there is nothing you can do about it."

Tirus shook his head, and smiled for the first time, more of a sneer.

"Have you not seen my forces lined up outside your walls? I've twice the men you have. All hardened Upper Islemen. All who have lived outdoors their entire lives in the freezing rain and cold, who have slept on rocks, who have tasted no luxuries. All who are deathly loyal to me."

"Yet another example of your kindness and fairness?" Godfrey asked wryly.

Tirus reddened, caught once again.

"These men will kill upon my command," he continued. "I have given you a generous offer. I will give it once. Abdicate the throne to me, and I will let all of you will live. Defy me, and our men will crush yours. You have one night to decide. You will give me my answer at sunrise, or you will witness the final destruction of your city, and I will take the Western Kingdom by force."

Tirus turned to go, but before he could, Gwendolyn stepped forward and called out:

"Uncle! You can have my answer now if you like."

Tirus stopped and turned back to her, a satisfied look on his face. He smiled, as he clearly prepared to accept her acquiescence.

"You are but a bully and a coward," she said. "My father looks down on you in disgrace. Do not ever enter these gates again. If you do, you will be met by an army of swords that will send you back to the Upper Isles in disgrace."

His face dropped in shock, clearly not expecting such strength and defiance from a woman. He shook his head disapprovingly.

"You speak hastily," he said. "That does not befit a ruler."

"Indecision does not befit a ruler, either," she retorted. "Nor, may I add, do greed and opportunism, especially when directed towards one's own family."

Tirus' expression darkened.

"You are a young, foolish girl. Out of courtesy to your father I will give you one night to contemplate your ill-spoken words and have your advisors talk sense into you. I look forward to receiving your apology and surrender in the morning."

Tirus turned with his entourage, re-mounted, and they all rode off. As they did, Gwen spotted a look on the faces of some of her cousins, as if they wanted to apologize for their father and be close to her, as they had when they were younger.

Their contingent soon rode out of view, passing through the gates of Silesia.

"Lower the gates," Gwendolyn commanded.

Several soldiers rushed forward and pulled down the heavy iron portcullis. Soon, all that was left in the silent, inner courtyard were hoof prints in the dust.

Gwendolyn turned and looked at the others, as they did to her, all of them stunned in the morning silence.

"You did well," Kendrick said. "You made our father proud."

"He is a pig," Reece said. "And a liar, and a braggart."

"He always sought to dethrone our father," Godfrey said. "Now that he is dead, and Andronicus on the way out, he sees an opening for the throne."

"He has no legal right," Aberthol said.

"But he has the men," Srog observed wisely. "Of course, we can defend. And we will. Our city is meant to withstand a siege. But after the Empire attack, our defenses are severely weakened. He, unfortunately, chose the perfect moment, when we are weak and vulnerable."

"What are the odds?" Gwendolyn asked.

Srog grimaced.

"We can hold back his ten thousand men," he said. "For a time. We can kill quite a number of them. But we shall lose most of ours, eventually. Strategically, right now, we cannot afford a war. We need time to rebuild, to heal, to re-fortify. Strategically, the wisest military move would be to accept his offer."

"Accept his offer!?" Godfrey said, outraged. "Have we then ousted Andronicus only to live as slaves to someone else?"

"What of Thor, and Mycoples?" Reece asked. "Are we forgetting them? Thor will return soon, after he has accepted Andronicus' surrender, and we will have all the might we need to repel our MacGil cousins."

"But what if the other MacGils attack before Thor returns?" Srog asked.

"What if Thor never returns?" Brom asked.

They all looked at Brom in horror.

"How can you say such a thing?" Godfrey asked.

Brom lowered his head.

"Forgive me. But we must plan for every contingency. Thor is not here right now to defend us. And we can't plan a battle around absent warriors."

Gwendolyn stood there and listened to everyone's opinion. She had learned from her father never to speak when others were talking, especially when they were giving counsel. It was advice she had taken to heart.

"I suppose, then, it is a matter of whether we choose liberty and death, or enslavement and life," Gwendolyn observed. "It is the same question we faced not long ago, with the Empire invasion. And we all know the answer. Life is important; but liberty is more important us than life."

There came a grunt of approval from all the men.

They all turned and headed back to the castle, and as they did, Gwendolyn looked up and watched the skies.

Thor, she wished silently. *Please come back.*

CHAPTER TWENTY ONE

Gwendolyn hurried down the corridors of the castle, reeling from her encounter with her uncle, debating what to do. She was not the same Gwendolyn she had once been, before her attack by Andronicus. She had been hardened by the world, had taken the worst it could give her, and she no longer feared men's threats. As she had faced down Tirus defiantly, she had meant every word she'd said. She was prepared to fight to the death. She was tired of running from danger, from fear of men. She wanted to make a stand—and she knew it was what her men wanted as well.

But at the same time, she also felt a tug of guilt knowing she was not just ruler of the armed forces, but also Queen of the people. The citizens, too, depended on her. Tirus' forces clearly outnumbered them, and they were better armed, and better rested. They had wisely sat out Andronicus' invasion on the Upper Isles, and had chosen their timing perfectly: now they arrived well-fed and well-armed, ready to wreak havoc on a besieged and broken city. That was her uncle: opportunistic to the last. It did not surprise her; he had been waiting his entire life for a chance at her father's throne, and he had found it, right when his brother's children were most vulnerable.

Gwendolyn needed someone to discuss this all with, someone outside her regular council of military advisors, someone politically shrewd and experienced in the affairs of men. As she marched through the corridors, she found herself craving, oddly enough, to speak to her mother, the former Queen. She wanted insight into the man who was her uncle, who was, after all, the former Queen's brother-in-law. She didn't necessarily want advice; she just wanted someone to sound off to. And since her own toughening, Gwendolyn found herself, in a strange way, relating to her mother more and more.

Servants stiffened and opened doors to her mother's chamber at her approach, and Gwendolyn entered to find her sitting there at her small table, playing a solitary game of chess, as she always did. It brought back memories of when Gwen would play with her. Now her mother was a woman alone, hardened and cold, not wanting anyone's company, but only that of a game.

Nearby stood her old and trusted servant, Hafold, who never seemed to be far away.

As Gwendolyn walked into the room, her mother turned and looked at her, which surprised Gwen, as her mother usually ignored her. Now, her mother actually looked at her with a whole new respect.

"Leave us," her mother commanded Hafold, and unlike times past, Hafold bowed and exited quickly. They both showed Gwen a respect she had never received before. It was as if her mother looked at her with whole new eyes.

The door closed behind her, and Gwendolyn stood there and faced her mother alone.

"Please, sit with me."

"I do not wish to play," Gwendolyn said.

Her mother shook her head.

"We do not need to play. Just sit. Like we used to."

Gwendolyn came and sat beside her mother, facing each other diagonally at the small chess table. She looked down and studied the ornate pieces, small military figures dressed in black and white robes, wielding magic weapons.

Gwendolyn sighed and looked out the window.

"I was pleased to hear of your return from the Tower," her mother said. "It did not sit well with me, you secluding yourself. You are part of the world and you need to be in it."

Gwendolyn nodded back. She was surprised to hear her mother cared for, and surprised to hear her being so kind. Clearly, losing her husband and her queenship had humbled her mother. This was not the same mother she had grown up with.

"The kingdom is happy to have you back," her mother said. She hesitated, then added: "And I am happy to have you back, too."

Gwendolyn looked over and saw her mother smiling at her with compassionate eyes, for the first time in her life. They were eyes lined with hardship, her face covered in lines and spots. Gwendolyn could not help but wonder if one day her face would look like that, too. She knew what it took for her mother to utter those words, and it meant a lot to her, even if it was too little, too late.

"Secluding yourself from the world is easy," her mother said. "Being a part of it—that is what is hard. And a queen's life is the hardest of all."

Gwendolyn thought about that. She was beginning to understand how her mother felt. As queen she could not help but feel the responsibility of all these people, feel it in the weight of every decision she made.

"We were paid a visit by Tirus this morning," Gwendolyn said.

"I heard."

Gwendolyn looked at her mother, surprised.

"How?"

Her mother smiled.

"I have my people still," she said.

Gwen surveyed her mother, impressed. She was an easy woman to underestimate; even in her state, she still had considerable resources.

"You did the right thing," her mother said. "Your father's younger brother is a pig. He always has been. Those MacGils have all the class of the Upper Isles, which is none. They are beneath you, beneath all of us. Tirus brought his family to the Upper Isles because he wanted a place to plot and build power and vie for the throne. If he had been a true brother, a loyal brother, he would have stayed in King's Court, at his brother's side.

"Do not accept any terms for surrender. He is ruthless. Regardless of what he promises, he will one day kill all of his brother's issue, so that no one else could have a claim to the throne. You are the one and only true ruler of this kingdom now; don't let anyone tell you otherwise. Not your uncle, and not anyone else. Fight for what you have; your father would want it no other way."

Gwen thought about all she said, and her mother's thoughts confirmed her own. She knew her mother would have wisdom to share, and she felt better already. In some ways, the two of them thought exactly alike.

Feeling resolved on the issue, Gwen sighed and looked away, and found her thoughts drifting back to Thor. It weighed on her even more than any of her other troubles. She wished she had never sent him away; it was nagging at her and would not go away. She wished she could take it back. But it was too late.

As she looked at her mother, she suddenly wondered how much her mother knew. She was starting to realize that maybe, deep down, that was why she had really come to her to begin with—not to discuss her uncle, but to discuss Thor.

"I made a grave mistake today," Gwen said, not looking at her, looking out through the window, her voice getting deeper and harder, sounding more and more like her mother's. "I sent away someone who loved me very much."

The former queen sighed.

"A mistake all of us are bound to make at one time. But the one thing you learn in life, as years turn into decades, is that it's never too late to rectify your mistakes. There is always a second chance. And if there's not, you can always *create* a second chance. The power to create it lies in your hands."

"I am afraid, in my case, it might be too late," Gwen said. "I may have just sent him to his death."

There was a long silence as her mother studied her.

"You speak of Thorgrin?" she asked.

Gwendolyn nodded back.

"Yes. I suppose you should be happy, mother. You hated him anyway."

Her mother sighed.

"I never hated him," she corrected. "I hated him for *you*."

"Because of who his father is?" Gwendolyn asked.

As she asked the question, she watched her mother's eyes closely. She saw them flicker, and she knew then that her mother knew. Gwen could not believe it.

"You *knew!*" Gwendolyn said, standing, outraged. "You knew all this time, and you never once told me!"

Her mother shook her head sadly.

"I told you to stay away from him. I tried to *force* you to stay away from him."

"But you still didn't tell me," Gwen insisted.

"I knew that one day you would find out," she said. "I wanted you to learn the news on your own. So you could decide for yourself to stay away from him."

"Because you think his father's blood runs in him? Because you think he will harm me?"

The Queen shook her head.

"No. You still don't understand. Not because there is any flaw in Thorgrin. But because there is a flaw in *you*."

Gwen looked back, confused.

"In me?" she asked.

"You are just like your father—you and all of the MacGils. You have always put so much credence on ancestry. But you are all wrong. There is much more to a person than who they descend from. How many countless tyrants descend from noble kings? And how many good kings descend from monsters? The son never equals the father."

Gwendolyn thought about that. Of course, her mother was correct. But it was still hard, emotionally, to accept it, especially after what Andronicus had done to her.

"You cannot blame sons for fathers' sins," the queen added.

"You should have told me," Gwendolyn said.

"I told you to stay away from him."

"But you should have told me *why*. You should have told me the truth, the whole truth, upfront."

"And what would you have done? Would you have stayed away from him?"

Gwendolyn thought about that, caught off guard. Her mother had a point.

"I ... might have."

"You would not have," her mother retorted. "You were blinded by love."

Gwendolyn pondered that.

"I never thought Thor would be a bad match for you," her mother said. "On the contrary, I knew he would be the perfect match."

Gwen furrowed her brow, confused.

"Then why did you so try so hard to keep us apart?" she asked.

She studied her mother, who seemed strangely silent.

"I sense there's something else you're not telling me, mother."

Her mother turned and looked away, and finally Gwen could sense that she was onto something. Her mother was withholding something from her.

After a long silence, her mother finally cleared her throat.

"There was a prophecy," her mother said slowly, tentatively. "I haven't spoke of it since you were a child. The night you were born, a stargazer came to your father. He proclaimed a prophecy about you. He proclaimed that you would be a great ruler—a greater ruler than your father ever was."

Gwendolyn's heart pounded as something made sense.

"Is that why he chose me to rule?" she asked. "Of all the children? Because of the prophecy?"

Her mother shrugged.

"Possibly. I don't think so. I think he saw something in you. I think he would have chosen you either way. He loved you the most. Even more than me."

Gwendolyn could feel her mother's jealousy, her sadness; for the first time, she felt sorry for her.

"I am sorry, mother," she said.

Her mother shrugged and looked away, yet by the way she was wringing her hands, Gwen could tell there was something more on her mind.

"What is it?" Gwen asked, puzzled.

Her mother would not meet her eyes and something occurred to Gwen.

"Was there something more to the prophecy?" Gwendolyn pressed, sensing that there was. "Surely that wasn't the only reason you scared Thor away?"

Her mother hesitated, reluctant. Finally, after an endless silence, her mother looked right at her, and Gwen could see the heaviness in her gaze.

"The prophecy foretold that you would marry," her mother said, her voice grave. "That you would bear a son. And that your husband would die young."

Gwendolyn gasped. She tried to catch her breath, feeling as if a bucket of cold water had been dumped on her head.

"That is why I did not want you to be with Thorgrin," her mother finally admitted. "I wanted to spare you that heartbreak."

Gwendolyn stood, numb. She was in a trance as she walked from the room and back into the hall, wishing her life was over.

CHAPTER TWENTY TWO

Thorgrin, gripping the Destiny Sword, rode on the back of Mycoples, her great wings flapping, taking them ever farther from Silesia. He felt hollowed out. As they soared through the clouds, racing into the early morning sun, he reflected on his encounter with Gwendolyn, and hardly knew what to think.

Thor kept replaying in his mind's eye the look she had given him when he had told her, when she had found out who his father was. It was a look of horror. He had watched her love for him grow cold in that glance, watched her eyes, once shining with love and devotion, become dull with anger and disappointment. The thought of it still left a pain in his chest.

Thor could not help but feel that their relationship had fallen apart, was lost forever. They had once been so close, he had been about to propose to her, to give her the ring. He only had left to tell her the news of his father.

But now…he didn't see how she would ever accept his proposal now. It was clear that she hated him.

Thor felt the ring inside his shirt pocket, and wondered what would become of it. A part of him felt like just throwing it away, dropping it down and letting it drift through the air, land somewhere in the Ring. But he thought of his mother and realized he could not.

Thor urged Mycoples faster, the wind whipping his face, needing to clear his mind of all these thoughts. Maybe it was not Thor's destiny to be with Gwen after all. Maybe his only destiny in this life was war and battle. Maybe he had been overreaching to think that he could be with a woman like Gwendolyn.

He forced himself to focus. Somewhere on the horizon lay his father, and he had to focus on the encounter ahead of him. As they raced across the Ring, getting ever closer to the great divide of the Highlands, the Destiny Sword throbbed in his hand. Thor felt both excitement and dread. On the one hand, he was excited to accept Andronicus' surrender, to rid the Empire of his men, and put an end to the war for good.

On the other hand, Thor dreaded meeting his father face-to-face, especially under these terms. He felt uncontrollable hatred for him, for what he had done to Gwendolyn, to the Ring. If Thor had his choice, he would kill him, and it burned him that he had to accept his surrender. But that's what had been decided by his people, and that is what he would do.

Thor tried to picture how it would go in his head, and he was having a hard time imagining it. Did Andronicus know he had a son? That it was Thor? Would he greet Thor as a father? As an adversary? Or both?

Meeting his father for the first time would be, in some ways, like meeting a part of himself. He needed to keep a cool head and not get caught up in his personal emotions. After all, he was representing his people.

They flew over the Highlands, the endless stretch of mountains rising in peaks below, covered in white from the snow, and finally there came into view the other side. Countless Empire troops filled the Eastern Kingdom, covering the ground like ants. Up ahead, in the distance, he spotted the center of their camp, saw a huge black and gold tent, and knew it must house Andronicus.

But suddenly Mycoples dove straight down, so steep that Thor nearly fell off.

"Mycoples, what is it?" Thor called out, surprised.

Mycoples dove down to one of the highest peaks on the mountain range, and set down beside a crystal-clear blue mountain lake.

As she sat there, beside this empty lake, so high they were nearly in the clouds, Thor looked down at her, puzzled. He had never seen her act this way before.

"Mycoples, tell me?" he asked.

She purred, blinking her eyes slowly.

"We must continue on," Thor urged. "We have no time to waste. Please. Fly!"

But Mycoples, for the first time, ignored his command.

Instead, she lowered her head down to the shore and rested her chin beside its waters. She dropped her head, and Thor sensed a great sadness in her.

Thor dismounted and came over to her; he stared at her, then reached up and slowly stroked her long, narrow face, running his hand along her scales. She blinked slowly as he did, purring deep inside her throat, and leaned over and nudged him with affection with the side of her nose.

"What is it, girl?" he asked.

She made a funny noise deep inside, almost like a whine, and Thor knew something was wrong. He felt as if she were trying to give him a message, as if she were trying to tell him not to go.

"But I must go!" Thor said.

She suddenly leaned back her head, aiming it up at the heavens, and shrieked. It was a loud, tortured shriek, like a wail, filling the entire highlands, echoing off them again and again.

Thor stepped back, shocked. It was a wail of desperation. It was as if she knew something terrible were about to happen.

Realizing that she was not willing to fly anywhere, Thor decided to give her some space. Perhaps she would calm, and her mood would change.

He took a few steps over to the crystal clear waters of the lake, a gust of wind rippling off it in this freezing weather, the only sound in this desolate place that of the pebbles crunching beneath his boots. Thor looked down at the icy waters and saw them reflecting the morning sky above, filled with purple and pink and crimson clouds. The sight took his breath away.

He was about to look away when suddenly he glanced at his own reflection. He looked twice.

He could not believe it.

There, in the waters, looking back up at him, was not his face. Rather, he saw, staring back, on his body, the face of Andronicus.

Thor turned away, agitated, breathing hard, not wanting to look back at the waters. Was it real? Who was he becoming?

CHAPTER TWENTY THREE

Gwendolyn stood on the upper parapets of Srog's castle, looking out at the swirling mists of the Canyon. The fog blew in fast and furious, enveloping her legions of men below within her walls. Beyond the outer wall, she saw the legions of Tirus' men, encamped like a plague, biding their time. She knew that when morning came, they would have a battle on their hands. Whether or not they chose to fight for their independence was not a question in her mind; now all that remained was *how* they chose to fight.

Beside her stood Srog, Kendrick, Brom, Atme, and all her generals, along with Godfrey, Reece, and several Silver, the small entourage walking the parapets together, looking out with her. They were all in preparation mode now, their battle faces on. Gwendolyn's stomach turned. She was not afraid of battle; what bothered her was the idea of killing her own people, especially when so many of Andronicus' men were still left within the Ring. After all, the other MacGils, however detestable, were people of her own blood, cousins she had once been friends with. At a time like this, they should all be sticking together.

But what choice did she have? They had forced her hand, and now it was live free or die. And freedom and honor were more important to her—and to all of them—than life.

As Gwendolyn looked down, she noticed a commotion inside the gate: a group of her attendants seemed to be arguing with a newly-arrived visitor. As she leaned over the edge and looked closely, she did a double-take. She recognized the man getting off the horse: he was short, with a twisted back, and carried an oversized bow. She knew that figure anywhere.

It couldn't be. Had Steffen made it back to Silesia? Or was her mind playing tricks on her?

Suddenly there came a commotion at the entrance to the parapets, and Gwen turned to see her chief attendant rushing for her.

"My lady," he said, agitated, sweating, "there is a commotion at the gate. We have a newcomer who claims he knows you; of course, given his appearance I assume it is a lie, and we are preparing to take him to the dungeons."

Gwendolyn's face flushed with embarrassment. She looked down and watched Steffen being led away from the main castle, toward the dungeon. She could see the look of shock and shame in his face.

"Bring him to me at once," she commanded firmly.

Her chief attendant's eyes opened wide in surprise, "You know him, my lady?"

"As well as I know myself. His name is Steffen, and you are to treat him with the highest honor and respect. If it were not for him, I would be dead today. He is my right hand, and he shall be afforded every privilege this kingdom has to offer. Go to him at once!" she said, her voice rising.

His eyes opened wide in surprise and he bowed and turn and ran back inside.

Gwen heard his footsteps echo and knew from the fear in his eyes that he would obey her orders right away.

She looked below and watched him run across the courtyard, to the group of servants, saw him stop them all, and watched as they looked at him in confusion, then fear. They bowed towards Steffen apologetically, and she watched with satisfaction as Steffen stood up a little straighter. He was led to the castle.

Moments later Steffen appeared at the roof, and without pausing, she ran towards him, bent over, and gave him a hug.

Steffen stood there, awkwardly, as if afraid to hug back someone in a position of royalty. But finally, hesitantly, he did. He pulled back and bowed low.

"My lady," he said. "When I heard you left the Tower, I came at once. If you decide to give me a position with the other servants, of course I will accept wherever it is you wish. But if you wish to have me once again by your side, I will fight to the death to protect you from any and all harm."

Gwen smiled back.

"Steffen, you are my right hand, and one of the few people I would trust with my life. You shall be afforded every honor this kingdom has to offer. Speak not of being a servant ever again."

Steffen's eyes opened wide and he broke into a smile as he stared back, then bowed his head low again.

"Yes, my lady."

"You've come just in time," she said. "Tomorrow, we face attack from my uncle. Believe it or not, Silesia is preparing for a siege once again."

"My lady," Steffen said, "whatever happens, I shall stay by your side."

Gwen turned and faced her men, determined.

"Let us go over our defenses again," she said. "Where are we most vulnerable?"

Srog cleared his throat.

"My lady, defending the outer wall will be a challenge," Srog said. "The damage Andronicus did was too extensive. Even if we were to hold one gate, there are too many other gates to secure. We just don't have the manpower. Tirus' men are veteran warriors—they will know that. They also have the manpower to test every gate."

"They probably scouted it all out before they approached," Kendrick added.

"What do you recommend then?" Gwendolyn asked.

Kendrick rubbed his chin.

"What they will expect," Kendrick began, "is for us to defend at the gates. I suggest that we surprise them. Let them overrun the gates. We can place our men at the inner wall, at the very edge of the Canyon, blocking the entrance to Lower Silesia. They will enter to find a vacant city courtyard, with no resistance, and they will be confused. Then we can attack them from all sides."

"It is a good plan," Srog said. He turned and faced the city courtyard. "We can place archers there," he added, pointing to various spots throughout the city walls. "And spears down below. We can take out the first thousand before they regroup."

"And after that?" Gwen asked.

Srog and the others exchanged a worried glance.

"After that, they will overrun our defenses. There is no way around it," Srog said. "But we can retreat to Lower Silesia, and hold out there as long as we can."

Gwen sighed.

"And if we retreat below," she asked, "how long until we all perish?"

They shook their heads, and Gwen saw the fear on their faces.

"With our current provisions, perhaps we can outlast them a week. Perhaps two." Srog cleared his throat. "I wish I had a better strategy, my lady. But we are vastly outnumbered, and our men are weakened and our provisions low."

Gwendolyn looked all around the city as she mulled over everything they'd said. She breathed deeply, hands on her hips, and examined the city walls, her warriors. She mulled over all her options and she didn't like any of them. Some inflicted damage, but none led to victory.

"There is another option," she said, "that none of you are considering."

They all watched her as she took several steps forward, and surveyed the walls and beyond.

"We can vacate the city altogether, and attack them beyond the walls, in the open field."

They all stood there, speechless, and looked at her as if she had gone mad.

"Vacate the city, my lady?"

Gwen nodded, feeling more confident in the plan the more she thought about it.

"In the morning, they will come for a decision. We will go out to greet them with an envoy, while our main forces will circle around them and flank their sides. We will surprise them with an attack in the open field."

"My lady," Brom said, "that would be suicide. Without the protection of these walls, we would all die."

She turned to Brom and felt a new strength course through her. She was hardening, becoming a queen, with no fears and no regrets.

"We will die anyway," she replied, matter-of-factly. "And if we're going to die, I'd rather die killing more of Tirus' men. I'd rather die now, with honor, than have our people suffer slowly."

They all looked at her, and she saw a new sense of awe and respect in their eyes.

"So it is decided, then," she said. "We will attack at first light. Prepare yourselves."

CHAPTER TWENTY FOUR

Erec led the Duke's army, thousands of men and growing, as they picked up men everywhere they went, freed men of the Ring eager to avenge themselves on the Empire. They had been marching for days, making the long trek from Savaria in the south to Silesia in the north, passing groups of armed survivors, hidden forts, groups of Silver that had outlasted the invasion. These men joined with the Duke's, and the size of their force had nearly doubled, now swelling to ten thousand men strong, all of them motivated, happy to be free, to have a cause, and to have a leader like Erec.

In these men's eyes there was no one better to follow than Erec, the most famed knight, the leader of the Silver, the champion of the Ring, the knight who had never been defeated by anyone. He drew people to him like a magnet, a natural leader, standing tall and proud, with a strong jaw and light gray eyes. He commanded respect wherever he went. Erec had become even more legendary since his single-handed defense at the gulch, his heroic smashing of the boulder to hold back the Empire.

They had marched steadily ever since Thor had flown over with Mycoples and saved them on the cliff. Erec knew they were heading north and had been determined to follow, to help. He followed the trail of charred Empire bodies, the path of destruction Thor had left, and knew he would catch up to them. It was a long and circuitous path, heading ever north, alongside the Canyon. Erec had thought it would end in King's Court and he would find them all there.

But when they had reached King's Court, the sight of it had gutted Erec. This place that had once been so dear to him, had once been the bastion of strength of the Ring, was now destroyed by the Empire, a remnant of what it once was. The trail of destruction continued north, through its gates, and Erec continued marching. He did not know where it ended, but he assumed it would lead them to the next northern city: Silesia. Perhaps they had all retreated there. Militarily, it would make sense.

Mounted on Erec's horse behind him, her arms wrapped tight around his chest, was his bride to be: Alistair. The warmth of her touch filled him with hope, with life, especially on this cold, snowy evening; she gave him purpose to live. He was filled with gratitude towards her, having been saved by her so many times, and he vowed to one day repay her.

They all rode at a slow pace to accommodate those on foot, more of a fast walk, heading slowly ever farther north as night began to fall. Near Erec rode his close friend, Brandt, and the Duke near him. They were a unified force, all determined to join Gwendolyn and the King's men. Erec did not know how he could be of service, given Thor's strength, yet he would offer he and his men in whatever way Gwendolyn needed them. After all, he owed that much to her father.

King MacGil had been like a father to Erec, too, and in some ways, Erec felt as if he were one of the MacGil siblings. He'd been like a brother to Kendrick and Gwendolyn and Reece and Godfrey. He had never been close to Gareth or Luanda, but certainly to the others. There had been many times when King MacGil had told him he wished he was his son, too, and he had seen it in his eyes.

Alistair squeezed him tight, and Erec was ecstatic with his choice of a bride; he only wished he could show her more gratitude, and he was determined to find a way. The mystery around her also persisted and deepened in his mind. Who was this woman, so unlike any woman he had ever met? How had she been able to save him—twice? He was dying to ask her, but he had promised not to pry, and he never broke his vows.

"You are wondering about me," Alistair whispered softly in his ear, out of earshot of the other men. "I can feel it."

Erec was amazed, as always, at her ability to read his thoughts.

"I would be lying, my lady, if I said I was not," he responded. "You saved my life too many times for me not to wonder how. You have a power I have never seen in battle, a power I do not understand."

"Does it make you love me less?" she asked.

"Even more, if possible," he said.

There came a long silence as they continued to ride, each comfortable in each other's silence. Erec thought they would continue that way for hours, when Alistair surprised him by speaking again.

"I've never told anyone of my lineage," she said. "I made a vow to myself."

"I understand," he replied.

"Yet I feel comfortable to share it with you."

They fell back into silence as they continued to ride, Erec's heart pounding as he waited for her to say more. But Alistair fell silent once again, and he wondered if she had changed her mind.

Then, she cleared her throat.

"My father was a monster. My mother, the most beautiful woman in the world. And the most powerful. All the powers I received, I received from her. There were many times when I did not want to go on living, when I discovered who my father was. I indentured myself as a servant to that innkeeper, when you found me, to blot out the pain of life. Yet now that I've met you, I feel ready to live again. Ready to face who I am."

Erec wanted to ask her a million questions, but forced himself not to pry, to be respectful of however much she wanted to share, whenever she felt comfortable.

"There is another reason I secluded myself," she said. "I was told of a powerful prophecy around my birth. It states that I would bring about both great healing and great destruction to those around me. I did not want to subject you—or anyone—to my destiny."

"Not all prophecies come true, my lady," Erec said, touched that she had shared so much and understanding the guilt she lived under. "Prophets see through a glass darkly. The entire vision is often obscured. You must not carry around this guilt. You are a beautiful soul. It does not matter who your father is. And any prophet who speaks otherwise is wrong."

She squeezed him tight, and Erec felt that, given what she shared, he should reciprocate. He had never told anyone much of his past, but he felt ready to share it with her, too.

"I know a little something about prophecies," he said.

She leaned forward and looked at him.

"You see, I hail from the Southern Isles of the Ring. Few people know this, but I am the son of a King myself."

Alistair gasped.

"You never said anything," she said.

Erec shrugged.

"I do not judge myself on who I come from, but on what I have done myself. When I was young, my father sent me to the Ring proper, to King MacGil, to be apprenticed in his service. The MacGils became an adopted family to me, and I so loved being with the Silver, that I have never returned home, nor seen my father or my people since."

"But are you then not heir to the throne of the Southern Isles?" she asked.

"Yes," he admitted. "They are a proud and great people, and they await my return. One day, perhaps, I shall. It would mean the world to my father and to my people. I delay, because I know that the day I return home, it will be hard to ever return to the Ring. I am an outsider here, but in many ways, the Ring has become my home. And loyalty is something I take very seriously, with all my heart."

They continued riding in a comfortable silence, when something occurred to him.

"If I ever do return there, would you come with me?" Erec asked, worried she might say no.

Alistair leaned forward and smiled.

"I would accompany you to the ends of the earth," she said. "Whether you are a prince or no, a decorated knight or a common soldier. I love you with everything that I am."

Erec's heart welled with a love stronger than he had ever felt, and he turned and leaned back, and the two of them kissed as they continued riding in the night.

The army suddenly came to a stop as they reached the top of a ridge, and Erec stopped with them. He looked out, following the Duke's finger as he pointed.

Erec saw it, too: before them lay a city made of a shining red stone, built right into the edge of the Canyon.

If they rode all night, by morning they would reach it.

Silesia.

CHAPTER TWENTY FIVE

Thorgrin rode on the back of Mycoples, lifting off from the top peak of the Highlands and finally flying again, diving down, heading east for Andronicus' camp. The second sun now sat low in the sky, as it had taken all day for Thor to convince Mycoples to stir, rise up, and fly again.

Mycoples flew reluctantly, flying in giant circles, getting a little closer, then circling back, farther away, screeching as she went. Thor could not understand her behavior. He had never seen her like this. He could feel her deep ambivalence to go forward, and he could not help but feel a sense of foreboding. Was she seeing some future he failed to see?

Thor looked below, and against the dramatic sunset sweeping over the Ring, casting a reddish pall over everything, he saw the endless soldiers of Andronicus' camp. As he managed to get Mycoples to fly ever closer to the center, he spotted what could only be Andronicus' tent, ten times the size of the others, with a wide clearing around it. They flew above it, circling low.

As they did, Thor could see the fear on all the faces of the Empire soldiers, looking up at the sky, watching him. They were right to be afraid: if Thor chose, he could dive down and have Mycoples burn them all alive, as she had their comrades. He could kill them all in one clean sweep, including his father. There was nothing he wanted more.

But he was obliged by duty, and he vowed to carry out orders and accept Andronicus' surrender.

As Thor circled, the clearing grew wider, Andronicus' men creating space for him and for Mycoples. Mycoples bucked and screamed as they neared the ground, lifting her head as if refusing to land. Thor looked at her, puzzled. He could feel her wanting to breathe fire, and it took all his will to get her to refrain.

"Do not be afraid, Mycoples," he said.

I fear not for myself, but for you, Thor could hear her thoughts.

"Do not fear for me," Thor said. "You are by my side, and the Destiny Sword lies in my hand. No one and nothing can harm us."

Mycoples grudgingly lowered her great talons down to the ground.

They set down in the midst of the hostile and foreign camp, and there came a dead silence. Not a soul stirred, all the Empire soldiers frozen in fear, as Mycoples landed on the dusty ground, and Thor dismounted before Andronicus' tent. All the Empire soldiers, faces etched in fear, kept a healthy distance.

Thor stood there, clutching the Sword, the tension thick in the air, and he looked all around, his heart pounding in anticipation. He was nervous to lay eyes upon his father, to speak to him for the first time. Mycoples, beside him, let out a noise, like a snarl or a growl, from deep within her throat. Clearly, she was very unhappy here; Thor could feel how on edge she was. Thor felt it himself. Something felt off to him.

Finally, there came a stir, and as Thor watched, the flap opened, and out came a figure.

His father.

Thor's heart pounded as he stood there, facing him. His whole world froze.

Andronicus walked out slowly and stepped towards him. Thor was taken aback by his father's height and breadth and size. He was a huge man, looked to be eight feet tall, as broad as a tree trunk, with muscles rippling on his red skin, long fangs, and curled yellow horns coming from his bald heads, glowing yellow eyes, and wearing a necklace that, Thor was horrified to see, was laced with shrunken heads.

Andronicus reached up and fingered the heads with his long talons, smiling back at Thor as he stopped but a few feet away from him. A deep purring noise came from deep within his chest.

Thor felt revolted at the sight of him. He felt ashamed. And he felt hatred. Looking at him, knowing what he had done to Gwendolyn, Thor felt, most of all, a burning desire for vengeance. Thor felt the Destiny Sword throbbing in his palm, and if his honor had not bound him, he would have lunged forward and killed him now.

But he could not. He had agreed to accept a surrender, and he had to honor his word.

"My son," Andronicus said. "Finally, we meet."

137

Thor did not know how to respond. He hated hearing the word "son" from this man. Thor felt nothing like a son to him; on the contrary, he was supremely disappointed in him, in having to meet his father for the first time, and to have him be a father such as this. He wanted more than anything to change it, to change who he came from, but he knew he could not.

"I've come to accept your surrender," Thor said formally, coldly. "Frankly, I would rather kill you. But that is not what my people agreed to. So you can dispense with the trivialities and command your men to exit the Ring, and kneel and announce your surrender. I don't want to speak to you a second longer than I have to."

As he spoke the words, Thor felt a newfound sense of confidence.

But Andronicus did not step forward or command his men, or kneel, or any such thing. Instead, he just stood there, his smile broadening. Thor sensed something was off.

"My son, you are in such a rush. We have all day for such formalities. Let us have a chance to get to know one another."

Thor felt a pit in his stomach at the thought.

"There is nothing I wish for less," Thor said. "I do not wish to know you. You are a murderer—and worse. Your time for speaking is through."

But Andronicus merely smiled and took a step forward.

"But our time for speaking has not yet even begun," Andronicus said, seeming amused. "You see, we will have a lifetime together. As much as you may wish to fight it, you are my son. Whose blood do you think you carry within you? It is mine. Who do you think you have to thank for being alive in this world? Me. You may fool yourself to think otherwise, but you know it's the truth. You and I are exactly the same. You might not know it yet, but you are just like me."

Thor's face reddened.

"I am *nothing* like you," Thor insisted. "And I will *never* be like you. You are a despicable excuse for a living thing. I regret the day I learned I hailed from you."

"It is a great honor to descend from me," Andronicus countered. "There is no man in the Empire more powerful than I, and one day, you will take my place."

Thor tightened his grip on the Destiny Sword.

"I will *never* take your place," Thor said, his anger rising, it getting harder to control himself. "I want nothing to do with you, and I'm through speaking with you. You can surrender yourself now to me, or if you refuse, then I shall kill you once and for all."

Thor was surprised to find Andronicus still unfazed, still standing there and grinning. He took another step closer to Thor, now but a few feet away.

"I am afraid you will have to kill me, then," Andronicus said.

Thor hardly knew what was happening.

"You withdraw your offer of surrender then?" Thor asked.

"I never intended to surrender," Andronicus smiled. "I did all of this to have a chance to see you. You are my son. I knew you would not let me down. I knew that once you were in front of me, you would see that you and I are the same. Join me, Thorgrin," Andronicus said, holding out a hand. "Come with me, and I can give you powers beyond what you ever dreamed. You will rule entire worlds. The Ring will be but a speck in the lands you will own, the peoples you control. You will have powers beyond what a simple human father could have given you. Join me. Stop resisting it. It is your destiny."

But Thor's eyes narrowed, as his rage began to overwhelm him. Had been duped by this man. They had all been duped.

"Take one step closer, and I will strike you down," Thor warned.

"You will not do so, Thorgrin," Andronicus said, staring into his eyes, as if hypnotizing him. "Because I am your father. Because you love me. Because you and I are one."

"I hate you!" Thor screamed.

Andronicus stepped forward, and Thor could restrain himself no more. He thought of Gwendolyn, of the damage done to her by this monster's hand, of all the people Andronicus had killed in the Ring, and he could hold back his rage no longer.

Thor lunged forward, raised the Destiny Sword high, let out a scream, and plunged it down with all his might, right for his father's chest, determined to show his father, to show himself, that he was nothing like him.

But Thor found himself stumbling forward, through thin air, his sword plunging through nothing but a cloud. His momentum carried him, and as his sword came down it found a target instead in a boulder. There was such strength to the blow that the Destiny Sword came down and lodged itself into the boulder, and kept sinking in until it was halfway through, filling the air with the awful noise of metal cutting through rock.

At the same time, Thor suddenly felt his entire body entangled in a light metal. He soon realized he was ensnared in a net. He tried to break free, but it was made of a material he'd never encountered, and he found himself unable.

Thor looked back to see Andronicus standing far away, a good thirty feet. He was confused. He turned and looked to where Andronicus had been and in his place, instead, was an evil creature, with a long scarlet cloak, and glowing yellow eyes.

Thor realized he had been tricked by some sort of spell of illusion. He had thought it had been his father in front of him, when all along it had really been this dark sorcerer.

The more Thor struggled against the net, the weaker he became. It was made of a material he had never seen before, a glowing, amber mesh, and whatever it was, it was draining the life out of him. He could not even manage to lift the Destiny Sword.

The sorcerer laughed at him, an awful, grating sound.

"That net is made of Akdon," the sorcerer said. "The more you struggle, the weaker you will become. It is the rarest metal on earth, a sorcerer's metal, forged in the lowest fires of hell. Not much of it exists—but enough to stop the likes of you. And your dragon."

Thor heard a roar, and he looked over to see Mycoples ensnared in a net of the same material. Dozens of Andronicus' men held the net, holding her down as she shrieked violently and tried to flap. But try as she did, her wings were constrained by the material.

Thor heard a noise and looked up to see Andronicus—the real Andronicus—standing over him, grinning down. He watched as Andronicus raised a fist high and brought it down, right for his face, and felt the impact of his knuckle on the bone of his cheek, snapping his head back. Thor found himself lying face first on the hard ground, and before he his world went black, he heard his father's final words:

"I told you you would join me, my son."

CHAPTER TWENTY SIX

Gwendolyn found herself standing atop the Tower of Refuge, confused as to how she got here. Dawn was just breaking, and surrounding her, facing her, stood the seven magical knights, frozen, in a perfect circle. As one, they all approached her, the sound of their plate armor clanking on the cobblestone, getting louder and louder as they closed in.

They reached out and were about to grab her when Gwendolyn, with nowhere to go, threw her head back and screamed.

Gwen blinked and found herself standing in the center of King's Court. The sky was black, filled with Winter Birds, cawing too loud. The city was but a remnant of what it had once been, scattered with rubble, charred from the dragon's breath. There was not a soul in it.

Gwendolyn stood in the city center, alone, looking for someone, anyone.

"Father?" she called out.

There came nothing but silence and the howling of the wind.

At the far end of the court a huge door began to open, perhaps a hundred feet tall, arched, made of iron. Towards her there walked a lone figure. He wore a royal mantle and a rusted crown, and as he approached she was thrilled to see it was her father. His body was wasted away, and he looked more skeleton than human being.

"Father!" she called out, reaching for him.

He held a long, golden scepter, and he raised one end out to her.

She reached out and clutched it, and as she did, her father disappeared.

Gwendolyn found herself walking on a path leading from King's Court, up a hill, to the former House of Scholars. Now it was burnt to the ground, nothing but a hole in the earth. She looked over the precipice and saw that inside was a tunnel, leading to blackness. She reached down, and picked up a book, now a heap of charred pages which turned to ash in her hands and blew away.

Gwen blinked and found herself in a rocky, barren wasteland, standing outside Argon's cottage. She examined the perfectly round, stone structure but saw no door.

"Argon!" she cried out.

"I am here," came the response.

Gwen spun and saw him standing there, facing her. She was so relieved.

"Why did you leave us?" she asked. "We need you more than ever."

Argon slowly shook his head.

"I live in a place of dreams now," he said. "I am trapped here. Save me, Gwendolyn. Save me!"

Gwendolyn blinked and found herself standing in the center of Silesia, surrounded by her uncle's army. They had swarmed through, filled every nook and cranny of the place, and they all marched towards her, in perfect unison, raising swords and spears and shields, preparing to attack her.

She turned every which way, looking for a way out, but there was none. Tirus led the group, and he raised a sword to stab her.

Mycoples swooped down and grabbed Gwen with her huge claws, cutting into Gwen's skin as she lifted her up and carried her away, over the men, up over the walls of Silesia. They flew across the countryside, and Gwen watched the Ring pass beneath her. Below were Andronicus' men, millions of them covering the ground, more than she could number.

Mycoples carried her over their encampment, and as she looked below, Gwen was horrified to see Thorgrin, a prisoner, chained by his hands and legs to a post. Over him stood Andronicus, and he raised a huge silver sword with both hands, and prepared to plunge it down into Thor's heart.

He stabbed Thor, who shrieked, and as he did, Mycoples dropped Gwendolyn.

She went hurling through the air, screaming, plunging right for Thorgrin's dead body.

"NO!" she screamed.

Gwendolyn sat up in bed, breathing hard, gasping for air. She looked around, trying to figure out where she was; she saw the torches burning in her castle chamber, saw the glow of the fireplace, and realized she was safe. It was a dream, and it was still night.

Gwen walked across the room, Krohn following at her heels, to a small stone washbasin at the far wall and reached down and splashed cold water on her face. She was still breathing hard as she surveyed

142

her room, so disturbed by her dream. She rubbed her stomach and felt cramps. The dream had felt too real. She felt certain she had witnessed Thor captured, dying at his father's hand. And she felt flooded with guilt.

She could not help but feel it was all real, that when the sun rose, she would be surrounded by her uncle's men, that Thor was captured and was to be killed.

Gwendolyn forced herself to catch her breath, to breathe slowly, regain her composure. She turned and went to the window, and looked out at the swirling mist of the Canyon in the pre-dawn light. The sky, still black, was beginning to break, to transform into dawn. The big day was almost upon them. The day when they would face Tirus. The day when Thor would face Andronicus.

The dream haunted Gwendolyn, and she felt a pit in her stomach, an awful feeling that something would go awry. She could feel it in her chest.

There came a sudden pounding on her door, too loud for this early in the morning. Something, she knew immediately, was wrong.

Gwen crossed the room and opened the door to find a messenger standing there, heaving, out of breath.

"My lady, I bear bad news," he gasped. "One of our spies has just ridden all the way from the Highlands to tell us: Thorgrin has been captured by Andronicus."

As she heard the words Gwen felt a sharp, shooting pain in her belly, felt the baby within her turn and flip, again and again. She dropped to her knees in pain, overwhelmed with cramps.

She heaved, gasping for air, fearing for the life of her child.

"My lady, are you well?" the messenger asked.

Gwen was unable to speak. She lay with one palm on the stone floor, as waves of pain rushed over her.

The attendant rushed from the room. With the news, she felt as if her whole life had been taken from her.

Thor, captured. How stupid she had been to let him go. And she had no one to blame but herself. She had driven him away.

Slowly, the waves of pain began to pass. The door burst open and Steffen entered, bringing an elderly physician who helped her to her feet.

"My lady, what has happened?" the physician asked.

Gwen stood, feeling better. She turned and faced the attendant.

"Summon my council at once," she commanded, using the strong, authoritative voice of a queen.

"Yes, my lady," he said, and turned and hurried off, the physician leaving with him. Only Steffen remained with her.

Gwendolyn turned and took one last look out the window. It was time to face the day.

*

Gwendolyn marched through the set of double doors, Steffen by her side, and into the council chamber, lit with torches in the pre-dawn light, met with the anxiety-ridden faces of all her top knights. There stood Srog, Kendrick, Brom, Atme, Godfrey, Reece, and two dozen others, all looking to her. They were all in their armor, and they all had their battle faces on. After all, dawn had nearly broken, and the time had come to confront them, to risk their lives for glory.

But with the news of Thor's capture, the mood was even more tense.

"Is it true?" Kendrick asked her.

The room fell silent, as Gwen nodded back gravely.

"It is," she said. "Our beloved Thorgrin is captured."

A collective groan escaped from the others, as several pounded their metal gauntlets on the table in anger and frustration.

"I knew we should not have let him go alone," Brom said.

"Andronicus was never to be trusted," Reece said.

"But how is it possible?" Kendrick asked the question on everyone's minds. "Thor had Mycoples. And the Destiny Sword. What could possibly lead to his capture?"

"Sorcery," came a voice.

Aberthol stepped forward, his cane clicking on the stone. "Only an act of magic could have done this."

"It matters not how it happened," Gwen said. "Now we are without Thor. Without Mycoples. Without the Destiny Sword. It is the few thousand of us against Andronicus' half-million men. And more pressing, we have Tirus surrounding our own city."

The room fell silent, and they all looked to Gwendolyn for her response.

144

"Now what, my lady?" Kendrick asked.

Gwendolyn looked at all the faces, and realized she was no longer the naïve, innocent girl she had once been. Now she felt hardened, perhaps even a bit callous. She was unafraid, despite the odds. And she was ready to lead these men. Indeed, they looked to her for leadership. She felt a sense of clarity and calm, even in the midst of the chaos.

"Nothing has changed," she said. "We deal with Tirus first. A small contingent of us will meet Tirus outside the gate. He will think we come with a message, that we come in peace. Meanwhile, the bulk of our army will flank them, and attack on my command. We may lose. But we will die on our feet—as warriors, not as cowards."

There came a collective cheer of approval in the room, as each man grabbed the hilt of his sword and rattled it.

The door burst open and several attendants rushed in, dragging Bronson by the arms as he thrashed and protested.

"Let me go!" he screamed.

"Here is the traitor who set up our Thorgrin," Brom said.

Gwendolyn turned to him, scowling.

Bronson looked back at the men in the room, wide-eyed with fear.

"I did nothing of the sort!" he protested. "I swear it! I knew nothing of Luanda's plot! She swore to me she had brokered a peace! I had no idea it was a trap!"

"I am sure you did not," Godfrey said sarcastically. "I am sure you have no interest in whatever deal your wife struck with Andronicus, no interest in sharing power with her."

"I do not!" Bronson insisted. "After what she has done today, I have no love for Luanda. This is my home now, and you are the ones I want to fight for!"

"To fight for?" Srog called out sarcastically. "Why? So you can deceive us once again?"

"We should execute him my lady," Atme said. "For what he did to Thor!"

There came a shout of approval from the others.

"FOR THOR!"

There came another shout of approval.

Bronson struggled, wide-eyed with panic.

145

"You must believe me!" he screamed. "If I had known, I would have never delivered her message!"

Gwendolyn stepped toward him and the room grew silent. She came close, until she was but a foot away, and looked deeply into Bronson's face, wanting to see for herself if he was lying.

She examined him, filled with rage at what happened to Thor; yet at the same time, she did not want to let it out on an innocent man. She summed him up, Bronson trembling, missing one eye, and some part of her told her that he was being truthful. She knew the depth of her sister's scheming treachery, and she would not put it past Luanda to dupe an innocent man like Bronson.

"You may have been set up indeed," Gwen said. "But that is something I shall never know for sure. Until I know that, I cannot trust you to ride with my men. I will not kill you, not without a fair trial. And since there is no one to stand witness for or against you, any trial would be unjust."

"Then what shall become of him, my lady?" Godfrey called out.

Gwendolyn looked Bronson over long and hard.

"I declare you banished," Gwendolyn said. "You shall leave our side of the Kingdom and never set foot on our soil again, by pain of death."

"My lady, you cannot!" Bronson called out in fear. "I have no home left on the McCloud side of the Ring. Sending me back there would be a death sentence!"

Gwendolyn slowly shook her head.

"You will have to fend for yourself," she said. "Like the rest of us."

She nodded, and the attendants took him away, yelling and screaming, until finally the doors closed on him and the room fell silent again.

Gwendolyn turned and faced her men, who looked back at her with increasing respect.

"Dawn nearly breaks," she said somberly. "We waste time. Raise your arms and follow me. It is time to meet our cousins."

146

CHAPTER TWENTY SEVEN

Gwendolyn, on horseback, led the small entourage of her finest warriors solemnly across the empty plaza of Silesia, heading for the northern gate, out to greet her uncle. She nodded, and as she did several soldiers raised the massive iron portcullis slowly.

They continued on through the open gate, Gwen flanked by Kendrick, Srog, Brom, Reece, Godfrey, Atme, and a dozen others. It was just a small group of them, riding out to face Tirus and his massive army, which stood lined up in the morning light, as if preparing to march on the city.

Gwendolyn's group seemed like a peace convoy, which was exactly how she wanted it to appear. She wanted to play to Tirus' ego, to make him think that they were going out to accept his terms. Surely he would assume that, as she would not come out with such a small entourage otherwise; and given Tirus' level of arrogance, she felt confident that he would.

Secretly, though, all of the Silesian forces were creeping around the sides of Tirus' men, flanking them, taking up positions in the woods, and preparing, on Gwen's signal, to attack.

Gwen's heart pounded as she walked forward slowly on her horse, with the others, in the silent morning, the tension so thick one could cut it with a knife. The swirling mists of the Canyon blew in and out of the battlefield, and as a horn sounded, a small convoy of Tirus' men rode her way, coming out to greet them in the middle of the empty field. Tirus rode out front, flanked by his four sons and a dozen generals.

As they approached, Gwendolyn felt the pain deep in her stomach, felt the baby turning again and again; it was overwhelming her, making her think of Thor. She could feel that he was captured, feel his helplessness. She did not understand how it had happened, but the thought of it tore her apart. She was crushed by guilt and remorse.

Gwendolyn shook these thoughts from her mind. Now was not the time. As soon as she finished with Tirus, assuming she lived, she would send every man she had to rescue Thor.

Gwendolyn focused on Tirus as his face appeared before her, a condescending smile etched into it, exuding bombast. They rode closer and closer, their chain mail jingling, their swords rattling on their hips, their spurs clinking, the smell of horses heavy in the air, mixed with the moist smell of the Canyon in the cold morning air.

Tirus and she stopped a few feet away from each other, and each stared at each other proudly. Tirus sat there, waiting for her to break the silence, clearly reveling in what he thought was his success, in the apology to come.

"You are a wise girl," he said, finally. "You have made the right decision to surrender to us. One must admit defeat when one is surrounded."

Gwendolyn's heart pounded as she sat there on her horse, her posture perfect, staring back into the ball of the rising first sun. Her eyes were cold and hardened, and she felt a new strength within her, the strength of the son she carried. Thor's son.

She no longer felt afraid. Not of these men, not of anyone, and not of death. Life felt less precious to her than it had, and no threats could get to her.

A heavy silence hung in the air, horses prancing and snorting, as Gwen took her time to respond. She was prepared to signal all of her men to charge, and knew that with the slightest gesture they would—and havoc would break loose.

"Whoever said we decided to surrender?" she responded coldly.

Gwendolyn's heart pounded, and she could feel the knuckles tightening on the hilts of the swords of her men. In just a moment she would wave her hand and mark the signal to begin the battle that would surely lead to her death, and to everyone else's. She was not afraid of death. Only of dying poorly. And this time, at least, she would die with her honor intact.

Slowly, Tirus' face fell, his arrogant smile beginning to drop as he realized from her expression that she was serious.

"Stupid girl," he said. "Have you come then to tell me that you have signed your death sentence?" he asked coldly, his voice filled with hostility.

As Gwendolyn raised her eyes to survey her men, to prepare to give the signal, she noticed something on the horizon, on the hills behind Tirus' men; something caught her eye, something she did not expect. Something gleamed in the light, where it shouldn't. It was the reflection of a shield. But it was not of her men. Or of Tirus'.

148

Then there came another shield.

Then another.

Over the ridge, there appeared several thousand shields, shining, gleaming in the light.

At first, Gwen was confused. Another army had arrived here, on this battlefield.

But as they got closer, as their banner hoisted over the hill and came into view, she recognized the emblem. Her heart soared. It couldn't be.

It was.

It was the banner of the Duke of Savaria. Those were his men—along with thousands of others. And leading the pack, she could recognize by his armor, the shiniest silver armor in the kingdom, was her father's champion. Erec.

Erec had returned. And he had brought with him thousands of men.

And Tirus had no idea.

Now it was Gwen's turn to smile. She looked back at Tirus and she realized she was going to enjoy this, very, very much.

"On the contrary," she said calmly back to Tirus, "I believe it is you who you who have signed your death sentence."

Tirus glowered in anger as his expression morphed into a scowl.

"You are a stupid girl," he said. "You are about to send many men to their deaths. And you are about to learn what it means to suffer."

"I have already learned far more about suffering than you will ever know," she countered. "I am through with trivialities. I will give you one chance to surrender."

Tirus looked at her in shock, then leaned back his head and laughed with derision.

"You mock me, girl. Either that, or you are completely mad." He laughed heartily, as did his men. "Why should I surrender when I outnumber you two to one? When your forces are weak, and mine are strong?"

Gwendolyn smiled wide.

"Because if you look behind you, you will see twice as many men as yours over that ridge behind you. You will recognize the armor: those shields belong to the Duke of Savaria and to the champion of the Silver, Erec, and all of his knights. He has returned home, to serve my father faithfully—something you have never done. And if that does not suffice, you can look to your right and to your left, and within those woods you will see thousands more of my men, flanking you from both sides, bows drawn and awaiting my signal."

Gwen smiled wide.

"So you see, my uncle, it is you who are completely surrounded."

Tirus grimaced.

"Do you think I'm stupid enough to turn and look at imaginary ghosts on the landscape? This is one last act of desperation on your part," he said.

But his four sons turned and looked, and as they did, their faces lit with fear, and their horses pranced.

"Father, she speaks the truth," one of them said.

Grudgingly, Tirus turned and saw himself surrounded, on all sides, by thousands and thousands of men. Erec held the high ground, his thousands of soldiers sitting proudly, lances held high—and at his sides Gwendolyn's men emerged two thousand archers at the ready.

Tirus turned and looked back at Gwen, this time with an expression of utter shock. His face turned pale, and he slumped a bit, losing his arrogant posture.

Kendrick and the others in her convoy drew their swords, the ring cutting through the morning air.

"Drop your weapons, all of you," Gwen commanded darkly. "If not, with the slightest wave of my hand I will have a thousand archers release their tension. Now it is you who has a choice to make."

Tirus' face finally crumpled in humility and fear. He dropped his weapons down to the ground and gestured for the others to do the same. All around them, his convoy dropped their arms, all hitting the cold ground with a clanging noise.

"I know when I've lost," he said. "You have outwitted me today. I surrender my forces to you."

"I know that you will," she said. "It is easy to surrender when you face a sure death. The question for me is whether I choose to accept your surrender, or whether I just take your life instead."

Tirus swallowed, for the first time seeming truly afraid.

"Please, my lady," he pleaded, his voice nearly cracking. "Do not kill us. We never meant you any harm."

Now it was Gwendolyn's turn to laugh.

"Never meant us any harm?" she asked. "You only sought to sack our city and destroy our men?"

Tirus nearly burst into tears.

"Please, my lady. We are family."

"*Family*?" Gwen echoed in derision. "Is this how you treat family?"

"Kill them, my lady," Kendrick said. "Tirus is a pig, and a traitor to his kin. He deserves to die. He has committed treason to the Ring, and violated our sacred law."

"Kill him, my lady," Srog said. "He is not to be trusted. If you let him live, he will kill us another day."

Gwendolyn sat there, and considered her options.

"Father, *do* something!" one of Tirus' sons called out. "Please, don't let us die!"

Gwen breathed deep.

"I should kill you uncle," she said. "And all your men with you. But I will not."

His face, and the faces of all his men, rose in relief.

"Like my father, I choose to be a gracious ruler, and to offer mercy even when it is undeserved. I also believe you can be of some use to us, and it is a shame to waste such good men, especially in these times. So, I will give you one chance. Either I will have all your men slaughtered here right now, or you can all join our forces, and become part of our army, answering to me, and to Kendrick and Srog and Brom. Your men will join us as we fight Andronicus and free Thorgrin. The choice is yours."

Tirus dismounted, dropped to his knees, and clasped his hands.

"I see what it means to be a true ruler here today," he said. "You have taught me, my lady. I am ashamed of my actions and grateful for your mercy. Thank you. Of course we shall join you. All of my men. And we shall ride anywhere you say."

Gwen looked down, saw the earnestness in his face, and decided. She raised one hand and motioned for her men to lower their arms.

A horn sounded, one of Tirus' men raised a white flag, and Tirus turned to his men and screamed out:

"WE SURRENDER!"

Flag bearers raised more white flags, and all up and down the ranks, men dropped their arms.

Shouts of joy erupted from all sides.

The battle was over.

*

Srog's huge castle chamber was packed with hundreds of people celebrating, members of MacGil's army, the Silver, the Legion, Silesians, the Duke's army, Erec and his men, and freed members of the Western Kingdom of the Ring. Joining them were Tirus and his elite warriors, along with his sons and all the MacGil cousins. Gwen, in her wisdom, had extended an olive branch and decided to let them join them; after all, if they were going to fight together, they were going to have to get to know and trust each other.

The mood in the room was jubilant, everyone relieved not to be at war with each other, and Gwen and the others so relieved to have Erec, after all these months, return home. Gwen had never expected to see him here again, and having him back was like having a piece of her father back with her. It brought back memories. Her father had loved Erec like a son, and in many ways he felt like a brother to her.

Among them stood Steffen, Srog, Brom, Kendrick, Reece, Godfrey, Elden, Conven, O'Connor, along with the women: Selese, Sandara, Indra. The woman who was commanding the most attention of all, though, was Erec's bride-to-be, Alistair. She was the most beautiful woman Gwendolyn had ever seen.

The tension of the battle behind them, Gwendolyn felt flooded with relief, though still on-edge about Thor and resolved to have him rescued as soon as her men regrouped. There was a stir in the room as Erec was being treated as the returning hero that he was, embracing Kendrick, Godfrey, Reece, and multiple members of the Silver. He was accompanied by Brandt, another hero of the Silver, and the room was filled with the satisfied shouts of reunion.

Gwendolyn held out her arms as Erec embraced her. It felt so good to see her father's champion again, after all these months. She felt as if a piece of King's Court had been restored.

"You have grown," Erec said, leaning back and studying her. "You are not the same girl you were when I left. Now, you are a woman. A queen. Your father would be very proud."

She studied him with a smile.

"As have you," she said. "You look to be twice the warrior you were." Gwen looked at Alistair, standing beside him. "And I see, most importantly, that your Selection Year has turned out to be a success."

Erec stepped back and realized.

"My lady," he said, bowing and clearing his throat, "may I present my bride-to-be, Alistair."

A curious crowd gathered as Alistair stepped forward.

Alistair smiled and curtsied to Gwendolyn, and Gwendolyn smiled back.

"It is a great pleasure, my lady," Alistair said. There was something about her voice that felt immediately familiar; Gwen could not explain it, but she felt as if she had known this woman her entire life.

Gwendolyn broke into a huge smile, stepped forward and clasped both of Alistair's palms.

"Erec has chosen well," she said. "A wife of Erec is a sister of mine."

Gwendolyn looked at Erec.

"Erec, you are still the Champion of my father, of the Silver, and you have saved us here on this day. We owe you a great debt."

Erec shook his head.

"The debt I owe your father is far greater," he replied. "And I intend to repay that debt by serving his daughter with the same loyalty I have reserved for him."

Erec turned and glanced about the room, the commingling of both sides of the MacGil family.

"Your wisdom is on display today," he added. "Your father chose wisely. Any other leader would have ended this day in bloodshed. We are fortunate to have you as ours."

Gwen surveyed the room and saw that her strategy was working: at first it had been an awkward commingling of both sides of the MacGils, but now the warriors merged happily, sharing drink and banter and battle stories. Looking at them, one could not tell the two sides apart. What could have been a day of bloodshed had turned into a celebration.

Now that the men had a chance to catch their breath and reunite, Gwen grew serious, thinking of Thor, imprisoned. She could hardly stand to be here while he was in danger, and she knew action had to be taken quickly.

"The time for idle talk has passed," she said to Kendrick and Erec, as the others crowded in and listened. "We must turn our attention to Thorgrin."

Her man gathered close, listening.

"We need a strategy for rescuing Thor," she stated.

The men looked at each other, grim.

"Would you expect the few thousand of us to battle Andronicus' half-million, my lady?" Tirus asked. "All for one man?"

"Thorgrin is more than just one man," she said, her face darkening. "And yes, I do. I would risk our men for any of our brothers and sisters."

Their faces grew grim.

"Even with the other MacGils here," Brom said, "Tirus is right: we stand vastly outnumbered. No simple attack can yield a victory, as much as I hate to say it."

"If we attack, we have little chance of surviving," Srog said.

"Yet if we stay here," Kendrick retorted, "we shall all surely die."

"Whether we live or die, none of that matters," Erec said.

All eyes fell to him, as his deep and confident voice commanded attention.

"All that matters is that we live and die with glory," he added.

There came a grunt of approval among the men. They all fell silent, contemplating, and Gwen cleared her throat.

"Battles are lost because missions are broad," Gwen said. "Our mission will be a narrow one: to liberate Thor and Mycoples. We will attack their main camp with a diversion, find out where Thor is, and free him. Once Thor is free, with the Destiny Sword and Mycoples on our side, the battle will turn. Do not think of this as a few thousand men against a half million; rather, think of it as a few thousand men liberating one man. The key will be to divide Andronicus' men, and to create a diversion."

"And how will we do that, my lady?" Brom asked.

"We will break our army into four smaller divisions, and attack them from all sides, creating a diversion and splitting their forces. Erec, you shall lead the Duke's men, and half the Silver. Kendrick, you shall lead the other half, along with half of MacGil's army. Tirus, you shall lead your men. And Godfrey, you shall lead the other half of the King's men."

Godfrey turned and looked at her, eyes wide in surprise.

"*Me*, my lady?" he asked.

She nodded back.

"I do not know if I'm fit for the task," he said, nervous. "I am not a warrior."

"You are fit," she said back firmly. "After all, it is you who saved us from Andronicus here in Silesia."

"What I did I accomplished through wit, not through strength."

"And it is wit that we will need to win this battle, especially in the face of greater strength," she answered. "You shall lead the fourth division. Do you accept it?"

All eyes turned to Godfrey, and finally, he nodded.

"Good," Gwendolyn said. "These four divisions will attack Andronicus' main camp from four different routes. We will confuse and divide his men just long enough to reach Thor."

"And you, my lady?" Steffen asked, turning to her. "Will you stay here?"

All eyes turned to Gwendolyn.

She shook her head.

"No. I cannot stay here, not with my Thorgrin out there. I will attack, too," she said. "But in a different way."

"How so, my lady?"

"They must be holding Thorgrin by some magical means," she said. "We will need magic to help free him. There is only one person I can turn to. I must find him. Argon."

"But Argon is gone from us, my lady," Aberthol said.

"He lives somewhere," Gwendolyn said. "I will find him. I will release him. And he will help us save Thor."

Gwendolyn turned to the others.

"Let us wait no longer," she said loudly, "Thorgrin awaits us!"

The crowd dispersed with a determined cheer, the men already breaking into divisions and preparing to leave.

As the room began to quiet and the crowd to thin, Gwen called out to Aberthol.

"Aberthol!"

He stopped and turned.

"You know all the ancient volumes," she said. "They are burnt, now, but they live in your memory. I recall some of them myself. The Cycle of the Sorcerers. There was a volume, I recall, on the legends on the trapped."

Aberthol nodded back.

"Your schooling serves you well," he said. "Part myth, part fact. No one knows how much each part is. But yes, there is a legend. That those trapped by magic are held in the Netherworld."

"The Netherworld," Steffen gasped, remaining by Gwen's side.

"Do you know of it?" Gwen asked.

Steffen nodded.

"It is a place rumored to make men's souls run cold. A place of ice and fog. One of the rings of the deepest hells."

"It is a place no humans are allowed," Aberthol added, "unless guided by a Druid. And since we have no Druid among us, I am afraid, even if it were true, we could not enter. Our journey would be for naught."

"I can lead you," came a voice.

Gwen, Steffen and Aberthol turned to see Alistair step forward. She looked back at Gwen with an earnest expression.

Krohn stepped forward and licked her hand. It was clear to Gwen that Krohn liked her—and Krohn rarely took a liking to people, especially strangers.

"But how can you?" Gwen asked. "Unless you are…"

Alistair nodded.

"You are correct," she said. "I am a Druid."

They looked back at her in wonder, and she lowered her head to the ground.

"I have never told anyone," she said. "But for you, I would do it. You mean the world to Erec. And for my lord, there is not a thing I would not do."

Gwendolyn stepped forward, close to her, smiling, feeling herself well with hope for the first time. If she could find Argon and free him, perhaps she could save Thor.

"From this day forward," Gwendolyn said to Alistair, "you are my sister."

Alistair smiled back.

"There is nothing I would like more."

CHAPTER TWENTY EIGHT

Thor braced himself as best he could, as yet another blow rained down on him. He tried to resist with all his might, but with his wrists bound behind him in Akdon shackles, there was little he could do. His energy had been sapped by this magical metal, and he found himself unable to fight back as a large group of Empire soldiers punched him in the face, the chest, the back, and finally knocked him face-first onto the ground.

The mob pounced on him, kicking him, blow after blow landing on his ribs, his back, his legs, his head. Thor tried to protect his face as best he could, but he already felt one eye starting to swell, to shut on him.

Not far away, Andronicus watched it all with a smile, clearly pleased to see his own son abused in this way.

What kind of father would allow something like this to happen to his son? Thor wondered. If Thor had had any confusion of whether he had any affection for his father, or whether his father had any for him, these blows certainly wiped them out.

The blows continued for so long that Thor lost count. Finally, Andronicus yelled:

"Enough!"

The soldiers parted as Andronicus walked forward. For a moment, Thor thought he would be getting a respite from the abuse—but instead, more soldiers approached and began to strip him of his clothing.

Thor felt the freezing winter winds cut into his raw skin. He tried again to resist with all he had, but he could not.

Thor screamed in protest as he felt his shirt being torn off his body and watched his mother's ring fall out, tumbling to the ground. He watched as a soldier grabbed it, holding it up and examining it.

"NO!" Thor screamed out, as he watched the ring he had reserved for Gwendolyn sink into the greedy palm of an Empire soldier. His face was distinctly recognizable, with a crooked nose, bulging eyes, and a scar running along his chin. The soldier put the ring on his pinky finger and held it up, laughing. Then he disappeared into the crowd.

More blows rained down on him as Thor felt his shirt stripped, then his boots. But all Thor could think of was his mother's ring, disappearing into the hands of that cretin, and his heart broke.

How could the fates be so cruel? Thor wondered. How can his mother allow this to happen to him? Couldn't she intercede somehow?

"Mother!" Thor screamed out, wishing she were here to help.

There came a deep, sinister laugh from above. He looked up to see Andronicus standing over him.

"Your mother won't help you now, boy," Andronicus said, glowering down.

He nodded, and another man stepped forward carrying a thick, coarse rope. Two soldiers went to work tying the rope around Thor's ankles. It cut into his skin, and just as Thor wondered what they were doing, suddenly, he heard a whip, a horse's neigh, and felt himself being dragged backwards.

Thor's body was dragged along the frozen winter ground, along the dirt and small pebbles; it tore at the bare skin of his back, as Empire soldiers jeered him. The horse gained speed, and he was paraded in circles around the Empire camp.

His body covered in bruises, exhausted, with no energy left, Thor began to lose consciousness. He tried to make this all go away, to imagine himself somewhere else, anywhere but here.

The dragging through the camp went on for he did not know how long, until finally he came to a stop, dust settling all around him. He lay there, face first on the ground, groaning, one eye swollen shut. With an effort, he opened his one good eye and saw he had been deposited a few feet away, ironically, from the Destiny Sword. Clearly, this had been done to rub it in. The Sword sat there, where he had left it, lodged inside the huge boulder.

"Here it is, this weapon that has plagued our Empire for centuries," Andronicus yelled out to a crowd of transfixed soldiers. "Thor may be the Chosen One—or the Chosen One might just be one of us. Who is to say that only a MacGil, only a member of the Ring, can wield it? Who is to say that is not a myth they have created to keep us down?"

The crowd cheered in approval.

"Whoever wields the sword," Andronicus yelled, "whoever can pull it from this boulder, will be named a general. Who will step forward and try?"

There came a cheer, followed by a rush of men, as one soldier after the next rushed forward, grabbed the Sword's hilt and yanked with all his might, trying desperately to get it out of the stone. Thor's could not bear to watch the Destiny Sword in the hands of these cretins. He did not know what he would do if one of them could wield it. That would mean that the legend had been wrong and that he, Thor, was not special after all.

But one at a time, the men tried and failed, one soldier after the next, pushing and shoving each other to get a try. Some tried two or three times.

But it was the same for all of them: nothing.

Finally, Andronicus himself approached the Sword, and the crowd parted ways. He knelt before it, then stood, wrapped his huge hands around its hilt, and with a great scream, he yanked the Sword with all he had. Thor worried for a moment. After all, Andronicus was his father, and a MacGil. Might that enable him to wield the Sword?

But though Andronicus' scream rose, higher and higher, eventually he collapsed, unable to make the Sword budge.

Thor felt a great sense of relief, as he realized that none of the Empire, even his father, could wield it. It also made him feel special.

Andronicus glowered down at the weapon, and Thor could see his face turning purple with rage.

"Bring me a hammer!" he commanded. "NOW!"

Several men rushed to his side with a two-handed war hammer. Andronicus snatched it, raised it high overhead, and with a scream, he brought it down on the rock.

Try as he did, the rock would not shatter. It would not even chip. Andronicus tried again and again, with always the same result: it was like hammering steel.

Finally, with a great groan of frustration, Andronicus turned and swung the hammer sideways, smashing in the heads of two soldiers and killing them on the spot. Then he spun the hammer again, and threw it into the crowd, killing another soldier as it hit him in mid-air.

"If the Sword cannot be wielded by myself, or any of my men," Andronicus called out, "then we have no use for it. It does us only harm while here in the Ring. It only keeps the Shield up, and keeps our men from reinforcing us. I command for the Sword to be removed from the Ring at once, taken back across the Canyon and destroyed for good. I want a dozen men to hoist this boulder on their shoulders and carry it back across the Canyon, to our ships. MOVE!" he screamed.

A dozen men rushed forward, jumping into action, heading to the boulder. They all tried to lift it, but it would barely budge.

More and more soldiers joined in, until finally, with two dozen men, they managed to get the boulder up high, on their shoulders. They all began to march, carrying the sword away.

Thor's heart was breaking inside.

"NO!" Thor screamed.

It was like watching a piece of himself being taken away.

As Thor watched it disappear from view, he did everything in his power to try to break free. But he could not. The Akdon shackles on his wrists would not allow him.

Andronicus turned towards Thor and stood over him.

"There is no weapon that you can wield than I cannot wield myself," Andronicus insisted.

Thor realized that it burned his father up that he was able to wield a weapon that his father could not.

"I am stronger than you, father," Thor said. "That is why you fear me."

Andronicus screamed, stepped forward, and kicked Thor so hard in the side he felt one of his ribs crack. Thor turned and coughed, lying on the ground, gasping for air.

"McCloud!" Andronicus yelled.

Thor looked up to see the former King McCloud step forward, missing on eye and with a huge burn on the side of his disfigured face, where he had been branded with the emblem of the Empire. He looked like a monster.

"I think it is time we teach our young Thorgrin what it feels like to be branded. Maybe we shall brand his face, the same way I did yours."

Thor's heart pounded at his words. McCloud's eyes opened wide with a smile of delight.

"It would be great pleasure, my master," McCloud said.

McCloud turned, grabbed a hot poker handed to him by an attendant, and examined the end of it, affixed with the large square emblem of the Empire, burning white-hot with fire.

"NO!" Thor screamed out, as McCloud reached down, the hot poker coming close to his face. Thor knew that within moments his face would be disfigured, just like McCloud's, branded with the Emblem of Andronicus. The thought tore him apart; he could think of nothing worse.

McCloud sneered in delight as he lowered the poker for Thor's exposed face.

Thor heard a screech, high in the sky. He looked up to see Estopheles; she dove down, her talons out, and McCloud looked up— but not in time. Estopheles clawed his face, leaving deep cuts across his nose and forehead and cheeks and lips. McCloud shrieked, dropping the iron, which landed on his foot, scalding it, and made him scream again. His face a bloody mess, he finally turned and ran, Estopheles chasing him across the camp.

Andronicus stepped forward and picked up the iron himself, holding it over Thor, sneering down.

"This is your last chance," Andronicus said. "Stop defying me, and accept my offer. Embrace me. Half the Empire will be yours. I am the only true father you have in this world. Embrace me and find relief."

Thor mustered just enough energy to lift his head, and spit at Andronicus.

"I would rather die a bastard than live as your son."

Andronicus grimaced, and with a grunt of supreme rage and frustration, he lowered the iron.

Thor turned, and at the last second, the poker missed his face and instead sunk into his shoulder. Thor shrieked, as the burning iron sunk into his shoulder and he experienced the worst pain of his life. The searing iron branded his flesh, leaving the emblem of the Empire on it. Smoke sizzled from his arm and filled his nostrils with the awful smell of burning flesh. Thor screamed until he could scream no more.

Finally, Andronicus stopped. Thor lay there weakly, limp, barely able to catch his breath. He couldn't take any more of this.

"Take him to the pit," Andronicus ordered.

Please God, let me die, Thor thought, drifting in and out of consciousness.

Thor felt himself being dragged by the rope binding his feet, paraded back through the camp. In the distance, he saw a round black pit coming into view, and he felt himself going over the edge, hurling down, sinking into the blackness.

CHAPTER TWENTY NINE

Silesia was awash in activity as Reece hurried through the courtyard, Elden, O'Connor and Conven at his side, all of them merging with the others, making their way from the hall of arms towards the main army in the city square. All around them thousands of knights were mobilizing, breaking up into four camps, one lead by Kendrick, one by Erec, one by Tirus and one by Godfrey. Reece and Conven and O'Connor and Elden stuck together, as they always had, and they were joined by the two other Legion members—Serna and Krog—along with Indra, who stayed by Elden's side. They decided to join Kendrick's division, as Reece wanted to be close to his eldest brother when battle came.

After so many months battling enemies alone in the Empire, with just their small group to rely on, it felt good to have the support of this vast army and to be fighting back home in the Ring. Even if the odds were worse, Reece felt more protected now than ever. He also felt more determined. Reece was devastated to hear that his best friend had been captured, and he had no reservations about riding into battle, whatever the odds. He would happily give his life for Thor's. He knew they were vastly outnumbered, but he felt as if that had always been the case, ever since he had joined the Legion. Battle was not easy. Nor was glory. But it was precisely these odds which made battle glorious.

The crowd swelled as they all reached the main gate of Silesia. They all began to funnel their way through, beneath the soaring arches, and hundreds of Silesian citizens stood there, waving banners, cheering them on.

"Return home to us!"

"Save the Ring!"

"Kill Andronicus!"

"Free Thorgrin!"

"Silesia awaits your return."

These citizens were brave: they cheered the soldiers, knowing full well that their departure would leave them unprotected and that Silesia would be vulnerable to attack once again.

Reece, fully dressed in his ring mail, prepared himself, feeling that nervous excitement and anticipation of battle in his gut, checking and tightening his weapons around his belt, testing his long sword, his short sword, making sure his daggers were there, feeling the shaft of his flail. He had more weapons on his horse, up ahead, and felt ready for every contingency.

"Were you just going to leave without saying goodbye then?" came a voice.

Reece turned to Selese standing there, in the midst of the crowd, but a few feet away, looking back at him sadly.

He forked away from his friends and went to her, lowering his head, ashamed. He hadn't known what to say to her. He felt bad leaving her, especially as they had grown close over these last two days and nights together. Reece was falling in love with her. He did not know what to make of his feelings. They had been inseparable, relaxing together by the bonfires, taking in the feasts and celebrations. He had hoped it would stay like that forever.

But once again he found his life upended, found himself back on the road to battle. Once again, he found himself leaving her, and hoping he would see her before long. Before, her love had been a fantasy; but now it was real, and that made it even more painful to leave her.

"I am sorry," he said to her. "I didn't know what to say. Or if I'd be coming back."

She looked into his eyes.

"All you had to say was that you cared about me."

Reece met her gaze.

"More than you shall ever know, my lady."

She smiled back, and her whole face lit up, covered in freckles.

"If I return," Reece added, "we shall marry."

Her eyes opened wide in surprise.

"*When* you return," she said, reaching out and fixing his breastplate, adjusting it, running her hands over. He saw a tear roll down her cheek.

"You have no choice," she said. "Return to me. We're not married, but if you die, I shall be a widow."

She looked up and met his eyes, and Reece met hers, and he felt his world melt. It meant the world to him to hear that she cared for him as much as he did for her. It was painful for him to leave, looking at that face, knowing she would be left here alone, unprotected. He felt more of a burden than ever to be victorious on this day, and he resolved that he would.

She grabbed his breastplate, leaned in and kissed him, and he held the kiss for as long as he possibly could.

Finally, jostled by his men, he turned and melted back into the parade of humanity heading out the gates. He turned back and watched her, and she him, for as long as he was able, until finally she receded from sight.

Reece saw he was not alone in saying goodbye to someone he loved: up ahead, Kendrick walked hand-in-hand with Sandara, and he watched them saying their goodbyes. She was tall, with broad shoulders, had a proud bearing, and the dark skin of the Empire. Reece could see that she and Kendrick were well-matched.

As he got closer, he overheard their conversation.

"I wish for you to stay here, behind the safety of these walls," Kendrick said to her.

"It is not my way, my lord," she replied. "I go with the men, as I've done my entire life. When the wounded fall, I shall be there to heal them. The same way I was there to heal you. It is what I do. It is who I am."

"I will be with my men, at the front of battle," Kendrick said. "I will not be able to protect you."

"I do not seek your protection," she said. "I have fended for myself my entire life."

They continued walking in silence. Kendrick turned to join his men, and she stopped and said to him:

"I don't know where we shall find each other. But promise me one thing."

Kendrick turned to her.

"You will not be among the wounded."

He smiled.

"That is one promise I cannot make."

They kissed.

As Reece rejoined his legion brothers, he found Elden embroiled in a similar conversation with Indra, who stood proudly by his side and who shook off his hand as he tried to hold hers. She was too masculine, too much of a warrior for that.

"You cannot fight with us," Elden insisted. "It is not safe."

"You are a woman," Krog said. "You should know your place."

She turned and have him a look of death.

"I am as good of warrior as you," she replied defiantly. "I carry weapons as fine as yours, my daggers are just as quick, and my arrows as fast. I can slice any man's throat as well as you. I may just slice yours. In fact, perhaps it is you who should stay behind."

Krog stared back, red-faced.

Indra turned back to Elden.

"I will fight by your side, or you will not see my face again. The decision is yours."

Elden sighed, and eventually shrugged. Indra was as strong-willed as they came, and there was no use trying to convince her. Besides, after all this time together with her in the Empire, after all the times she had saved their lives, she had become like a member of the legion. Indra was a survivor, and he had no worries about her.

Reece came up beside Conven, who looked as morose as ever; he blended in well, with all the somber faces around him, the men mentally preparing for battle. Reece could see in his eyes that he had nothing to lose, that he was ready to throw down his life, and Reece seriously wondered if Conven would survive this battle. He could sense that he did not want to. Not without his twin brother.

O'Connor oiled his new long bow and wore his ever present smile, in his chipper mood, as always. Whether he was in the Empire or back in the Ring, O'Connor seemed at home everywhere. Reece was glad to have his steady hand at his side as they all rode into battle.

Serna and Krog walked tentatively beside them. Reece could see the anxiety in their strides; they had not undergone the quest they had in the Empire, had not faced the same travails that they had undergone. Reece could recognize in them their anxiety, the way he'd once felt. It made Reece feel like a veteran.

There was Godfrey, not far off, his older brother, and Reece was proud to see him in a suit of armor, even if it did not seem to fit him quite perfectly. Godfrey marched with a swagger, flanked by Akorth and Fulton, leading several hundred men. Reece wondered if they were drunk; certainly Akorth and Fulton were, obvious from their gait.

It was funny to see Godfrey in charge: on the one hand, it didn't quite fit him, yet at the same time, somehow it did. Reece thought that he could see something of their father in him. Godfrey might not be a warrior, but he was a survivor, and a crafty one. Reece felt that Godfrey could outwit anyone. And he had a feeling that no matter what, he would find a way to survive, even if he did it his own way.

They all finally reached their horses, Reece picking out his in the vast sea of animals.

Reece stood there, about to mount his horse, when he spotted something out of the corner of his eye that made him turn. It was a face, staring back at him from the sea of onlookers. He did a double-take, assuming he was imagining it.

But as he looked closer, his heart stopped as he saw who it was. Standing there, in the midst of the people, was a girl whose face he had etched into his mind for most of his childhood. A girl who had never been far from his thoughts, at least not until he met Selese. Standing there was his cousin, Tirus' only daughter.

Stara.

She stared back at him, her glowing green eyes clearly locked just on his, even in the mass of people. She was too far away to speak to, and with the tide of soldiers coming in and out, he lost sight of her, then regained her again. She looked like an apparition, floating in a sea.

It pained him to see her. Why did she have to be here? Why now? After he had already fallen in love with someone else? It had taken him years to let her go. But seeing her brought it all back again, the pain fresh.

Reece forced himself to turn and look away. He loved Selese now; it wouldn't be fair to her to look at anyone else.

As he mounted his horse, despite himself, he turned and glanced back for Stara. He was flooded with both relief and upset to see that she was gone.

A horn sounded, and a messenger came galloping across the landscape, racing right up to Kendrick. Reece and the others gathered close, listening.

"My Lord," the messenger said, gasping for breath. "I have news...the Destiny Sword—Andronicus has sent it away."

There came a horrified gasp from the men as the messenger stood there, heaving, catching his breath.

"Speak clearly," Kendrick ordered. "What do you mean, 'sent it away'?"

"It is being sent now to the other side of the Canyon. If it crosses, the Shield will be down. All will be lost!"

"We must retrieve it at once!" Tirus, close by, called out.

"It must be out foremost objective," Erec called out.

"But we cannot spare the men," Kendrick said.

"We need but a small group to go after the Sword," Godfrey said. "Not an entire division."

"I will go," Reece volunteered, stepping forward.

Immediately, Elden, Conven and O'Connor stepped forward by his side.

"And we," they said.

"After all," Reece added, "it is we who chased that Sword halfway across the Empire. If anyone should know how to get it back, it should be us."

"Let our small group of legion go," Elden said. "That way you will not detract from the main battle, from saving Thor."

Kendrick looked Reece up and down with a new look of respect. He nodded back solemnly.

"You make our father proud," Kendrick said.

Reece felt a swelling of pride, elated to be so raised up in Kendrick's eyes.

"We will meet again, my brother," Reece said.

"I know that we will," answered Kendrick.

Without a word, Reece and the other legion mounted their horses and were the first to ride, following the messenger as he led them down a separate road, forking off to the side, away from the road the army would take.

Reece felt the wind in his hair, the ground moving fast beneath him, and knew already that battle had begun.

CHAPTER THIRTY

Thor lay deep in the blackness of the pit, the smell of earth in his nose, his entire body aching. Somewhere up above he heard the muffled shouts of soldiers. He managed to open his one good eye, the other swollen shut, as he strayed in and out of consciousness. It was dark and cold down here, at least a dozen feet below ground, and the light that filtered down, although not bright, made him squint. He tried to move, but every part of his body felt too bruised and broken. He had never known what aching was until this moment. He felt as if he had battled a million men.

He tried to move his wrists but felt them still shackled by the Akdon cuffs; all the strength he'd once had sapped from his body. He could feel all of his energy leaving him, right at the spot where the shackles held his wrists together tight. There was something about this metal—he'd never felt so weak, so vulnerable, in his life.

As Thor squinted, looking up into the sky, he dimly saw soldiers up above, jeering down, throwing clumps of dirt. He closed his eyes and lowered his head, unable to expend the effort.

Thor shut his eyes and saw himself standing in a land far away. He was in the Land of the Dragons, back in the Empire, and he stood atop the highest peak. Sitting on a mountain across from him was Mycoples. She looked at him and flapped her massive wings, then leapt from the peak and flew towards him. He could read her thoughts, and could feel that she was coming to rescue him.

She flew closer, and as she flew beside him, he reached out for her.

But as he did, he looked up to see his hands were clasped in the Akdon shackles; he could not summon the strength to reach her.

A huge net suddenly fell, entangling Mycoples, and she tumbled down through the sky, falling end over end, screeching. She called out for him, needing his help as much as he needed hers.

Thor blinked and found himself in a vast desert, baking under the sun. He looked down and saw the desert floor, blanketed in thousands of snakes. Stretched before him was an endless trail that weaved through the snakes; he knew instinctively that he had to stay on that trail if he wanted to live. It was a trail made up of ossified dragon bones.

Thor walked down the trail, deeper and deeper into the desert, feeling as if he were walking to the end of the world. On the horizon a stone cottage came into view, and as he came closer, he looked up, and was surprised to see Argon's face.

"Argon, help me," Thor whispered, gasping for air, reaching out for him with his shackled hands.

But Argon stood behind a protective wall, an invisible shield, and Thor could not get closer. Argon stared back from the other side, staff in hand, concern etched across his face.

"I wish I could," Argon replied. "But I am of help to no one now."

"Teach me," Thor said. "Teach me to be free."

Argon shook his head.

"I have already trained you," he said. "All the powers you have left, they lie deep within you. Now, you must train yourself."

Argon's eyes lit up, a fiery glow so intense that Thor nearly had to look away.

"Search within yourself, Thorgrin. Therein lies the last frontier. You must come to know who you are. Not who your father is, not who your mother is. But who *you* are."

Thor reached out for him, trying to get through, but found himself falling backwards.

Thor was lying face down on a long, narrow footbridge, spanning a massive Canyon. The footbridge crossed the sky, stretching for miles, and he lay there in the middle. It rose in an arc and led to a cliff, on top of which sat a castle, shining blue. He rolled over, looked to one side, and saw the Destiny Sword. He reached for it, grasping its hilt. He held it up high, and as he did, he was horrified to see the Sword had been snapped in half. He examined it, hardly comprehending.

It was now just a useless piece of metal.

Thor turned and hurled the Sword, and it went flying over the edge. He watched it tumble through the sky, drop down to nothingness.

"Thorgrin," came a woman's voice.

171

Thor looked up. In the distance, atop the castle, stood his mother, arms wide at her sides, smiling down compassionately at him.

"Mother!" Thor called out.

"I am here, my son," she said back, her voice filled with love.

"Why didn't you tell me?" Thor said. "Why didn't you tell me who my father was?"

She shook her head.

"None of that matters now, Thorgrin," she said. "Come home. Come home to me. Come and gain powers greater than you ever knew. Learn the secret of who you are. Only then will you be free. Only then can you overcome your father."

With a supreme effort, Thor got to his hands and knees and began to crawl his way down the bridge, towards her. But the bridge was so long, and she seemed to stand in another realm, getting farther away from him the more he crawled.

"Mother!" he screamed.

The footbridge suddenly snapped, and Thor went tumbling, end over end, screaming as he plunged downward, towards the depths of the world.

Thor woke screaming.

He was still in the darkness of the pit, his face still swollen, one eye swollen shut, and his arm still throbbed where he had been branded. He wondered how long he'd slept; from the pain throbbing all over his face and body, he figured it wasn't long enough.

He looked up to see Empire men still jeering down at him. Nothing had changed.

He was disappointed. He thought he had died, and a part of him wished that he had, and as he looked up at all these men, he had a sinking feeling that the worst of his suffering was yet to come.

CHAPTER THIRTY ONE

Gwendolyn hiked down the dense forest trail, accompanied by Steffen, Aberthol, and Alistair—and, of course, Krohn, who would not leave her side, nearly clinging to her, his fur brushing up against her leg. It was an unlikely group, the four of them and a leopard: Gwendolyn the Queen, Steffen the hunchback, Aberthol the scholar, and Alistair the mysterious Druid. Two beautiful, young women, one old man, and one hunchback. From an outside perspective, they must have seemed to be a vulnerable group of travelers taking this remote road this far north, in the notorious Thornwood Forest, no less. But appearances were deceiving: Steffen was adroit with a bow, Gwendolyn, raised with the King's guard, was confident of her own fighting skills, and while Aberthol was frail, she sensed that Alistair carried a hidden power that would be at least equal to Steffen's fighting skills.

Gwen surveyed the beautiful, thick forest all around her, the trees made of an ancient, white bark. A winter forest, they called it. The northern reaches of the Ring were filled with them. Leaves sprouted here in winter, fell off in the summer, and began to bloom in fall. Now that it was winter, they were in full bloom, huge white leaves everywhere, covered in frost. It looked like a white wonderland, the frost on the leaves crunching beneath their feet. Gwendolyn felt the cold grow more intense, more biting, with every step they took. This place looked so pure, so untouched, as if nothing evil could ever happen here; yet Gwen knew some of the worst criminals lurked amidst these trees.

Gwendolyn had been relieved when Steffen, Aberthol, and Alistair had insisted on accompanying her on her quest to the Netherworld. Aberthol had tried to dissuade her, reminding her that no human had ever entered the Netherworld and returned alive, but it had done no good. She knew it had to be done, that this is what Thor needed most. She sensed that Thor could never have been captured—nor could have Mycoples—unless by magic, and she knew they would need an equally strong magic to counteract it. It was her way of aiding in the battle. This was her front.

Gwendolyn also desperately missed Argon, felt guilty for him being punished on her account. She wanted to bring him back, regardless. She sensed, in her dreams, that he needed her, and she was determined to go to him, even it meant risking her life. After all, he had risked his life for her.

Gwendolyn had expected Steffen to accompany her, but she had been surprised by Alistair's insistence upon coming. Ever since meeting Erec's wife-to-be, Gwendolyn had felt a special connection to her; the two of them had bonded instantly, like sisters. In some ways, she was like the sister that Gwendolyn had never really had, considering Luanda had hardly been there for her.

"The Netherworld is a place of magic and trapped souls," Aberthol said, in his old raspy voice, his cane clicking in the icy leaves as they continued marching endlessly through the forest. It was getting so dark in here, Gwen could no longer tell if it was day or night.

"It is not a place fit for a lady," he added. "And most certainly not for a Queen."

Aberthol had been trying to talk her out of it the entire way, trying to convince her to turn around. She didn't want to hear any more.

"I believe our course is ill-advised, my lady," he continued. "Argon has served the MacGils for generations; perhaps his time has come to move on. We cannot understand the way of sorcerers. In any case, I don't see how you can rescue him."

"Argon was my father's trusted advisor," Gwendolyn answered, "and he has been a good and faithful friend. If he is meant to stay where he is, then neither I nor the gods can stop it. But I shall not let him wallow there without at least trying."

"These trees are ancient," Aberthol prattled on. "This wood has seen centuries of battle. But there has never been a city here. Why?"

Gwendolyn noticed that the older he became, the more prone Aberthol had become to speaking to himself, to rattling on with old stories and lessons, whether or not anyone was listening. He talked more and more in his old age, and Gwen sometimes had to tune him out.

"Of course, the land could not tolerate it," Aberthol continued. "This land has been relegated throughout the history of the Ring to a place of abandon. It is the road to the Netherworld, that is all. No one lives here. Except of course, for ne'er-do-wells and thieves of the night. It's a haven for derelicts, do you understand? No one crosses Thornwood without a proper entourage. And we enter with just the four of us." He shook his head. "A recipe for disaster. Now, if you had listened to me…"

Gwendolyn tried to tune him out, as Aberthol continued mumbling.

"Does he always go on like this?" Alistair asked Gwendolyn, coming up beside her, with a smile. She nodded towards Aberthol as he continued his monologue.

Gwendolyn smiled back.

"More than he used to," she said.

Alistair smiled.

"Do you fear the Netherworld?" Gwendolyn asked the question foremost in her mind.

Alistair continued to walk beside her, silent and expressionless, until finally, she shook her head.

"I have to be honest and say that I do not," she said.

Gwendolyn was intrigued. It was not the answer she had expected.

"Why?"

"I have seen some of the worst things this world has to offer," Alistair said. "I have suffered enough to learn that fear is a waste of energy. What will come, will come. And what will not, will not."

As they continued to walk, Gwendolyn sensed there was something more Alistair wanted to tell her. Gwen found her so mysterious, and there were many questions she wanted to ask. Who was this woman, this Druid, who feared nothing?

But Gwen didn't want to pry. So instead she respected her silence, waiting until she was ready.

Finally, Alistair sighed.

"I once worked in a tavern," Alistair said. "One night, as I was serving drinks, a patron grabbed my wrist and when no one was looking and pulled me inside a room. He was a strong man, with a warrior's grip, and I didn't have the strength to resist. I cried out for help, but either no one heard, or no one cared."

Alistair continued walking, staring into space as if reliving it.

175

"Something happened," Alistair finally said. "I still don't fully understand it. I reached up to push him off of me, and a burst of energy came from my palm. It struck his chest and he flew across the room. He lay there, frozen in fear, staring back at me with a look of wonder. I didn't wait: I turned and walked out the door."

Alistair sighed.

"I'm different from others. I don't know how. But I am. I don't feel this world the same way you do. I didn't seek to harm that man. But I couldn't have stopped it if I tried."

Gwendolyn was more impressed with Alistair each time she spoke to her. Alistair was so humble, so soft-spoken; and despite her beauty, Gwen could tell she bore great strength. Gwen also felt a sense of camaraderie with her: she had found someone who had suffered, like she had, someone who understood what it was like to go to the other side and back.

Gwen didn't want to pry, but she couldn't help herself; she felt compelled to ask the next question:

"Where do you hail from?" she asked.

Before Alistair could answer, there came a twig snap in the forest, and they all turned to see a dozen men appear behind them. Krohn snarled, a vicious noise, his hairs on end as he stood out front of the group and took a few steps forward.

Gwendolyn immediately recalled her ambush in the Southern Forest. These men were thieves, too, it was obvious from their expressions—yet they were more somber looking. Dressed in chain mail from head to toe, they had new arms, seemed impervious to the cold, and were well-organized, camouflaged in all-white. They did not look like amateur thieves, as the ones in the Southern Forest. They looked like professional killers.

She feared for Krohn, who was snarling louder and louder, especially as the thief raised a crossbow for his head.

"Krohn, come back here," Gwendolyn said.

But Krohn had other ideas. Krohn, fearless, leapt into the air and, with a horrific snarl, laid his fangs into one of the thieves' throat before he could get off a shot. The thief screamed as Krohn pinned him down on the ground. Krohn thrashed left and right, and in moments, the thief was dead.

There came the noise of a crossbow firing, and an arrow sailed through the air before any of them could react.

"KROHN!" Gwen cried out.

Krohn yelped as the arrow embedded in his side, knocking him down.

The thieves expected that to be all, but Krohn surprised them. He was not done yet.

Krohn bounced back to his feet and leapt again, snarling. He took down another thief, killing him, before yet another arrow sailed through the air and knocked Krohn down for good.

"KROHN!" Gwen cried, stepping forward for him.

The lead thief stepped forward and pointed his sword at Gwendolyn's throat.

She and the others froze.

"I will say this but once," the lead soldier said, in a raspy voice, empty of warmth. "Each of you strip. Take off all your clothes, everything you have. Then lie face down in the snow. We will kill you either way, but this way your death will be quick and painless. If you resist, it will be long and torturous."

"And what sort of choice is that?" Aberthol asked. "I don't see why we should allow you to kill us."

The lead soldier stepped up and backhanded Aberthol, who cried out and stumbled, clutching his face.

"I won't say it again," he said, stepping forward and holding up a hooked knife. "You have three seconds, so make your decision quickly."

"You can have our decision now if you like," Gwendolyn said.

Gwen glanced at Steffen, who broke into action. He raised his bow faster than she could blink, and within moments fired off three arrows, killing three of the thieves on the spot.

Gwen drew a small dagger she had in her waist, stepped forward and stabbed the lead thief in the throat; his eyes opened wide in surprise as he clutched his bleeding throat then sank down to the ground, dead.

But that left only four dead, and eight more determined thieves charged, weapons raised high. Gwen realized there was nothing left they could do to defend themselves; there were too many of them, looming too fast, and she knew that they were going to die.

177

As the thieves were but a few feet away, Alistair stepped forward, before them all, closed her eyes calmly, and raised a palm.

The eight charging thieves suddenly stopped short, as if hitting an invisible wall. They ran into it headfirst, and dropped their arms.

A blue light then flew from her palm, striking each one of them and sending them flying dozens of feet through the air at an impossible speed, until each struck a tree and collapsed to the ground, dead.

Gwendolyn turned and looked at Alistair in awe, as did the others. She had never seen anything like that in her life.

Alistair then took several steps forward, knelt by Krohn's side, who was whimpering, bleeding, on the verge of death, and laid her palms on his wound.

Gwen watched, transfixed, as a white light emanated from them and as Krohn's wounds were healed before her eyes.

In moments, Krohn regained his feet. He blinked several times, as if confused. Then he stepped forward and licked Alistair. Gwen could not believe it: Krohn was revived.

Gwen examined Alistair closely, with her beautiful blonde hair and blue eyes, and she could not help but wonder:

What secrets was she hiding?

CHAPTER THIRTY TWO

Reece galloped across the countryside, flanked by O'Connor, Elden, Conven, Indra, Serna, and Krog, all of them heading east, racing in the direction of the stolen Sword. Reece felt odd to be on a quest, to be riding into battle, and not have Thor by his side. He was determined to find his best friend and free him; if he had his choice, he would be riding with the main army right for Andronicus' camp right now.

But Reece knew he had to serve the army, serve the Ring first, and he knew that right now, where he was most needed was in tracking down the Destiny Sword before it left, before it brought down the Shield and exposed all his countrymen to death. He knew it would be what Thor would want him to do as well.

Their small group, seven in all, galloped hard, passing all the charred Empire corpses that Mycoples had wiped out along the way. The countryside was in ruins, the Ring caught up in a wave of destruction from both directions. Reece did not know exactly where the Sword was at this moment—none of them did—but he knew it was somewhere on the other side of the Highlands.

They had crossed the peaks of the Highlands hours ago, and they all charged down the descent. It felt funny to be here, on the McCloud side of the Ring. Reece had never been this far east, spending his entire life on the Western side of the Ring, but he had heard stories of the McClouds, and he'd had no desire to venture this far. Crossing the Highlands was like crossing an invisible barrier in his mind, and a part of him already felt as if he were behind a wall, with no way back.

The tension was thick in the air here. When they had crested the Highlands they had spotted, on the horizon, a half-million of Andronicus' men, swarming like ants across the countryside. They had all paused, and felt the gravity of it. In some ways, this felt like a suicide mission.

As they continued on the road, charging ever East, as they came closer to the body of troops, they forked off into a smaller trail that took them through dense woods. They could no longer ride the main roads, with so many troops swarming about. They would have to use stealth, speed, and cunning.

"We need to know exactly where they have taken the Sword," Reece called out to the others.

"And how do you propose we do that?" Krog asked back.

"We will have to interrogate an Empire soldier," Reece responded.

"We can hardly just go up to one and ask him," Krog said, skeptical.

"We will capture one," Reece replied.

"The seven of us, confront an Empire division?" Krog pressed.

Reece was growing impatient with Krog's skepticism and his lack of respect in the face of command.

"We don't need to confront a division," Reece explained. "We need only ambush a smaller group. That's why we took the woods. All armies send out scouts, on the periphery of the main camp."

They continued riding in a tense silence, header deeper into the woods for several minutes, until finally Reece spotted movement.

Reece raised his hand in a signal, and they all came to a stop. They all sat there on their horses, very still, waiting and watching the trees.

There came a muffled noise, then movement of branches, then around the bend, there came into view a small patrol of Empire soldiers. There were seven of them—exactly as many as Reece's group—all hardened warriors from the looks of them, wearing the black and gold of the Empire, the intimidating helmets, the brand-new glistening weapons. They rode strong horses and scanned the forest carefully. It would not be an easy ambush. But they had no choice. If they did not, they would be discovered anyway. Reece felt confident in his own skills; he only hoped that Indra and the two new legion could hold their own. At a moment like this, he desperately wished Thor was by his side.

"On my signal," he whispered to the others, "ready your weapons."

They all sat there on their horses, watching as the troops came closer. Reece could feel his horse want to prance and held her in check, his palms sweating, despite the cold.

"And who put you in charge here?" Krog asked Reece.

Reece turned and saw Krog staring back defiantly. Reece and his friends had fought together so seamlessly for so long that Reece had never expected division amongst them.

"Thor is in charge," Reece corrected. "But he's not here. In his absence, I am leading. Now be silent or leave!" Reece snapped, afraid the voices would give them away.

But Krog would not relent.

"I'm as much a Legion member as you," Krog said.

Reece flushed with rage. Krog was going to give them away. Reece was going to rush over to him and slap him silent.

But it was already too late: all the bickering caught the attention of the Empire troops, who suddenly looked their way.

Before any of them could react, Conven let out a battle cry, kicked his horse and charged forward through the woods. He raised his sword and rode recklessly right into the thick of the Empire patrol. He was fearless—or suicidal.

Reece was quickly losing control, watching his plan fall apart all around him.

Conven, sword raised, charged into the startled group of soldiers, slashing wildly and managing to knock a few of them off their horses with his wild blows. He didn't even bother to raise his shield as blows rained down upon him. He charged through the group so fast, that somehow he did not get killed. A final blow, however, knocked him off his horse, and he fell down and hit the ground with a clank of metal, rolling.

Reece could wait no longer.

"ATTACK!" he screamed.

O'Connor, disciplined, awaited the command, then fired off two arrows with perfect precision, killing two soldiers—the two that Conven had knocked to the ground, killing them as they tried to get back up.

That left five Empire, two of whom were going for the exposed Conven.

Reece led the charge, racing to save Conven's life, and he slashed at one of them. But the soldier wheeled, blocked the blow and swung back at Reece. Reece blocked it with his shield, and the two went back and forth, locked in a fierce battle.

Finally, his arm getting tired, Reece found an opening, reached around and smashed the soldier in the side of the head with his shield, knocking him off his horse. Kolk's old lesson came back to him: one does not always need a sword to do the most damage.

Elden charged forward with his spear and stabbed a soldier in the gut—but that left his side exposed, and another soldier brought down an axe for his shoulder.

Indra raced forward, screamed, drew her dagger and stabbed the soldier in the throat. He dropped his axe limply, right before it hit Elden.

That left three more Empire soldiers, and Serna and Krog charged forward, Krog going blow for blow with a soldier while Serna jumped off his horse, tackled a soldier down to the ground, and wrestled with him. Reece watched as he fought hand to hand, expertly knocking him out with his elbows and fists. He was impressed.

But Krog raised his sword to bring it down on the other Empire soldier, and he was outfought. The Empire soldier dodged, then wheeled around and knocked Krog off his horse with an elbow strike.

Krog lay supine on the ground, startled, and turned to see the Empire soldier bring his sword down for his throat.

There came a clang, as Indra leapt forward and used her dagger to block the soldier's blow. She then swung around and slashed the soldier's leg. The soldier fell, screaming.

Indra scowled down at Krog.

"You still object to a woman joining the group?" she asked derisively.

Reece looked and saw there was but one soldier left alive—the one Indra had wounded in the leg. He lay on the ground, groaning.

Reece hurried over to him, yanked off his helmet, and looked down at his Empire face. He looked different than the men of the Ring, with his darker skin and yellow eyes.

Reece reached down and grabbed his throat, scowling.

"Where have they taken the Sword?" he asked urgently.

The Empire soldier said something to him in a language he did not understand.

Reece turned to Indra.

"What's he saying?" he asked her.

Indra stepped forward, knelt down beside him, and looked down into the soldier's face.

"He speaks an Empire tongue. He says he does not understand your language."

"Ask him," Reece said.

Indra spoke to the soldier in a language Reece did not understand.

The soldier looked at her and they exchanged a banter back and forth.

"What is he saying?" Reece finally asked, impatient.

Indra leaned back, hands on her hips.

"His words don't make any sense...." she said. "He's saying something about the Sword being in a boulder....that the boulder is being taken across the sea...that they will cross a bridge....towards the ships."

Reece's eyes opened wide.

"The Eastern Crossing," he said. "So it is true. They are taking the Sword across the Eastern crossing of the Canyon."

Reece stood, knowing all he needed to, ready to hunt down the Sword.

But as he did, the soldier surprised him by reaching up, grabbing his ankle and twisting it, catching him off guard. Reece cried out in pain, as the soldier pulled a hidden dagger from his belt and raised it, preparing to impale Reece's calf.

Conven appeared with his spear, and before anyone else could react, he plunged it into the soldier's chest, pinning him to the ground.

Reece looked up at Conven, and saw madness in his eyes. He was so grateful to him for saving his life, yet also worried for him. If Conven didn't get over mourning his brother soon, Reece feared he would not be with them for long.

Reece got up, his ankle throbbing in pain, and stormed over to Krog, who was still lying on the ground and trying to work his way up.

Reece stepped forward and planted a foot on his chest, pinning him down.

"You gave us away," Reece said, fuming. "You want to go home, go home now. You want to stay with us, you will follow orders. You defy my command again, and it will be *you* that I kill. You understand?"

Krog stared back, defiance in his eyes; but finally he relented, and nodded back in agreement.

Reece stepped off him and re-mounted his horse, as did all the others. He screamed and kicked, and soon they were galloping back through the forest. He rode with all he had: the Eastern Crossing was far, and if they were going to save the Sword, there was little time left to lose.

CHAPTER THIRTY THREE

Kendrick, leading thousands of men, paused atop the highest peak of the Highlands, as thousands of horses came to a halt behind him. He looked down at the rolling valleys below, on the Eastern side of the Ring, saw Andronicus' half-million men stretched out in companies as far as the eye could see, glistening in the sun, and knew, as a warrior, that their chances were slim. But they had no choice. Thor needed them, and the Ring needed Thor. With Thor and Mycoples and the Destiny Sword back, they would stand a chance again. If not, all would be lost. More importantly, Kendrick felt that Thor was like a brother to him, and whatever the odds, Kendrick's honor forbade him from turning an eye to his capture.

Kendrick huddled together with Erec, Godfrey, and Tirus, the four division commanders, unlikely bedfellows, convening before their masses of men. Kendrick was elated to be back in battle with Erec, the champion of the Silver, the greatest warrior the Ring had ever known; with him by his side, he felt that anything was possible.

Erec, a natural leader, raised a finger and pointed.

"Between here and Andronicus' camp lie those two valleys," Erec said. "At the easternmost point, they all converge to a chokepoint. In an area so narrow, we will have the advantage. There are two roads before us. Kendrick, you and I can lead the bulk of the attack straight down the middle, while Godfrey, you join us, and Tirus you can flank to the right. We will divide the frontline of Andronicus' men. Then we can converge beyond the valleys and attack as a unified force, aiming for the most narrow point of his eastern flank. If we hit them all together, we can create a funnel effect, and enough of us will be able to slip beyond them to find Thor."

Kendrick nodded.

"I agree," Kendrick said. "Our driving goal is to hit them fast and quick, not to get embroiled in battle, and to get a small group moving forward, deep into their camp."

"Then we waste time talking here," Tirus yelled out. He screamed and kicked his horse, and he forked off to the right, and his men of the Upper Isles, distinct in their scarlet and blue armor, obediently followed on his heels.

Kendrick and Erec kicked their horses and charged, too, taking the mountain roads before them, forking left, their forces charging after them with a shout.

But Godfrey merely sat on his horse, watching it all.

"Sire, shall we not follow them?" came the surprised voice of Godfrey's general, his horse prancing beside him.

Godfrey sat there and watched the horizon, other plans in mind. He turned and nodded to Akorth and Fulton, who each raised a horn. They blew them in alternating fashion, in staccato notes.

After waiting ten seconds, the sound of their horns was repeated back to them, echoing from somewhere in the distant valley, off to the left.

"What was that, my Liege?" his general asked, confused.

Godfrey smiled wide, satisfied.

"You'll see," he answered.

Kendrick and Erec had their strengths, and Godfrey had his. He might not be as great a warrior as they, but he had cunning. And he had made contingency plans of his own.

Godfrey screamed and kicked his horse, and his men followed as they all turned away from the other divisions and charged down the left side of the mountain.

As they followed him blindly, Godfrey only prayed that his scheme would work.

*

Erec held his sword high, nearly standing on his horse as he galloped, his face fierce, in battle mode. He gained more and more speed and was closing in on the large group of Empire men waiting to greet them at the base of the lower valley. Between he and Kendrick they had perhaps five thousand men at their disposal, all hardened warriors, all of whom he would trust with their lives.

But waiting to greet them there appeared to be twice as many men, fierce warriors each. Still, Erec was undeterred. As was Kendrick, who rode valiantly by his side, leading his own division of men. Erec took comfort knowing that Kendrick would fight to the death, just as he was prepared to do himself.

Erec heard the passing screech of an eagle high overhead and he looked up and saw Estopheles, circling. Erec raised his sword high and met his cry. It was days like this that he had been born for. He had not been born to merely survive. He had been born to live. To *truly* live.

Erec raced forward, wanting to be the first to engage in battle, and brought his silver sword down on the lead empire soldier, slashing the soldier's sword in half, then spinning around in the same motion and slashing the soldier across his back, knocking him face-first off his horse.

The soldier landed on the ground in a great clang of plate armor, the first casualty of the day. The battle had begun.

Erec was a one-man fighting machine, darting like a fish through a lake filled with slow-moving creatures. Ever since Alistair had healed him, he felt filled with energy, more than he'd ever had, and at the top of his fighting game. He attacked left and right, going blow for blow as he cut through the ranks of Empire soldiers, never pausing, receiving some blows, but most of them bouncing harmlessly off his plate armor, merely bruising or scratching him. He, on the other hand, inflicted deadly force, killing a wide swath of soldiers to his left and to his right, striking with lethal precision and moving faster than any of them could react. There was a reason he was the Silver's champion—nobody fought quicker than he. While Empire soldiers raised their swords, Erec had already punctured their armor. He was a thing of beauty to watch, and it was clear this is what he had been born to do.

Nearby, Kendrick fought just as brilliantly, forking his men off to attack the other contingent of Empire men, going blow for blow with a host of them, taking down nearly as many as Erec. He was a fearless leader, and his men rallied around him, charging into the thick of the fight.

Men began to fall on both sides, as the Empire warriors were fierce in their own right, well-rested and well-trained. The clang of metal rose up, reverberated in Kendrick's ears, as men fought for their lives in both directions. The battle grew thick, horses bumping into each other, nowhere left to move. Both sides swayed, giving to and fro, and it reminded Kendrick of the waves of the sea, pushing back and forth, breathing in and out. At some moments, Kendrick and

Erec's men were gaining momentum, pushing forward; at other times, they were being pushed back.

As the battle grew even thicker, soldiers began to dismount from their horses, and the fighting became hand-to-hand. The fighting was fierce and bloody, soldiers using swords and spears and hammers and axes, others fighting with daggers and even with their hands. Cries of men and horses rose up all around him, and the winter ground grew slick with men's blood.

Kendrick, unable to maneuver, soon found himself knocked off his horse. On foot, surrounded by hostile troops, he raised sword and shield and met a group of Empire soldiers. A soldier raised a halberd and brought it down for his face and Kendrick dodged, aiming at the shaft and slashed the halberd in two. He then butted the soldier in the face with the hilt of the sword, knocking him out.

In the same motion, Kendrick blocked a sword blow meant for his shoulder, then reached up and kicked his attacker in the stomach, knocking him back into the crowd, where he was trampled by a horse.

Another soldier charged with a spear. This blow came in too fast; Kendrick, distracted by his other attackers, braced himself for the deadly blow.

There came the distinct clang of a shield, and Kendrick looked over to see Erec, beside him, deflecting the spear; Erec then wheeled around with his shield and bashed the soldier in the face.

Another soldier came at Erec with a flail, and in the same motion, Erec pulled back his shield and threw it: it spun through the air, its sharpened edge slicing the soldier's throat.

Two more Empire soldiers attacked from behind Kendrick and Erec, ambushing them, wielding spears. It happened so fast, there was no time to react. There came another clang of metal, and Kendrick turned to see Atme and Brandt. They had stepped forward and blocked the spear thrusts meant for Erec and Kendrick, Atme with his shield and Brandt with his gauntlet. Atme stabbed the attacker with his sword, while Brandt backhanded the other attacker, sending him to the ground.

Kendrick was inspired fighting beside Erec, Atme and Brandt, just like old times, and he grabbed the soldier's flail off the ground and swung it high, creating a wide perimeter around the four of them, and taking out a half-dozen Empire soldiers.

The fighting grew fiercer and fiercer, thicker and thicker, going on for what felt like hours. No matter how hard they all fought, Kendrick felt they were not gaining momentum. It was like fighting against a never-ending tide. He was beginning to seriously doubt they would be able to execute their plan of getting a small group through quickly and furtively to liberate Thor in the center of the camp.

There came a blast of horns, and Kendrick looked up to the valley's end to see a sight which worried him: several thousand more of Andronicus' men were pouring into the far end of the valley, coming to assist their fellow soldiers.

The momentum was just enough to push the tide back. Kendrick, Erec and their men began to be pushed further and further back by the crush of soldiers. More of their men were beginning to fall, and Kendrick was starting to realize they were losing. The Empire men were just too strong for them, and too many. He knew that unless something happened soon, he and his men would be slaughtered on this field.

Kendrick spotted something out of the corner of his eye, up high, at the side of the valley, reflecting light. He glanced over and saw something which puzzled him. There, atop a cliff, were several thousand soldiers mounted on horseback, dressed in the distinctive armor and flying the banner of the McClouds. They charged down the slope, heading for the flank of the battle.

At first Kendrick thought they were charging to abet the Empire cause; but as he watched he realized they were not aiming for them, but instead, were charging for the Empire. They were not attacking his men—they were helping them.

The new fighting force opened up a second front, causing mass confusion up and down the Empire ranks. It was exactly what Kendrick needed. But he could not understand what was happening: why would the McClouds, their sworn enemy, want to help them?

As Kendrick looked closely, he saw, with shock, who was leading them, and it all made sense:

Bronson.

Bronson rode out front, before the thousands of McCloud soldiers, and charged with all his might, right for the Empire. They came like a thunderstorm, using their downhill momentum to create a wave of destruction.

They impacted with a clash as loud as thunder.

In moments, they began to cut a path right through the terrified and confused Empire forces. In a panic, many Empire began to turn and flee, trampling each other.

Erec and Kendrick took advantage of the moment, redoubling their efforts, and began to gain new momentum. Empire soldiers fell in every direction, as they pushed them back further and further.

Soon, Empire men were turning and running, and the MacGils pushed them back, all the way out of the valley.

Finally, with a great cheer, Erec's and Kendrick's men met up with Bronson's at the valley's end. The valley now belonged to them. They had won.

Kendrick came over to Bronson, who stood there breathing heavily, covered in blood, grinning.

"I told you I am a MacGil," Bronson said.

Kendrick and Erec shook their heads.

"We were wrong about you," Kendrick said.

"You have saved our forces here on this day," Erec said.

Bronson's grin widened.

"The day is not done yet," he replied, "and I don't know about you, but I don't plan on stopping until we drive the Empire all the way back to the sea."

Godfrey rode with his men, forking down to the side of the valley, away from the main battle, Akorth and Fulton by his side and several thousand men behind them. Godfrey kept in his sights the huge group of Empire soldiers before them as he galloped straight ahead fearlessly. The soldiers before them outnumbered them, at least five to one, a massive Empire division waiting to face them.

"My Lord!"

Godfrey's general caught up behind, riding fast, terror in his voice.

"Where are you leading us?! We are outnumbered and ride to instant death. Your bravery borders on recklessness! We must turn around, go back and join the others. Surely, they do not expect us to meet so many men here. Your plan, whatever it was, has gone awry.

We ride to our deaths. We must turn back! I am all for chivalry, but this is suicide!"

But Godfrey only smiled wider as he rode, never slowing.

"Funny, I am all for chivalry myself," Godfrey said, "yet, I prefer a different sort of chivalry."

"My lord, I do not understand!" his general persisted. "Are you such a reckless leader that you would lead all these men to their deaths?"

"Sometimes leaders need to be reckless, don't they?" Godfrey asked with a smile. He then turned, kicked his horse and rode even faster.

Godfrey rode and rode, praying and hoping his plan worked out. Of course, his general was right; they were vastly outnumbered. There were far more men facing them than Kendrick had ever dreamed. It was a massive division of Empire men. And in conventional battle, they would all certainly die.

But Godfrey, for the first time in his life, was unafraid. He knew that he could outwit the sword, and he was relying on his wit to save this day. This would be the supreme test of it.

As they neared, hardly fifty yards away, Godfrey raised a hand and slowed to a walk. Akorth and Fulton blew their horns and waved the banner meant for all to stop.

Behind them, Godfrey's thousands of men came to a halt, a mere thirty yards away from the Empire men, who stood there frozen, lined up in perfect ranks, silent.

"Why did we stop, my lord?" his general asked, his voice shaking in fear.

But Godfrey ignored him.

Godfrey dismounted, his armor clanging, and Akorth and Fulton dismounted beside him. The three of them, armor and spurs clanging, walked across the gap between them, each leading their horses by the reins, and the Empire soldiers, who also sat there, on horseback, unmoving.

The Empire general, out front, dismounted, along with two other warriors, and walked out to meet them. They met in the middle, in a tense silence.

Godfrey, Akorth and Fulton turned to their horses and unstrapped dozens of huge bags from the harnesses. They dropped them down at the Empire commander's feet where they landed with a metallic clang that any soldier anywhere in the world would recognize.

It was the clang of gold.

The Empire general reached down, hoisted a bag, pried it open, and reached in and held up a gold coin. He examined it, and finally he nodded, satisfied.

"Our men are yours," he said.

A huge cheer came up among the Empire men.

Realizing what had happened, a cheer arose among Godfrey's men.

Godfrey's general came up beside them, staring down at the huge mound of gleaming gold, his mouth open in shock.

Godfrey smiled over at him.

"As you get to know me," Godfrey said with a smile, laying a palm on his shoulder, "you'll discover there are many ways to win a battle."

CHAPTER THIRTY FOUR

Romulus strutted down the marble corridor of the capitol building, making his way toward the vast doors to the Grand Council's chamber. His footsteps echoed as he marched alone, passing row after row of decorated Empire soldiers, who stood silently at attention. The Grand Council had summoned him this time, he knew, to depose him, to strip him of all title and rank, to question him about his activities, and to try him for treason. He had spies everywhere, and he already knew what each and every one of them would say. This was their moment to imprison him once and for all and seal Andronicus' power.

Romulus had other plans. Now that he had the velvet cloak in hand, he would soon be departing from the Empire, crossing the great sea, entering the Ring, destroying the Shield, and deposing Andronicus for good. But before he embarked on his final quest to make himself the greatest ruler of the Empire, he had one last matter left to attend. The Council. A perpetual thorn in his side. He would have come on his own to seek them out, to tie up loose ends—but they had summoned him first. He had his own matters he wished to discuss. And he did not think they would be very pleased.

Romulus marched through the open doors, several soldiers yanking them open deferentially and bowing their heads as they stepped out of his way. Romulus marched right into the chamber.

Staring back at him were the two dozen dissatisfied faces of the councilmen, representing all provinces of the Empire, looking up at him with distaste and scorn.

The door was slammed behind him.

"You can stand where you are, because you won't be here long," one of them said, as he barely stepped into the room.

Romulus froze, staring back. He urged himself to restraint.

"Word has reached us that you shut off reinforcements for the great Andronicus. We are not interested in your explanation. In the name of the Grand Council of the Empire, you are hereby tried and sentenced for treason. You will be imprisoned and executed on the morrow. You will hang on the highest tree, for all would-be traitors to see."

Romulus breathed deep, expecting as much.

He then smiled wide, and took a step forward in defiance.

"I am glad to hear that you have plans for me," Romulus said. "Because I have plans for you as well."

"We have no interest in your plans," said another councilman. "You are only lucky that the Great Andronicus himself is not here to torture you slowly. We will have mercy and execute you quickly."

"Guards, arrest him!" another councilman called out.

He stood there, waiting, and nothing happened. The old men looked baffled.

And Romulus' smile widened.

"GUARDS!" they screamed.

Romulus grinned wider, and took another step forward.

"It is no longer the Great Andronicus. Now, it is the Great Romulus."

As he nodded, from out of the shadows, from all corners of the room, there suddenly appeared two dozen of Romulus' finest assassins. They rushed forward silently, short swords held high.

The councilmen barely had time to react, to meet death in the face. Romulus's men came down like a sudden plague and stabbed and hacked to death each and every one of them. Their screams filled the room, the pathetic screams of these pathetic old men, as they all slumped onto the very table where they had tried to pass judgment on Romulus.

Romulus stood there, taking in the sight, holding his hands out at his side, breathing it in like fresh air.

When his men finished, they all snapped back to attention, awaiting his command.

It was a beautiful sight. There was no one left to oppose him in the Empire now. He breathed deep, feeling his power rise. Finally, there were no more obstacles.

There was but one man left in his way, and he would soon meet the wrath of the Great Romulus. Soon he would enter the Ring. And soon, it would all be his.

CHAPTER THIRTY FIVE

Reece galloped alongside Conven, O'Connor, Elden, Indra, Serna and Krog, the seven of them racing down narrow trails, up and down hills as they charged through the thick wood, staying out of sight of Andronicus' main army. Reece knew they had to avoid the bulk of Andronicus' men if they were to have any chance of getting there safely—and before it was too late. They rode and rode, his arm scratched by branches, avoiding the open plains and meadows that could tip them off. They were cutting through McCloud territory, taking a huge shortcut, and they had been riding hard for hours.

Finally, they broke free of the forest, finding themselves deposited in a rocky, open field, with the Canyon in view on the horizon. Reece's heart soared in excitement. They had made it.

Reece could smell the ocean air, the sea was but miles beyond the Canyon. As he rode, Elden charged up beside him. He pointed:

"There!" Elden screamed. "The Crossing!"

Reece looked and saw that he was right: there on the horizon, amidst the swirling mists of the Canyon, lay the Eastern Crossing, the massive bridge spanning the Canyon, glistening in the sun. It let travelers out on the Eastern side, and the crossing, once manned with McCloud's men, now sat empty. Of course it would: all of McCloud's men were in Andronicus' service now, and with the Shield back up, there was no need for Andronicus to have the crossing manned. No one else could get in, so there was no one left to defend against.

Reece searched desperately for any sign of the Empire entourage who had taken the sword.

"There!" O'Connor screamed, pointing.

Reece squinted against the sun and saw the entourage of about two dozen Empire warriors, marching under the burden of a huge Boulder, carrying it slowly towards the bridge. They were just setting foot on it.

Reece kicked his horse and screamed, doubling his efforts.

"RIDE!" he screamed. They had caught them in time, but it would still be close. If they crossed to the other side, the Shield would go down for all time. Either way, it was a losing proposition.

They charged and charged, the cold wind whipping Reece's face, galloping until he was out of breath. Beside him his Legion brothers did the same, all of them feeling the urgency of their mission.

Luckily, the Empire group was slow-moving, weighed down by the boulder, and as they were crossing the bridge, Reece and his men narrowed the gap quickly.

Reece and the others reached the bridge and rode onto it, not slowing, catching up with the Empire men as they were nearly halfway across.

The Empire men heard the commotion, and they all turned and faced Reece and the others, surprised expressions on their faces. They set down the boulder, and prepared to fight.

Reece realized they were badly outnumbered, just the seven of them against twenty-plus hardened Empire warriors. But the Sword was in his sights, and there was no turning back now.

"FIRE!" Reece screamed again.

O'Connor, beside him, fired two arrows, taking down two soldiers, Elden hurled his spear, Indra threw her dagger, and Conven his small throwing axe. They each hit their mark, taking down five of them, narrowing the odds.

Reece charged out in front of the others, drew his sword, and galloped into the thick of the group. He rode between two Empire soldiers and leapt off his horse in mid-air, knocking them both down with his arms.

They all tumbled together to the ground, and Reece landed in a roll, turned, took a knee and slashed each of them both before they had a chance to regain their feet.

His Legion brothers were fighting all around him, hand-to-hand, as the fighting grew fierce. The surprised Empire soldiers seemed wary of losing the Sword, intent on crossing the Canyon with it, and they were distracted in their fighting, huddling around it. They were also clearly exhausted from carrying the boulder so far, giving Reece and his men the advantage.

Reece, fighting for his life, for Thor's life, for the Sword's life, and for the life of the Ring, gave it everything he had. He had never fought with such abandon, slashing and stabbing and parrying, and he took down several soldiers, as did Conven beside him, who also battled in a reckless rage. Elden used his sheer strength to overpower them, wielding a battle axe and using his strong legs to kick several soldiers in the chest, onto their backs. O'Connor fired arrow after arrow, most of them finding their mark, and Indra, too, was a force to be reckoned with, weaving in and out of the men and slashing with her dagger. Serna and Krog were an impressive addition to the group, Serna wielding a flail, knocking swords from Empire soldiers' hands before they attacked, and Krog using his shield as a weapon, blocking blows for others, and smashing soldiers in the face and in the throat, sending them down to the ground. He followed up with his big studded gauntlet, knocking them out for good.

Soon, the odds were even. There stood seven of them against seven of the Empire, all of them covered in blood and breathing hard.

One Empire soldier yelled a command to another, in a language Reece did not understand. He was looking at the Sword and gesturing wildly at it.

That was when Reece realized: he was ordering his fellow soldiers to destroy the Sword.

Reece's eyes opened wide as he watched three of the largest Empire soldiers hoist the boulder up off the ground with all their might, while the other four circled around them, a wall to defend them.

Reece and the others fought hand-to-hand with the four soldiers, trying to cut their way through to the three soldiers carrying the Sword towards the bridge's edge. They went blow for blow, clang for clang, but it was not easy—these remaining four soldiers were better than the others, and more determined. They were losing precious time.

Conven charged forward and threw himself onto the lead soldier, tackling him to the ground. It was a move no one had expected, and it turned the tide in their favor. While the other Empire soldiers, distracted, turned to pry Conven off, Reece and the others attacked fearlessly. The seven of them fought as one, overwhelming the four Empire soldiers and killing them on the spot.

Reece, kneeling over a soldier he had just killed, looked up to watch the boulder feet away from the edge. The three Empire soldiers were lifting it, higher and higher, preparing to send it over the railing, to hurl it over the precipice. They already had it sitting on the ledge of the stone railing, teetering, about to be pushed over. In moments the Sword would be lost forever. He could not let that happen.

"NO!" Reece screamed.

Reece charged forward, the others right behind him, raised his sword and attacked the four soldiers. They turned and raised their swords—but too late. Reece deftly killed two of them on his own, and before the others could raise a defense, Elden, with his axe, and Conven, wielding a short spear, stepped forward and finished them off.

The Empire men were all dead, but there was no time for Reece and the others to rest on their heels. The boulder was rocking, teetering over the edge, the Sword swaying both ways.

Reece and the others rushed forward, and they all grabbed hold of the boulder. It was so heavy, so precarious, and already leaning over the edge.

As they grabbed on with all they had, their knuckles turning white, the boulder began to slide over the edge; Reece grabbed onto the hilt of the Sword, while the others grabbed the rock. He pulled with everything he had, pulled so hard that he felt his back and stomach muscles tearing. All of the others pulled just as hard, the sky filling with the sound of their screams. Even Elden, with all his strength, holding on with two hands, groaned.

But their hands were slick with the blood of men, and they were beyond exhausted. With whatever strength they had left, they pulled, but no matter how hard they pulled, the boulder just continued to sink lower and lower.

Finally, after one last desperate effort, Reece watched, horrified, as the hilt of the Sword slipped from his grip—and as the boulder slipped from all of their hands.

"NO!" Reece screamed.

He looked down and watched, wide-eyed, as if in a nightmare, as the boulder, the Sword still lodged in it, hurled down over the edge of the Canyon bridge. It spun and spun, plummeting down into the mist, into the bottomless Canyon.

Reece felt his whole life caving in, all hope being lost, as he watched everything he cared for in the world slipping before his eyes, the Sword hurling into nothingness, lost forever.

The Ring, he knew, was finished.

CHAPTER THIRTY SIX

Thor peeled open his eyes as he felt his wrists being dragged, his arms being raised and hoisted above his head. He felt himself yanked up, his body scraping against the hard, dirt wall of the pit, in and out of consciousness as his body scraped against mud, roots and rock.

Thor opened his one good eye, the other still swollen shut, and found himself laying face-first on the cold winter ground. He squinted at the harsh light of day, shivered from the cold gust of wind that struck his bare back and chest. He looked up to see an Empire soldier standing over him, scowling down.

"The Great Andronicus wishes to see you now," the man said coldly.

Thor felt several sets of strong hands grab him from behind, and set him on his feet. Thor stood on unsteady legs, his wrists still shackled with Akdon, still feeling weak, and wondered how long he'd been out.

He felt himself shoved hard from behind and he stumbled forward, dragged by several men, across the Empire camp. Thousands of soldiers gawked at him as he went. He felt every bump and bruise in his body, felt like he weighed a million pounds with every step he took. He felt more dead than alive.

Thor looked up to see he was being led to a small, ancient octagon-shaped structure, adorned with marble fluted columns. It was the ruins of an ancient temple. It sat alone in the camp, the Empire soldiers keeping a safe distance from it. Its huge iron doors were bolted shut, and Thor could sense an intense evil energy coming from inside as an attendant unlocked the door and swung it open.

Thor was shoved inside, and the door slammed behind him, echoing in the silence. It was colder in here than outdoors and something in the air made his hairs stand on end.

Thor stood alone in the octagon-shaped building; it was dim in here, lit only by a circular opening in the ceiling through which streamed a shaft of sunlight, tinged with scarlet, near day's end.

Thor sensed someone else in here with him. He looked up and saw with dread that, standing in the center of the empty circle, was his father. Andronicus.

He stood alone, as tall as a mountain, smiling down at Thor, as Thor stood across him. It was just the two of them now, facing each other in this empty, ancient ruin of a temple. Thor could hardly believe that he issued from this man. It was like a nightmare that would not go away.

"You have tasted the strength of the Great Andronicus," he began, his voice ancient, booming, echoing through the hall. "You have begun to learn the price of defying me."

Thor felt his shoulder throbbing and burning where he had been branded by Andronicus, and he hated this man with a hatred greater than he ever thought possible. He thought of Gwendolyn, of what Andronicus had done to her, and he ached for vengeance for her, too. He was so livid, he could barely breathe.

"I can feel your hatred for me," Andronicus said. "That is good. Your hatred will serve you will in this life."

Thor felt exhausted by his own hatred, felt barely able to stand anymore. He felt as if he were being broken by this man.

"Thorgrin," came the voice.

Thor looked up, shocked by the voice, and saw standing across from him now was Argon. It was a voice he loved, a man he missed dearly. Argon looked back, his eyes glowing with a fatherly love. It was a love that Thor had never experienced in his life.

"Join Andronicus," Argon said. "He is your father. Embrace who you are. Embrace your destiny."

Thor shook his head, confused. He stepped forward.

"Argon?" he asked. "It can't be you."

Thor blinked, and the figure before him became someone else. His mother.

"Thorgrin," she said sweetly. "Your time in the Ring is over. It is time for you to go someplace greater. Choose life. No one will fault you. Join him. I want you to join him."

Thor stumbled towards her.

"Mother!" he screamed.

Thor blinked to find Andronicus standing before him again. Thor shook his head, trying to shake off the visions. He knew Andronicus was using some sort of dark sorcery to play with his mind. But he could not understand what.

"Those shackles," Andronicus said. "There is an easy way to get them off, to regain all your strength, to become the warrior you once were."

"How?" Thor asked, his voice weak.

"Join me. That is all you have to do. Join me, and the two of us will rule the Empire together. Join me, and you will be stronger than you've ever been. Strong enough, even, to kill me if you choose. That is what you want, isn't it? To kill me? Yes, it is…I can feel it. Join me, and you will be strong enough to."

Thor breathed heard, his mind muddled, trying to make sense of it all. Strong enough to kill Andronicus?

"All you have to do is decide, inside your heart, that you are my son. That you are ready to embrace who you are. Once you do, those shackles on your wrists will fall off by themselves. It is the only way to get them off. You will be reborn as one of *us*. As my son. And you will reach a level of strength you could never comprehend. You will become the greatest warrior of all time. All you have to do is accept me. Accept me as your father."

Thor shook his head again and again, trying to get the voices out of his head. They seemed to spiral into his brain, to lodge deep in his mind like a foreign entity he could not shake out. Thor felt as if some force were invading his thoughts, making him unable to think, to decide, for himself.

Was it all true? Was Andronicus really his father? Would he really be wrong to defy his own father? He was starting to feel that if he said no, somehow he would be betraying his father. Betraying himself. He couldn't understand his own thoughts. It was as if they were turning on him, as if everything Andronicus said was starting to make sense.

"Thorgrin," Andronicus said, stepping closer to him, hardly a foot away. He reached out and lay a hand on his shoulder.

"You know I speak the truth," he continued. "You've never had a father in this world. And, aside from me, you never will. I am the only one who claims you. Now you must claim me. I am a part of you. A part that will never leave you. If you want to make all this go away, to silence that voice in your head, then claim me. Claim me as I have claimed you."

"NO!" Thor shrieked, sinking to his knees, trying to raise his hands to his head to blot it all out.

Andronicus' words circled inside his head, making clear thoughts impossible.

"Join me, and together, we will crush the Ring. The Ring that never embraced you. Join me, and become unstoppable."

"NO!" Thor shrieked, so loud, his voice echoed off the walls, blotted out all his thoughts.

He leaned back and roared in agony.

Thor heard a noise, felt something lift, and he raised his wrists and stared at them in shock: the Akdon shackles snapped.

They dropped harmlessly from his wrists, and landed on the floor with a clang.

Thor looked up at Andronicus, and saw his own eyes looking down at him.

"Father," Thor said, feeling a new strength begin to well within him.

Andronicus smiled wide with satisfaction.

"My son."

CHAPTER THIRTY SEVEN

Kendrick felt a renewed sense of optimism as he rode beside Bronson and Erec. Ever since Bronson's arrival, they had wiped out the Empire division. Together, they had all crossed the valley, their thousands of men merging seamlessly with one another. The size of their forces had doubled, thanks to Bronson, and momentum was finally on their side.

Kendrick knew that they owed Bronson a great debt. Bronson would have a friend in him for life now, and if they all ever survived this, Kendrick would make sure Bronson was given a position of honor and power. He marveled at how wrong they had all been about him. He should have known all along that it was his sister, Luanda, who had duped him. She had always been that way: conniving, power-hungry, and willing to stop at nothing until she had her way. Much, in a way, like Gareth.

With their newfound momentum, Kendrick felt they had a renewed chance to burst through enemy lines, rescue Thorgrin, and get him out. They had weakened the Empire army, or at least a sliver of it, a sliver wide enough to allow them to achieve their goal. Their plan was working. Now, before the Empire could regroup, all they needed was to press through the crack in the men they had created.

Kendrick recalled the olden days, when King MacGil had been alive; when the Silver had been all together, there was nothing in the world that could stop them. He felt something like the olden days returning once again, and felt that they were on the verge of achieving one of the greatest conquests of their lives, one that would be sung of for generations.

The valley narrowed, leading them on a path between two steep cliffs, and as they rounded a bend, a new vista opened up before them—and Kendrick's heart fell.

Blocking off their path in the narrow valley, facing them in combat, waiting to ambush them, were tens of thousands of men. More Empire soldiers than he had ever seen. These were led by thousands more. Men he recognized at once from their armor, from their banners.

Tirus' men.

At first, Kendrick was confused. Why would Tirus' men be joined with the Empire's, one unified force facing him? Then he realized: they had been sold out by Tirus.

As all of his men came to a sudden stop, Kendrick sat there on his horse, dumbfounded, hardly able to breathe. Tirus sat there, grinning back with a huge look of satisfaction. The battlefield was thick with a tense silence of anticipation.

Kendrick finally cleared his throat and called out to Tirus across the battlefield:

"You have betrayed the better half of the MacGils," Kendrick called out to him.

"Whoever said you were the better half?" Tirus answered.

"Why have you betrayed us?" Erec asked.

"You MacGils have always been fools," Tirus called back. "You take men for their word. You still believe in chivalry. And that is your great downfall. I believe in gold. It hasn't failed me yet."

"We were gracious to you," Ere called out. "Gwendolyn offered you control of the Northern half of the Ring."

Tirus beamed widely.

"But Luanda offered us the *entire* Western Kingdom of the Ring. Her sister, it seems, is the smarter of the two."

"Does your word mean nothing, then?" Kendrick called out.

Tirus smiled back.

"It does," he answered. "But not nearly as much as gold."

CHAPTER THIRTY EIGHT

Mycoples thrashed furiously against the Akdon net that entangled her, unable to flap her wings, to release her claws, to arch back her neck and breathe fire. Filled with rage, she thrashed again and again, trying her best to breathe or at least claw her handlers. Dozens of Empire soldiers grabbed onto the rope trailing the net and dragged her, thrashing, towards the long plank leading to a ship.

Mycoples scraped against the white sand of the Empire beach, feeling helpless for the first time in her life. The Empire ship was looming before her eyes, and there was nothing she could do about it.

Mycoples closed her eyes and saw Thorgrin, her master. The one person left in the world that she cared for. She tried to summon him, to share his thoughts as she often did.

But as she closed her eyes, she saw Thorgrin in a darkened building, beside his father. She saw him transforming. He was becoming something else. He was no longer the same man she once knew.

Mycoples' heart broke. Thorgrin, the one she would die for, was fading away from her.

Mycoples arched back her neck and shrieked to the heavens, again and again. It was a shriek so piercing that it shattered the ship's mast. But shriek as she did, nothing could prevent her from being dragged on board, tied down to this ship, and taken far, far away from here.

Thor, she thought. *Save me.*

CHAPTER THIRTY NINE

Gwendolyn shivered against the cold and lowered her head against the snow as she walked with Steffen, Aberthol, and Alistair, with Krohn whining by her side, the group heading ever-deeper into the wood. A snowstorm had picked up, whipping large flakes into her face, and she clutched her furs around her shoulders, all of them shivering violently against the freezing gale. Icy snow clung to everything and it had become an effort to walk. The deeper they went, the more Gwendolyn was starting to wonder if Aberthol had been right all along, if this was a journey they could never fulfill.

As the snow grew thicker, her legs heavier, the wind so loud she could hardly hear Krohn's panting beside her, finally, they turned a bend and Gwen saw light up ahead, peeking through the thick forest. With renewed hope, they marched faster, and they all came to the very precipice of the wood.

They stepped forward, out into the open, and were met with a gale of wind even stronger. The world opened up before them, a world of white, desolate, never-ending.

Before them lay the great divide of the Canyon, and spanning it, the Northern Crossing. It was a place Gwendolyn had heard about, but had never gone herself. It was spanned by a narrow footbridge, wide enough to hold one person at a time, shaped in a high arch, rising up over the Canyon like a rainbow. On the far side of the Canyon, there was a wall of white. Snow whipped about in a frenzy, mixed with waves of fog that rose up. Indeed, as the footbridge arched down toward the other side, it was entirely covered in ice, hanging below and off its sides.

They all stopped and stared in wonder. Krohn whined.

"The Netherworld," Aberthol said. "A world of ice and snow and desolation. A world of illusions and traps."

Gwendolyn swallowed.

"No one has ever crossed and returned," Aberthol added.

Gwendolyn stared out into the witness, the desolation, and knew it would be a long, hard quest. Perhaps an impossible one. She did not know if she would be able to even find Argon, and if she did, she had no idea if she'd be able to free him. Most of all, she knew that she would probably not even survive this journey herself.

Yet despite all of this, Gwendolyn had no doubt in her mind. She thought only of Thorgrin. She had to save him. Whatever it took. However remote, however impossible.

"Well," she said, turning to Aberthol, "there has to be a first."

Aberthol turned to her.

"Are you certain, my lady?" he asked softly.

They all stared at her, awaiting her answer.

She put her hands on her hips and stared out confidently.

"More certain than I've ever been of anything in my life," Gwendolyn replied.

With that, she took her first step, heading across the empty plane, into the howling winds, towards the iced-over footbridge, fully prepared to enter the abyss of the Netherworld.

CHAPTER FORTY

Thorgrin, free of his shackles, dressed again, feeling stronger than he'd ever had, walked together with Andronicus up a small knoll, the two of them heading towards the high point of the camp. As they crested the top they looked out together, and there sat the Empire army, a half-million soldiers looking back.

The Empire soldiers stared back in suspense, waiting. Andronicus stood beside Thorgrin, father and son. Thor was now fully dressed in the clothing of the Empire, wearing the same black and gold, the same uniform of his father, his breastplate emblazed with their symbol: a lion with an eagle in its mouth. Thor's eyes were cold and hard, and as he looked out, he looked more like his father than ever. He was unrecognizable from the boy he once was.

Thor stood atop the hill, gripping his new sword, the one that had once belonged to his father, long and black and evil, with a silver hilt, glistening in the scarlet sun like a snake ready to strike.

"MEN OF THE EMPIRE!" Andronicus yelled out. "Meet your new commander. My son. Thornicus!"

Thorgrin stepped forward and looked down. Then he raised his new sword high above his head with a single arm.

There came a huge shout of approval, and Thor drank it in. He was ready to lead these men, to crush the Ring. He was ready to embrace who he really was. He was ready to do as his father commanded him. He was ready for the final destruction of the Ring.

"Thornicus!" echoed the army, a half million voices rising to the sky.

Thor turned slowly, raising the sword ever higher.

"THORNICUS!"

"THORNICUS!!"

NOW AVAILABLE!

A GRANT OF ARMS
(BOOK #8 IN THE SORCERER'S RING)

"A breathtaking new epic fantasy series. Morgan Rice does it again! This magical sorcery saga reminds me of the best of J.K. Rowling, George R.R. Martin, Rick Riordan, Christopher Paolini and J.R.R. Tolkien. I couldn't put it down!"
--Allegra Skye, Bestselling author of SAVED

In A GRANT OF ARMS (Book #8 in the Sorcerer's Ring), Thor is caught between titanic forces of good and evil, as Andronicus and Rafi use all of their dark sorcery to attempt to crush Thor's identity and take control of his very soul. Under their spell, Thor will have to battle a greater fight than he has ever known, as he struggles to cast off his father and free himself from their chains. But it may already be too late.

Gwendolyn, with Alistair, Steffen and Aberthol, ventures deep into the Netherworld, on her quest to find Argon and free him from his magical trap. She sees him as the only hope to save Thor and to save the Ring, but the Netherworld is vast and treacherous, and even finding Argon may be a lost cause.

Reece leads the Legion members as they embark on a near-impossible quest to do what has never been done before: to descend into the depths of the Canyon and find and retrieve the lost Sword. As they descend, they enter another world, filled with monsters and exotic races—all of them bent on keeping the Sword for their own purposes.

Romulus, armed with his magical cloak, proceeds with his sinister plan to cross into the Ring and destroy the Shield; Kendrick, Erec, Bronson and Godfrey fight to free themselves from their betrayal; Tirus and Luanda learn what it means to be traitors and to serve Andronicus; Mycoples struggles to break free; and in a final, shocking twist, Alistair's secret is finally revealed.

Will Thor return to himself? Will Gwendolyn find Argon? Will Reece find the Sword? Will Romulus succeed in his plan? Will Kendrick, Erec, Bronson and Godfrey succeed in the face of overwhelming odds? And will Mycoples return? Or will the Ring fall into complete and final destruction?

With its sophisticated world-building and characterization, A GRANT OF ARMS is an epic tale of friends and lovers, of rivals and suitors, of knights and dragons, of intrigues and political machinations, of coming of age, of broken hearts, of deception, ambition and betrayal. It is a tale of honor and courage, of fate and destiny, of sorcery. It is a fantasy that brings us into a world we will never forget, and which will appeal to all ages and genders.

About Morgan Rice

Morgan is author of the #1 Bestselling THE SORCERER'S RING, a new epic fantasy series, currently comprising eleven books and counting, which has been translated into five languages. The newest title, A REIGN OF STEEL (#11) is now available! Morgan Rice is also author of the #1 Bestselling series THE VAMPIRE JOURNALS, comprising ten books (and counting), which has been translated into six languages. Book #1 in the series, TURNED, is now available as a FREE download!

Morgan is also author of the #1 Bestselling ARENA ONE and ARENA TWO, the first two books in THE SURVIVAL TRILOGY, a post-apocalyptic action thriller set in the future. Among Morgan's many influences are Suzanne Collins, Anne Rice and Stephenie Meyer, along with classics like Shakespeare and the Bible. Morgan lives in New York City.

Please visit www.morganricebooks.com to get exclusive news, get a free book, contact Morgan, and find links to stay in touch with Morgan via Facebook, Twitter, Goodreads, the blog, and a whole bunch of other places. Morgan loves to hear from you, so don't be shy and check back often!

Books by Morgan Rice

THE SORCERER'S RING
A QUEST OF HEROES (BOOK #1)
A MARCH OF KINGS (BOOK #2)
A FEAST OF DRAGONS (BOOK #3)
A CLASH OF HONOR (BOOK #4)
A VOW OF GLORY (BOOK #5)
A CHARGE OF VALOR (BOOK #6)
A RITE OF SWORDS (BOOK #7)
A GRANT OF ARMS (BOOK #8)
A SKY OF SPELLS (BOOK #9)
A SEA OF SHIELDS (BOOK #10)
A REIGN OF STEEL (BOOK #11)

THE SURVIVAL TRILOGY
ARENA ONE (Book #1)
ARENA TWO (Book #2)

the Vampire Journals
turned (book #1)
loved (book #2)
betrayed (book #3)
destined (book #4)
desired (book #5)
betrothed (book #6)
vowed (book #7)
found (book #8)
resurrected (book #9)
craved (book #10)